The Death Catchers

The Death Catchers

JENNIFER ANNE KOGLER

WALKER & COMPANY

New York

First published in the United States of America in August 2011
by Walker Publishing Company, Inc., a division of Bloomsbury Publishing, Inc.
www.bloomsburyteens.com

For information about permission to reproduce selections from this book, write to
Permissions, Walker BFYR, 175 Fifth Avenue, New York, New York 10010

Library of Congress Cataloging-in-Publication Data
Kogler, Jennifer Anne.
The Death Catchers / by Jennifer Anne Kogler.
p.   cm.
ISBN 978-0-8027-2184-6
[1. Death—Fiction.   2. Grandmothers—Fiction.   3. Supernatural—Fiction.   4. Lady
of the Lake (Legendary character)—Fiction.   5. Morgan le Fay (Legendary
character)—Fiction.   6. California—Fiction.   7. Letters.]   I. Title.
PZ7.K8215De 2011   [Fic]—dc22   2010031904

Book design by Nicole Gastonguay
Typeset by Westchester Book Composition
Printed in the U.S.A. by Quad/Graphics, Fairfield, Pennsylvania
2 4 6 8 10 9 7 5 3 1

All papers used by Bloomsbury Publishing, Inc., are natural, recyclable products
made from wood grown in well-managed forests. The manufacturing processes
conform to the environmental regulations of the country of origin.

For Mom and Dad

Darcy mentioned his letter. "Did it," said he, "did it soon make you think better of me? Did you, on reading it, give any credit to its contents?"

She explained what its effect on her had been, and how gradually all her former prejudices had been removed.

—Jane Austen, *Pride and Prejudice*

The Prologue

Mrs. Vicky Tweedy
Room 122, English Building
Crabapple High School
Crabapple, CA 91292

Dear Mrs. Tweedy,

    I know that a letter may not be what you had in mind when you said I could save myself from flunking your class by writing a defense paper on the topic *Why I Should Still Pass English Even Though I Did Not Turn in My Final Project*. By the way, I honestly could've given you a big hug right on the spot if I didn't think word would spread that weirdo Lizzy Mortimer had stepped one foot closer to crazy and bear-hugged her English teacher.

    I've got to admit, though, my heart sank when you said that, in my paper, I had to find a way to "adequately demonstrate my mastery of the literary devices and techniques" we'd learned about in class this semester. Sure, I can recite all the terms I've learned—allegories and alliteration and climax and character-ization and conflict—and you get the picture. But whenever I try to write something that's any good, it's like I downshift into auto-horrible-cliché-pilot.

My grandma Bizzy is always saying the same thing to me: "You have such a gift with words, Lizzy-Loo . . . a way of throwin' 'em together like the most unexpectedly tasty word casserole." When I began to puzzle over why my grandma thinks I'm a supergenius with words and a lot of my teachers think I'm an idiot with them, I realized something. I'm pretty sure I can talk with the best of them. Ask around. I only get really mixed up when I *write* words down.

After Jodi's letter worked so well, I decided to make my defense paper a letter. What I'm really doing is pretending I'm having a conversation with you, except I'm the only one doing any talking.

I know you may not believe any of it. Two months ago, I sure wouldn't have. I seriously thought about making up some-thing that you'd be more likely to believe.

But I'm so tired of lying to everyone about everything. Besides, it's like Bizzy always says—sticking to the truth is the only guarantee that you'll keep your story straight.

†HE SE††IΠG

Before I learned my best friend was going to die, I never understood why writers went on and on about setting. It didn't make sense to me when Mom would go hog wild if a book was set someplace exotic like Turkey or Malawi or Canada. The way I figured it, *people* were what moved a story forward, you know? I realized the time and place where events occurred were important, but whenever I read a book, I usually skimmed the background stuff because it made my eyes droop. You can do a lot of things when your eyes are drooping, but concentrating on a book is not one of them.

Of course, I was dead wrong about setting. Don't get me wrong. I know people are really important to any story—especially mine, where most everybody turned out to be totally different than I thought they were. But I'm now sure none of this sinister stuff could've happened anywhere but Crabapple. So, though I'll try not to bore you, Mrs. Tweedy, there are certain things about this town that aren't at all what they seem.

The official name on the welcome sign is Crabapple-by-the-Sea, but the town is just plain old Crabapple to everyone except the occasional tourist.

Let's be honest: Crabapple is an odd name for a town. What's even odder, though, is that there are no crabs here at all and the only apples are the ones at Miss Mora's Market. That doesn't really seem like anything worth naming a town over, now does it?

Crabapple is a little blotch of a village. When you fly over it in an airplane, that's exactly what it looks like—a tiny hunk of civilization resting on towering, jagged cliffs above the Pacific. There's one two-lane road leading in and out of town. Some say Crabapple sprang up as a coastal mining town between Oregon and San Francisco and later became a retreat for progressives and freethinkers in the 1920s. I used to think that explained why there were so many peculiar people living here. Of course I don't mean you, Mrs. Tweedy—but peculiar doesn't even begin to cover it.

Take, for example, Crabapple's monthly town "Round Table" meetings. On the first Monday evening of every month, the whole town crams into the Crabapple Community Center and votes on proclamations like, *"Commuting by bicycle shall be encouraged whenever possible"* (in fact, lots of people, including me, ride their bikes around town). I've never seen you at a meeting, Mrs. Tweedy—you probably have a life—but I'm sure you're well aware that all house names must be approved by a majority of citizens at town meetings.

Many of the houses in Crabapple are stone cottages that look like they've been here forever. They all have name placards out front. There are no street addresses at all. Some house names are historic, some are geographic, some descriptive, and others nobody's quite sure about. It's supposed to be quaint, but I find it confusing more than anything else (as does the postman, Mr. Westerberg, I'm sure). Our house is named Beside the Point because it's on a cliff right next to a lookout over the whole Pacific. On the south side of us is The House of Six Gables (the Dandos planned on the traditional seven gables but ran out of money) and to the north, Periwinkle (repainted an eye-popping blue violet color every summer by the McGraw brothers).

At a Round Table town meeting a few years ago, Bizzy almost got into a shoving match with the head of the Crabapple Historical Preservation Society, Mr. Primrose. The grouchiest man in Crabapple, Mr. Nettles, wanted to change the name of his house from Windbreaker to Breaking Wind, in recognition of his newfound habit of public flatulence. Mr. Primrose, outraged, argued "the name would bring shame and dishonor to each of Crabapple's citizens." My grandma Bizzy yelled out that Mr. Primrose should consider renaming his own home The Cranky Cottage. I didn't think it was *that* funny, but it got a big laugh from the crowd. Things got heated and Bizzy and Mr. Primrose eventually had to be separated. Obviously, Mr. Primrose is one of Bizzy's many detractors.

I'm no expert on what's normal, but I've watched enough television to know that most towns aren't anything like

Crabapple. Which is why I should've realized how strange (and terrifying) Crabapple was long before I did.

Even the weather here is unusual. Bizzy says that Crabapple doesn't have air, it has fog. It's true. Large, soggy cotton fingers of fog creep in from the Pacific at night, seize Crabapple, and don't let go until midafternoon when the sun finally slaps them away from above.

Anyway, Crabapple is really where everything in this story happens. Except, of course, if you want to get really technical, some of it happened a long, long time ago, in a place called the Isle of Avalon.

But I really should tell you about the horror at the cemetery before I get into all that history stuff.

The Mood

Mrs. Tweedy, don't think I haven't noticed that you're always trying to get your students to discuss the mood of the books we read. *"What kind of mood or atmosphere is the author creating with the setting and figurative language?"* you ask each time we begin a new book. Since I'm the author here (a scary thought, I know) and I'm no genius when it comes to figurative language, I'm just going to go ahead and tell you the mood of this story.

Creepy.

I don't know how else to put it. Unless shocking counts as a mood. Because that might work, too. If I had to pinpoint exactly when things *got* creepy or shocking or whatever, I'd say it was the moment I laid eyes on Vivienne le Mort in the Crabapple Cemetery. Of course, I didn't know she was Vivienne le Mort then—I thought she was your run-of-the-mill loon who had wandered off from the senior center on Mission Avenue.

You're probably wondering why I was at the Crabapple Cemetery in the first place. Well, I spend a lot of time there for one reason: Jodi Sanchez. You know Jodi Sanchez, Mrs. Tweedy. She's my best friend, but you may not like her. She's not exactly a teacher's pet.

Mom says she's "mouthy."

Jodi is fourteen—a freshman just like me—but that's where our similarities end. Unlike me, Jodi doesn't seem to care what people think of her. Her wardrobe is filled with punk-rock staples like pencil-thin suspenders and skinny black jeans, though she claims she's more "mod" than punk rock. Either way, she sticks out like a sore thumb in Crabapple, whereas I just try to blend in.

As soon as she graduates, Jodi plans on forming a new-wave punk band. She says the band will be a cross between the Clash and Beyoncé, called the Destiny Strummers. Though she's out there, Jodi is very thoughtful. For instance, when she talks about the Destiny Strummers' first nationwide tour, she always mentions that she's reserved a place for me and my flute in the band, even though everyone knows that a flute is the opposite of punk rock.

Jodi's vowed that she'll never wear a backpack as long as she lives. Apparently, she thinks backpacks are too "institutional." I'm not even sure what she means, but I have no doubt she'll stick to her guns. Instead of a backpack, she has this large shoulder bag that looks as if it's made from pieces of a burlap sack sewn together. A hand-drawn, black-and-white-checkered pattern covers the outside flap, along with all sorts of quotes and pictures Jodi sketched.

Anyway, Jodi's a constant reminder of how two people can be very different and still be best friends.

If you knew Jodi as well as I do, you'd be able to guess that Crabapple Cemetery is her kind of place—she's convinced the graveyard is filled with adventures waiting to be had and mysteries waiting to be solved. Personally, I think she likes feeling as if, at any moment, her life could turn into a horror film. Regardless, when we're bored after school, her first suggestion is to head to the cemetery.

One afternoon near the end of October, when the sun had just made its first cameo of the day, peeking beneath a bank of cumulus clouds on its way down to the horizon, Jodi and I decided to pay the cemetery a visit.

I still wish we hadn't.

But it's like Bizzy says—you can never outfox the past, so there's no use thinking about it. After pushing open the wrought-iron gate, Jodi and I weaved our way through the row of white fir trees and collection of different-sized tombstones. Many of the headstones belonged to deceased relatives of current Crabapple residents. The long shadows of dusk seemed to be moving with us.

Jodi was headed toward the stone cottage at the top of Cemetery Hill, the sloping knoll where the cemetery's caretaker, Agatha Cantare, lives. Agatha supervises the cemetery, and from her cottage on top of Cemetery Hill she can see most of Crabapple.

Before we reached the cottage, Jodi stopped next to the

most ornate tombstone. It was known as the oldest grave in the cemetery and looked like a miniature pyramid, coming to a polished marble point. A name was engraved at the top in large cursive letters.

Arthur Pendragon

Jodi traced the writing below the engraved name with her finger.

The Most Righteous Knight of Them All
Rest in Peace
687

"Hey, Lizzy, what if Old Arthur really did die in the year 687?" Jodi asked, referring to the long-buried Crabapple resident by the nickname he'd acquired.

"Crabapple's been around a long time . . . but not *that* long," I said, moving on to a tombstone, bathed in orange light, with the name *Gawain Orkney* carved on it. "I'm sure one of the Cantares forgot to add the one at the front of the year. *Sixteen* eighty seven seems more reasonable, no?" I sounded confident, but no one was exactly sure how old Crabapple was.

Both Jodi and I knew the legend surrounding the dates on the older tombstones. The Cantare family had been caretakers of the graveyard for as long as Crabapple had existed. In fact, not far from Old Arthur's headstone was the cemetery's lone statue, depicting Ambrosius Cantare, the first of the Cantares. Apparently, Ambrosius was a bearded man in long robes and a cone-shaped hat. Now his stone figure is mostly hidden behind the bushes that have grown up around it. Ambrosius Cantare had been not only famously illiterate, the story went, but also incredibly careless with regard to engraving the headstones.

The graveyard was littered with inaccuracies and mistakes— the oldest granite tombstones had dates that went as far back as the sixth century. After Ambrosius passed on, generations of Cantares came and went, but not one bothered to fix the dates on the older tombstones. Agatha is the latest in this long line of careless Cantare caretakers.

She may also be the strangest.

Agatha has two tangled gray braids and wears only white linen trousers and shirts. Most everyone in town, at one time or another, has seen Agatha talking to herself among the long grass and jagged tombstones. People assume she's completely bonkers. There are rumors she belongs to a cult. I even heard Mr. Primrose whisper at a town meeting that she was a *pagan*, whatever that means.

All of this, I suppose, is why Jodi's so fascinated with her.

That afternoon, I trailed behind Jodi, worrying that it was only a matter of time before we got caught snooping around Agatha's cottage.

The cemetery grew darker with each passing minute and I grew more frightened.

"Her light's on," Jodi said, as the sun sank farther below

the horizon. She crept up Cemetery Hill, moving from one gravestone to the next. "That means she's home."

Jodi and I crawled up to the cabin, peeking above the windowsill. We had a partial view of Agatha's living room. Agatha swayed back and forth in a rocking chair, watching a fire blaze, her feet on the brick hearth in front of her.

"She's just staring into space," I whispered.

"Shhh!" Jodi commanded.

"Agatha is crazy, Jodi. This is a waste of time."

"Hold on one minute," Jodi said softly. "She's about to say something."

Sure enough, Agatha seemed to be talking to someone on the other side of the room. The half-closed drapes blocked our view.

"It's not that I don't appreciate the visit, Vivienne," Agatha said, her voice soft and sweet, "but I'm afraid your presence here is a violation of the Great Truce."

"Why do you continue to stay in this drab village, Agatha, with petrified Merlin as your only companion?" a voice responded. "You can live anywhere in the mortal world you choose."

"I have a lot of fond memories of this place," Agatha said.

"Doomsday is close, dear sister," the voice responded. "The Last Descendant walks among mortals."

"*What's this?*" Agatha asked. The slight tremor in her voice betrayed her calm appearance.

A woman stepped into the middle of the room in plain

view. At least six feet tall, wearing a long, black satin robe, she towered over Agatha. Her mouth was stuffed full of crooked yellow teeth. Her midnight frock and harsh facial features made her resemble a sinister judge who only ruled in favor of the guilty and the wicked.

"I have had a vision that the Last Descendant is here in Crabapple."

"A vision? You should not be dabbling in arts for which you have no skill," Agatha said. She held a pair of knitting needles, moving her hands in a precise rhythmic pattern in her lap. "Why are you here, Vivienne? Avalon is where you belong."

I wanted to leave immediately. But Jodi was still, seemingly transfixed by the unsettling scene.

"You haven't had *any* visions yourself? You haven't seen a boy with the Mark of Arthur?" Vivienne asked.

"I have very limited contact with mortals," Agatha said. "And you know very well that since I journeyed here, I no longer have visions."

"We all had to make sacrifices," Vivienne replied.

"Indeed," Agatha said. She continued to stare at her knitting, slowly rocking in her chair.

"You must take solace in the fact that with each breath, Doomsday nears."

Agatha raised her hand, waving it dismissively at her sister before responding. "I have been hearing you prattle on century after century about Doomsday, and, yet, it has never come."

"Perhaps, dearest sister," Vivienne said, her voice oozing

sarcasm, "you have grown too comfortable here to listen to reason. But take note: the last Pendragon lives. In fulfillment of the final prophecy *you* made, after he is dead, I will finally be in control." Vivienne's voice approached a screech. "You would be well advised to join me before it is too late."

"I will not listen to another moment of this nonsense," Agatha responded. "Go."

"We must first deal with the two mortals spying on us right outside your window," Vivienne responded.

I looked over at Jodi. As soon as I attempted to turn my head, I felt a strange stiffness. I wanted to tap Jodi on the shoulder to get her attention, but I couldn't raise my arm. I tried to stand up but was frozen on my knees. The connection between my mind and my muscles had been severed. I attempted to scream for help, but my mouth wouldn't move either.

"I hadn't noticed," Agatha said.

"You have grown careless, then. There are, in fact, two mortals outside your cottage. One of them is due to have her thread cut shortly," Vivienne added. "But I will not take any chances and allow their eavesdropping to alter destiny. Their minds will be cleansed."

"Do what you must. But should you fail to return directly to Avalon, I will inform the others," Agatha threatened.

"*Adieu*, dear sister," Vivienne said. Though my head was frozen in place facing Jodi, out of the corner of my eye, I spotted the vile flash of Vivienne's crimson eyes. "We shall meet again very soon."

With one fluid motion, Vivienne flung the hood of her cloak over her head, covering her long golden hair.

Terrified, my mind raced inside my stonelike body.

Jodi was as still as I was.

Vivienne strode toward the door.

Then, an incredible thing happened—something more unbelievable than the mind-boggling conversation between Agatha and her frightening sister.

Vivienne walked right through the front door, without opening it. It was as if the cottage door was a hologram. Either that, or Vivienne was. I stared at my arm, half-outstretched toward Jodi, willing it to move. Nothing happened.

Jodi remained in a trance beside me.

Vivienne came around the side of the house and into my petrified view. She approached us quickly and stopped, looming directly above us. Her red eyes gleamed in the half darkness of the cemetery. They seized on us. Reaching out, the tall robed woman placed one spindly hand on each of our heads. Her hand was as cold as if it were made of solid ice. My head felt numb. Vivienne's eyes turned from gleaming red to spinning black whirlpools of terror. I looked into them and swore my heart stopped beating. Vivienne let her hand linger on our heads. Jodi's eyes flashed white with fear.

A damp, swirling black cloud rose from the ground where Vivienne stood, blocking her figure.

In an instant, she was gone. The thick midnight-colored vapor engulfed us.

I gasped as if I had been holding my breath underwater for a minute. I tried to speak. This time, I could.

"Jodi!" I said, reaching for her. "Can you hear me? Jodi, are you okay?"

Jodi, as still and mute as the tombstones surrounding us, didn't budge. She looked dead. I reached for her stiff wrist, desperately hoping I'd feel a pulse.

Foreshadowing

Maybe it's just me, but I think some English teachers go out of their way to make things overly complicated. One of the things I really love about you, Mrs. Tweedy, is that you try to keep things simple. The whole idea of foreshadowing confused me until you explained it as a hint that the author gives a reader about what will happen next.

I'm telling you, that day in the cemetery with Jodi was a foreshadow the size of Texas. What happened there hinted at every single thing that would occur later on.

It's amazing how slowly time passes when you're panicking. As we crouched outside Agatha's cottage atop Cemetery Hill, I thought Jodi was dead. She wasn't moving. After pressing my index finger to the underside of her wrist, I finally felt a pulse. Seconds later, her eyelids fluttered. She stood upright and stepped away from the windowsill. Agatha was still inside. I squinted through the fog. If Agatha was in any way related to the frightening woman who had just touched our heads before disappearing into thin air, I wasn't taking any chances.

"Ruuuuuuun!" I shouted.

Half stunned, Jodi stumbled after me, wide-eyed. We zigged and zagged between the rows of tombstones, past Old Arthur and Ambrosius Cantare, finally bursting out of the cemetery gate. We didn't stop sprinting until we got to Delores Avenue, two full blocks from the cemetery.

Breathless, Jodi collapsed onto the lawn in front of the Camelot Theater. Clutching my chest, I joined her on the wet grass.

"What was *that* all about? Why did you freak?" Jodi asked, still panting.

"What?" I responded, not understanding why Jodi wasn't as horrified as I was by being frozen solid by Vivienne. Jodi was flat on her back, looking up at the starry sky. She smiled at me.

"No offense, but aren't you a little old to be spooked by Agatha? Maybe you can't handle the cemetery anymore."

At first, I thought Jodi was playing some kind of cruel joke on me—trying to act cool even though she was as scared out of her mind as I was. I recounted exactly what I'd seen in Agatha's cottage.

"Look, you don't have to rub it in, Lizzy," Jodi said, slightly annoyed. "You were *right*, okay? Agatha was talking *to herself* about somebody named Vivienne and some truce and who-knows-what-else. She's totally crazy."

"You swear you didn't see a woman in black walk through the door like a ghost? Agatha's sister or something? You didn't hear her talk about the Last Descendant and Pendragon and Doomsday?"

"Okay, Lizster. It's time to give this up," Jodi said, sitting upright. "It's just not funny anymore."

"I'm not *trying* to be funny. You don't remember being frozen? That Vivienne woman touched our heads, Jodi! I saw it!"

Jodi put her hand to my forehead. "Are you feeling okay?" she said. "Because you are starting to sound, like, straitjacket crazy. Agatha started muttering, I was calmly listening to her, and then you started freaking out, grabbing my wrist. The next thing I know you're yelling 'run' at the top of your lungs."

The whole incident—the conversation between Vivienne and Agatha, the way Vivienne put her hand on our heads—was so vivid. But I began to doubt myself. Was it possible I imagined the whole thing?

"Your forehead's a little hot," Jodi concluded, withdrawing her hand. "High fevers cause delusions, you know. Maybe you're getting sick."

"You think I imagined the whole thing?"

"Let's get you some OJ and Tylenol from the market," Jodi offered, ignoring my question.

"Orange juice? For a fever?" I questioned.

"Sure. OJ is like chicken soup . . . it helps whatever ails you."

Jodi didn't wait for me to agree. Instead, she began walking toward downtown Crabapple. I followed, wondering why Jodi was so anxious to change the subject. I started to think that the tall witch-woman, Vivienne, had cast some evil spell on us by touching our heads. What had she meant when she said one of our threads was going to get cut? I knew it was a little insane, but what if she was real and Jodi was under some kind of hex? Maybe it hadn't worked on me. Worse still, maybe it had. Could Jodi be pretending she hadn't seen Vivienne? What if Jodi wasn't Jodi at all anymore, but some kind of zombie? Maybe we both were.

"What's your favorite kind of candy?" I asked as we walked down Delores Avenue.

"Um, you know the answer to that already, Lizzy."

"Well, what is it?" I insisted.

"Gummy bears. But not the imitation kind, only the real kind."

"What's your favorite color?"

"Turquoise."

"What's the name of your band going to be?"

Jodi stopped and grabbed my arm. "Seriously, Lizzy. You are acting really weird. Are you okay?"

"Are *you*?" I asked.

"Yes."

"What I saw seemed so real, Jodi."

"Listen. A few years ago, I *swore* I saw an alien on the Dandos' roof when I was leaving your house. In the span of a minute, I convinced myself Crabapple was being invaded. Turns out it was a green kite stuck on a shingle."

"So?" I wasn't sure what Jodi was implying.

"So, everyone's brain goes a little haywire sometimes. But you didn't see a witch in Agatha's house and no one touched our heads, okay?" Jodi's brown eyes pleaded with mine. She certainly wasn't acting like she was under a hex.

"All right," I said, feeling I had no choice but to drop the whole thing. Jodi released my arm and we began moving toward town again.

Before long, we were inside Miss Mora's Market. Jodi went behind the counter into the back of the store. I waited until she reappeared with her mother by her side and a cold quart of fresh-squeezed orange juice in her hands.

"Hiya, Lizzy!" Miss Mora said.

Part of the reason I loved Jodi so much was because of her mom, Mora Sanchez. Jodi's mom is known around town as Miss Mora, owner of the local grocery store, Miss Mora's Market. Miss Mora is a sturdy woman with a long dark braid and a nice word for just about every customer who comes into her store. Truly, she is one of those people whom everyone likes to the point that it is almost annoying—except how can you be annoyed when someone's that nice?

Miss Mora's Market is five blocks down the hill from our house. Which means that whenever Mom forgets to pick up something, she sends me there.

"What did your mother forget now?" Miss Mora always says when I drop in around dinnertime. Sometimes it's green onions or butter or milk. If the market's busy, Jodi is usually there helping behind the counter.

Every time before I leave, Miss Mora whistles me back to the counter and hands me a dark chocolate square wrapped in bright green foil and says, "It helps with digestion." Like most people in Crabapple, she knows Mom's reputation for turning perfectly good meats and vegetables into heaping burned piles of tastelessness. When it's especially bad, like when Mom cooks her tuna casserole, so wet and mushy you can barely use a fork to eat it because it's more like soup, Bizzy winks at me, smiling devilishly, and says, "Rita, you've simply outdone yourself this time. Just divine!" Later, Bizzy whispers something in my ear like, "Those green beans should press charges against your mama for what she did to 'em. Mutilation!"

It would be one thing if Mom only inflicted her cooking on the immediate family. But she loves doing things for other people. This includes dropping off books and baked goods on a weekly basis for Jodi and Miss Mora at their apartment, which is on the floor above the market.

Now, Miss Mora was staring at me curiously.

"Honey," Miss Mora said, "Jodi tells me you're feeling under the weather."

"Her head is hot," Jodi said.

"You should probably go home and rest," Miss Mora said sympathetically. "It may be a touch of the flu."

"Maybe," I said. Physically, I felt absolutely fine. Mentally, I was a mess. I couldn't get the harrowing figure of Vivienne out of my head. I looked at Jodi. I didn't know if I was imagining it, but she seemed different somehow.

Miss Mora took the fresh-squeezed orange juice out of Jodi's hands and placed it in mine.

"Take this with you," she said. "There's nothing better in this world than a glass of freshly squeezed orange juice."

I reached into my pocket, pulling out some single dollars to pay for the orange juice.

"Oh, no, no, honey," Miss Mora explained. "It's on the house."

I hesitated, clutching the quart of orange juice. Mom had told me over and over again that I was *never* to accept any freebies from Miss Mora. "It's hard enough being a single mother in this world . . . ," I overheard Mom explain to Dad after she chided me for bringing home a free loaf of olive bread, "but Miss Mora, bless her heart, would give away everything in that store of hers if she felt someone was in need."

No matter what I said, Miss Mora wouldn't take my money. I put the wad of singles back in my pocket.

"Can I ask you a question, Miss Mora?"

"Anything," Miss Mora replied.

"You know Agatha from the cemetery? Is she crazy like everyone says she is?"

Jodi rolled her eyes and then smiled at me. "Lizzy is convinced that we saw Agatha talking to a witch."

"I am not," I defended. "I just wondered if the rumors about Agatha are true."

Miss Mora put both her hands on the counter and leaned toward me. "Agatha Cantare may be a little eccentric, Lizzy, but she's no more unhinged than half the people in this town." Miss Mora reached behind her into a wicker basket lined with a red kerchief. She held a foil-wrapped dark chocolate square in her hand.

"I feel sorry for the poor woman," Miss Mora said, frowning. "The only person I've ever seen even talk to her is your grandmother."

"Bizzy?"

"Sure, in the past couple weeks, I've seen Bizzy coming and going from Agatha's cottage a lot. I think they've recently become friends. They're about the same age, aren't they?"

Questions spiraled through my head. Bizzy . . . friends with Agatha from the cemetery? Did she know that awful Vivienne woman? Was Bizzy a witch, too? It seemed ridiculous. Jodi raised an eyebrow at me suspiciously. I wondered if she could tell what I was thinking.

Miss Mora unfolded my hand and placed the dark chocolate square inside it. "Insurance in case your mother makes her legendary tuna casserole tonight," she said, smiling brightly.

"Thank you," I responded.

Jodi turned to her mother. "How come you never give me chocolate?" she whined.

"Because you were blessed with a mother who can cook," Miss Mora said, winking at me. "Not to offend you, Lizzy. Rita is wonderful, but the woman can't cook canned soup."

I laughed. "I know. Thanks again, Miss Mora." I took one last look at Jodi, to see if there was any trace of whatever it was Vivienne had done to us. Jodi appeared to be completely normal. I knew I couldn't stand there and watch her all night. "See you tomorrow," I added, reaching back into my pocket. I set the wad of one-dollar bills on the counter. I jumped toward the door, cradling the quart of orange juice.

"But—," I heard Miss Mora object.

"Keep the change!" I shouted as the door to Miss Mora's closed behind me. I sped home in the soggy Crabapple night, sure that Bizzy was the only one who could explain what had really happened in the cemetery.

The Protagonist

Here's the first curveball in my story, Mrs. Tweedy: this story really isn't mine. Like a lot of narrators, I kind of found myself caught in the cross fire. The real driving force of this story is my grandma, Beatrice Mildred Mortimer.

Nobody calls her that, though.

People call her Bizzy Bea or just Bizzy because she's always buzzing around when strange things happen in Crabapple. She's the town gossip who knows everybody's business. Bizzy Bea is more a term of endearment than anything else, though, and my grandma doesn't seem to mind it. She's had the nickname since she was a teenager.

Bizzy is a better protagonist than I am. She's the real center of the story. Even if you're convinced the main character of this story is me (I'm pretty darn sure it isn't), there are still a few things you need to know about Bizzy before I tell you what happened when I asked her about Agatha and the cemetery.

Now, Bizzy was born in 1936 in West Monroe, Louisiana,

which is right smack-dab on the Ouachita River. I guess that's only important because she's got this great southern accent that makes everything she says sound better. Like the word "for" is "fow" and when she says "golf" she just drops the "l" completely and it's "gof."

My grandma loves to tell me that I remind her of an "adolescent Beatrice Mortimer." This, of course, just means that I remind Old Bizzy of Young Bizzy. Bizzy has this habit of talking like she's the narrator of a documentary about her own life. For instance, when describing herself growing up she once proclaimed, "In her teens, there were two words most often used to describe Beatrice Mildred Mortimer: 'wild' and 'child.'" Only the way she said it, "wild child" sounded more like "while" and "chi-ull" (and as far as I can tell, Bizzy still is a bit of a "while chi-ull"). Whenever Bizzy tells me I remind her of herself, I try not to be rude and frown. The truth is, I love Bizzy, but she's not exactly the person I want to grow up to be. Now that I know we share the same curse, I may not have much choice in the matter.

But I'm getting ahead of myself again.

As the most opinionated person in our small town of Crabapple, Bizzy has quite a few critics, ranging from Mr. Primrose, the head of the Historical Preservation Society, to Mrs. Frackle, the owner of the Camelot Theater.

Also, Bizzy looks different, to put it nicely. Her hair reminds me of a large mound of crumpled Kleenex. It's always a messy pile of white. But she has these magnificent eyes that resemble blue-green algae at the bottom of two pools of crystal clear water.

Bizzy loves wearing pearls (she wears a string around her neck and so many around her left wrist that they cover half her palm and look like a thick pearl wristband); fishing off the Crabapple Cliffs (I swear she hasn't caught anything living or larger than an index finger in four years); and putting Konriko Creole Seasoning in just about everything she eats (she even sprinkles some into her morning coffee).

Though she moves pretty darn well for a seventy-four-year-old woman, Bizzy fell down some stairs a few years ago and now she mostly gets around using one of those combination walker-stools. But it's not just any old walker-stool. When she got it, she had it painted fire-engine red so it sparkles in the sunlight. It has extralarge wheels, a cushioned seat in the front, and patriotic streamers on its handles. She also attached small side-view mirrors to each handlebar so it was "highway ready." By far, though, the best part is that Bizzy named her walker-stool: Dixie. Strangely enough, almost everyone in Crabapple refers to Bizzy's walker by name as well.

There is one last thing about Bizzy I'm sure you don't know that is a key piece of this story. When I was younger, Bizzy used to tell me she was part fish. For a while, I believed her. See, each morning, Bizzy ignored the warning signs posted all along the beach below our house and went for a swim in the dangerous waters of Crabapple Cove. Sometimes, as a little kid, I would stand on Lookout Point on the cliffs above and watch Bizzy.

Her ritual was always the same.

First, she stripped off her sandals, slacks, and blouse, revealing an old black wet suit underneath. While the thick mat of coastal fog slept lazily on the shallow waters of the cove, Bizzy waded into the surf. She swam out, ducking under the large surface-skimming water logs rolling in from the Pacific. Then, she flopped over and floated on her back, her legs and arms stretched out to her sides. She let the waves crash over her and toss her body like a rag doll in the surf, slowly returning her to shore. When Bizzy reached shallow water again, she walked up to the beach, her hair looking like a janitor's old mop. When she reached her pile of clothes, she wrote in a journal she always brought along.

Dad guessed Bizzy's ritual had something to do with the death of her older brother, Henry. Bizzy was five years old when she witnessed Henry clonk his head on a rock and drown in the swimming hole near their house. He was much bigger than she was and there was no way for her to save him. Dad says Bizzy never got over it.

Her morning routine never changed . . . until recently. I first noticed that Bizzy had stopped going for her swim at the beginning of this past October. Mom chalked it up to Bizzy getting older. Dad was simply relieved that she wasn't putting herself in danger every morning. After she stopped, I detected a lingering sadness in Bizzy's face—like something important had been taken from her.

When I thought about what Miss Mora had said about

Bizzy visiting Agatha, I began to wonder if there was a connection between her visits and why Bizzy stopped swimming. The two changes coincided with each other almost exactly. That night, I worked up the courage to ask her.

Bizzy's room was on the first floor of the house. I knocked on the door. Bizzy opened it.

"Why, hello, Sweet Pea!" When Bizzy smiled, you could see every wrinkle on her face.

"Hi."

"What brings you to my door on this fine evenin'?"

"Do you know Agatha Cantare?"

"What's all this now?" Bizzy leaned on Dixie and stared at me blankly.

"Agatha from the cemetery . . . are you friends with her?"

"Who's askin'?" Bizzy scanned the hallway. I couldn't tell if she was scowling or smiling. Her lips formed a straight line across her face.

"Miss Mora said that you've been visiting her lately."

"Oh, I see," Bizzy said. I could sense her body relax. "Can't say Agatha and I got much in common 'cept the aches and pains of old age, but every so often, I go over and play a little gin rummy. Some older folks ain't as fortunate as me, Lizzy-Loo. They got no family around."

"She's not crazy, is she?" I asked.

"Agatha? Heavens no! She's just a mite lonely. And not much of a gin rummy player. A' course, I let her win now and again to keep her morals up."

"You mean *morale*?" I said, laughing at Bizzy. Sometimes I wondered if she mixed up words on purpose.

"You say potato, I say spuds," Bizzy said, winking at me with a crooked smile. She studied my face.

"Have you ever heard of Doomsday?"

Bizzy eyed me curiously. "Is somethin' troublin' ya, Sweet Pea?"

I considered telling Bizzy everything. But Jodi already thought I'd hallucinated and was borderline bananas. I certainly didn't need Bizzy worrying about me, too.

"I think I'm just a little tired," I answered.

"Well, now, that brings to mind one a' my best pearls of wisdom," Bizzy said. "The early bird may catch all the worms, but why eat worms when you can sleep in!"

In case you were wondering, Mrs. Tweedy, Bizzy has a habit of interrupting a person, sometimes midsentence, to interject what she calls "Bizzy's Pearls of Wisdom." For instance, if you were in the middle of telling a long-winded story (not that *you* would tell a long-winded story, but this is just an example), Bizzy would probably shout out, "Best way to make a long story short is to shut your darn mouth," clutching the string of pearls around her neck. She always follows these outbursts with, "That there is one of Bizzy's pearls, free a' charge."

Anyhow, after saying good night to Bizzy, I made my way up the stairs to my bedroom, somewhat guilt-ridden. In the span of a few hours, I'd actually been deluded enough to believe Bizzy was some sort of witch—all because my grandma had shown kindness by playing cards with a lonely cemetery keeper.

It turned out, however, I wasn't nuts at all.

Two days later, for the first time, Bizzy would admit she'd been lying to me. But it wasn't only me, of course. Bizzy had been lying to us all.

Conflict

If you have the gift (or, depending on your outlook, curse) of second sight, you see your first death-specter on your fourteenth Halloween. And after I saw mine, the real conflict began.

See, Mrs. Tweedy, this past Halloween, I learned that Halloween isn't just Halloween—it's also the start of the Celtic New Year. There used to be this big feast every Halloween, called Samhain, to celebrate the end of summer and beginning of winter. The feast supposedly also recognized the brief period each year when the mortal world and the spiritual world became united.

You probably remember this past Halloween, too, Mrs. Tweedy, because you promised to give anyone who dressed up in a literary-themed costume extra credit on that week's vocabulary quiz.

I'm sure you remember Opal Greenstone's costume, don't you?

Opal made a cardboard cube with fake tinfoil burners on

top and knobs on the front, and cut a hole in the bottom for her head. She wore the cube around her head, drew dark circles around her eyes, and told everyone she was that young writer who committed suicide by putting her head in an oven, Sylvia Something-or-other. I heard the whole school was buzzing about it. Principal Gladroy sent Opal home before recess even started.

My costume wasn't half-bad, if I do say so myself. I wore a bright pink elephant trunk on my head that my mom made and stuffed with Styrofoam so it stuck straight out, a large bow tie from an old clown costume, army pants, a red tuxedo vest, sparkly silver gloves from my Madonna costume a few years back, and ballet shoes. For the finishing touch, I hung a sign around my neck that said CRISIS OF IDENTITY. Except I'm positive you don't remember my costume, Mrs. Tweedy.

I never made it to school that day.

It wasn't my fault. I was sitting at the breakfast table in all my Halloween finery, reading the paper as I ate my oatmeal with golden raisins. Mom and Dad were there, too, on each side of me. They were watching a story on *Good Morning America* about cooking with applesauce in place of vegetable oil. My grandma raised her eyebrows at me—we were both thinking of what kind of cooking crimes Mom would commit using this new cooking tip. I imagined Mom pouring a whole jar of applesauce into her already dreadfully runny mashed potatoes.

Bizzy was sitting on her walker-stool, Dixie, which put her almost a foot higher than the rest of us. Normally, Bizzy read one of her medical books at the breakfast table as she slurped some concoction of Konriko Creole Seasoning, raw eggs, coffee, and carrot juice. I always considered this reading habit very odd, especially when drinking something so revolting, but Bizzy loved reading about strange illnesses, odd injuries, and morose facts.

"Did you know that more than two thousand five hundred people die every year from gangrene in this country?" she'd ask. Or, "A few years ago, a man drivin' while suckin' on a lollipop kicked the bucket when his air bag inflated. Why, it was only a fender bender, but the force of the air bag caused the lollipop to lodge in his throat. Cause of death? Suffocation."

Today, she wasn't reciting peculiar, morbid tidbits from one of her medical tomes. Instead, she was paying close attention to me. I was reading the Life & Style section, but I could feel the burn of Bizzy's eyes on my forehead. Instead of glancing up at her, I concentrated on the paper.

That's when it happened . . . everything went topsy-turvy.

I was looking at the paper, skimming the picture captions. All at once, every printed letter jumped off the ashen gray background, like a thousand tiny black crickets hopping up and down. The letters landed back on the page, all mixed up. I blinked furiously, worried that my contacts were melting in my eyes. I couldn't possibly be seeing what I was seeing. The letters swiggled on the page. Round and round *L*s, *K*s, *E*s, *O*s, and the other letters went in a circle, getting smaller and smaller like the water in a toilet that had been flushed. Finally they disappeared. The paper faded to a blank page and new letters bubbled to the surface, gradually. Soon I could make out the headline.

JODI SANCHEZ, 14, DIES IN TRAGIC ACCIDENT

I could hear my mom's voice in the distance.

"Are you all right, honey? You look like death!"

My fingers tingled as I tried to smooth out the paper, hoping that the alarming words would disappear. Instead, more appeared. A faded picture of Jodi, standing in front of the green awning of her mother's store, appeared next to the article about her death. She was smiling, revealing the small gap between her two front teeth. She was wearing a tight black T-shirt, her long hair in a ponytail slightly off-center.

Jodi Sanchez, beloved daughter of Mora Sanchez and freshman at Crabapple High, died yesterday at County General Memorial Hospital after sustaining fatal injuries from a car accident.

I could hear Mom chattering in the background, echoed by mounting concern on the part of Dad. But I couldn't stop reading.

A reckless morning commuter hit the girl while she was crossing the street at the corner of Ocean Avenue and Delores

Avenue. Though emergency medical technicians tried to revive her at the scene, she died two hours later during surgery.

Jodi stared at me from the paper and I could've sworn her brown eyes blinked at me. "Oh. My. Good—"

Bizzy bounced off Dixie and, with one step, was at my side, clawing at my shoulder. I could feel her knee dig into my hip as she shoved me off my chair. I thought of Jodi and almost vomited.

"Ow!" I yelped in pain.

"Oh my word, chi-ull!" Bizzy howled, even louder. "You're lookin' mighty green around the gills! You must have gone a little spotty and fallen right over!" Her clear eyes peered into mine intently. She swept her index finger to her lips and signaled for me to *shhhh*. With a surprising amount of force for a septuagenarian, Bizzy pulled on my arm, yanked me up by my elephant trunk, and dragged me toward the living room.

"We're gonna get you horizontal right away, Lizzy-Loo! Off to the couch we go!" Bizzy yelled for my parents' benefit more than mine.

I glimpsed Mom with my left eye. She scrunched her eyebrows together, completely befuddled by all the commotion.

"Is she all right?" I heard her say. Bizzy kept pulling me forward. I staggered and lurched along with her as she pushed through the swinging kitchen door.

I'd heard that sometimes older people get a little loopy as they age. But as far as I could tell, Bizzy had gone suddenly senile. She was acting like a complete maniac. I looked at her as she pushed me onto the living room couch, my hip still throbbing from the crush of her bony knee, my elephant trunk lopsided and my clown bow tie up around my chin.

I was afraid of my own grandmother. What in the world had come over her? Why was she trying to isolate me from Mom and Dad?

"Sit here, and hush up until I return. *Please.*" The *please* was more of a command than a polite request. She hobbled back into the kitchen and pushed the door wide open.

"'Fraid it's the sudden inset of the flu," I could hear Bizzy explain in a voice louder than necessary to my parents in the kitchen. For a moment, I thought maybe it *was* the flu. After all, out of nowhere, I'd seen my best friend appear in the paper and imagined a headline describing her death. Maybe the delusional fever I'd had at the cemetery was back in full force.

During one of her breakfast medical information sessions, Bizzy had told us that hallucinations were sometimes an early sign of a brain tumor. I considered the possibility. I put my hand on my forehead. It felt normal. I wondered if I was the one who was going suddenly senile.

Though I hadn't heard her return to the living room, Bizzy was now standing over me. She was leaning on Dixie.

"You need to listen to me, Sweet Pea, like you've never listened to me before."

"What's going on?" was all I could manage to mutter.

"What did you see?"

"What did I *see*?"

Bizzy's eyes were clear.

"In the paper. Did somethin' appear?"

"How do you know I saw something in the paper?" I began to push back against the couch, away from Bizzy, scared.

"Now ain't the time for questions," Bizzy said urgently. I was confused. If there was *any* time for questions, I was sure *this* was it.

Though my trust in her was shaken, I wanted an explanation and she seemed to have one. So I told Bizzy about the spooky picture of Jodi, the headline to match, and what the paper said about her dying in a car accident on the corner of Dolores Avenue and Ocean Avenue.

"When?"

"Just now, at the table."

Bizzy skootched Dixie closer to the couch so her whole head was floating above mine.

"*When* did the article say she passed on? Was there a date?" Her voice turned hard, as if her throat was made of steel.

"I don't know."

"You don't know because it didn't say? Or because you didn't notice?"

"I don't know."

Mrs. Tweedy, I don't want to admit this—it's embarrassing and I'm not sure why it happened—but I began to cry. The tears welled up silently, but when they gushed out, it was a pathetic display of general wussiness.

Now that I think about it, I know exactly why I started crying. Bizzy had never spoken like that to me. All the customary kindness in her voice had drained away. She was behaving like I had done something awful. Though she called me Sweet Pea, she was grilling me like I was a rotten pea who had given her a bad case of food poisoning. It didn't help that I began to think that Jodi was actually dead.

Bizzy saw the tears pool in my eyes and her face softened immediately. She took her crinkled thumb and slowly wiped my eyes. The tears spilled out and collected on her thumbnail.

"I promise it'll be okay, Lizzy-Loo. Jodi's gonna be all right."

"The paper changed, Bizzy," I said, wiping away more tears. "The article on Jodi appeared out of nowhere on the page I was reading."

"I know it did, Sweet Pea."

"You do?"

"Been expectin' this day for a long time now," Bizzy said. She wasn't happy when she said it.

"What day?"

"The day you saw your first death-specter." She looked at me, her mossy eyes filled with resignation.

"My first *what*?" I asked.

"Death-specter. It's a fancy way of sayin' you had a vision of what's to come."

"*What's to come?* You mean the future?" My mind reeled. Did that mean Jodi was set to die?

"Yes, child," Bizzy said.

"How do you know that?" My voice was filled with doubt and mistrust because I didn't want to believe it. "Maybe I just imagined the whole thing . . . because I have a fever. Or a tumor."

I began wishing it *was* a tumor. A tumor was something a doctor could explain. "Visions" of the future, however, were not something that could be explained by any doctor I knew, unless he or she was of the witch variety. Better still, a tumor would mean that the headline I'd seen about Jodi wasn't true.

"What about Jodi? Is she okay? If what you say is right, we need to go warn her before it happens!"

"We can't do that, Sweet Pea," Bizzy said. "You have to trust me when I say that if we warn her, it'll only cause what you saw in the paper to happen sooner."

"How do you know all this?"

"I have death-specters, too," Bizzy said. "Since I was your age. You inherited this from me, Lizzy-Loo."

"But . . . how do I know that you're not just making all of this up . . . that . . ."

"Look at your left hand," Bizzy said, motioning with her head toward my arm, which rested limp at my side. I held my hand in front of my face, almost expecting to see another vision.

"The other side," Bizzy said.

I flipped my left hand over so that my palm was facing me. As I started to gasp, Bizzy grabbed a pillow from the couch and placed it across my mouth to stifle my startled cry.

Right above where my wrist joined my hand were the words JODI SANCHEZ. The name was as red as my own blood and as small as if it'd been written with a typewriter. But there was sloppiness to it. The letters were hot and raised, like a stinging nettle had scratched me in the exact formation of each letter, inflaming my skin.

I lay there, transfixed by the sight of Jodi's name at the bottom of my hand.

"When you have a death-specter, the person's name appears on your left hand." Bizzy placed her own hand next to mine. She twisted her wrist and jangled the dozens of pearls covering it. "Why do you think I wear so many pearls on my left hand, Sweet Pea?"

I looked at Bizzy blankly.

"It certainly ain't because it makes eatin' any easier," she said, laughing.

"I don't understand. I mean, *how* is this even possible? Dad and Mom don't have death-specters, do they?"

"It's passed on through generations of the womenfolk on your father's side of the family. Somethin' about the ability to make a life's connected to the ability to see when it'll end. The trait skipped right past your father because he's a man."

"But why? Why you? Why me?"

"That's like askin' why you're as tall as you are or why your feet ain't smaller. It's somethin' you inherited and there ain't no reason why other than fate."

Stunned doesn't even begin to cover it, Mrs. Tweedy. You

know that vocab word you're so fond of—*ineffable*—that describes what there aren't words for? That moment taught me the limits of the English language, because they haven't invented the word yet that explains how I was feeling right then. The feeling was kind of like jittery-painful-nausea-headache-dread. The whole situation was ineffable. And it was about to get a lot worse.

"One thing's for sure," Bizzy continued, "there's no doubt left in my mind that you're a card-carrying member of the Hands a' Fate."

"The Hands of Fate?"

The room began to spin. My grandma eyed me curiously. She swung around her walker and sat down on the edge of the couch. Taking my whole head in one of her arms, she squeezed. Using her free arm, she took my Hand of Fate and put her fingers over Jodi's name.

"That's what we've been callin' ourselves for hundreds of years. I know it's a lot to take in all at once, but you'll get used to it in time," she said. "I promise you, as sure as the sun'll shine, you will. I'll be with you every step."

"It's not possible."

"The one thing I've learned in all this is that anything's possible . . . First things first, though. We gotta figger out a way to save your friend before that headline you saw turns true."

Man (or, in This Case, Old Lady) vs Machine

This bit of advice will probably never be much use to you, Mrs. Tweedy, but let me give it to you anyway: if you suddenly tell your granddaughter that she had a vision of death and is part of a strange cult called the Hands of Fate, don't just leave her all alone.

At least, not right away.

Almost as soon as Bizzy told me that I'd seen my first death-specter, she left me lying on the couch. I was about to ask if Jodi's name would ever disappear from my hand when Bizzy told me she had to "go gather her materials, lightnin' quick."

Those minutes alone were absolute misery. At first, I weighed the possibility that my grandma, Beatrice Mildred Mortimer, was legitimately unbalanced. People had all sorts of mental "breaks" that came on all at once. Just last year, in fact, Mrs. Frackle, owner of the Camelot Theater, refused to get dressed and started living in pajamas in the crawl space above the theater. Maybe I'd imagined some strange thing appearing in the paper exactly like I'd imagined the woman in the cemetery. Maybe the raised bloodred letters on my hand were a figment of my imagination, too. Or maybe Bizzy had drawn them in my sleep when I wasn't looking. I was unable to take my eyes off my hand. It was as if it had been replaced with someone else's.

But maybe it was real. After all, Bizzy was eccentric, but surely she wasn't deranged.

Somehow, it seemed to be the only scenario that *was* possible. Because it was certainly Jodi's name, spelled correctly, right there, engraved on my palm. I grew incredibly sad, thinking about Jodi and her plans for the Destiny Strummers. I wasn't sure I'd be able to survive Crabapple High without her.

I looked at the clock—6:32 a.m. Miss Mora would have just arrived in her store. Jodi would be right beside her, helping her open up the market. If Jodi were alive, I'd be able to spot her through the front store window. Bizzy said I couldn't warn her, but I *could* make sure she didn't cross Ocean Avenue without me. Heck, I'd tackle her if I had to.

If I could lay eyes on her, at least, I wouldn't feel so terrible inside.

I stripped off my elephant trunk, sparkly gloves, and big rubber bow tie. I didn't look normal, but I wouldn't be completely conspicuous. I ran out the screen door toward Miss Mora's Market.

The ballet slippers made negotiating the mist-slicked pavement harder than normal. I raced down the hill anyway. The shortcut through the Ramblings' yard would get me there quicker, so I took it. I nearly tripped on their Oregon or Bust house name placard, sticking up in the middle of their lawn.

I reached the corner of Dolores and Ocean Avenue in no time. I bent over, trying to catch my breath before dashing on.

Crabapple was dark and damp at dawn. And empty. There wasn't a person or car anywhere. The streetlights were still glimmering. One shone on Miss Mora's green awning across the street. I was positioned diagonally from the entrance to the store.

The lights were on. I squinted, trying to locate Miss Mora or Jodi through the store's plate-glass window.

Magically, there she was.

Jodi came through the front door of the store, wearing a red apron that matched her red Converse high-tops. She was wheeling crates of fruit on a dolly.

"Jodi!" I exclaimed.

I couldn't help it. I was overjoyed. Jodi turned around and saw me across the street. She smiled widely, the slight gap in her two front teeth on display.

She walked toward me, stepping down from the curb and into the street with her hands on her hips.

"You're up early!" She shook her head in surprise. "Did you run out of eggs or something?"

I had to get ahold of her—to make sure she got out of the street.

What happened next was a blur.

I still can't be sure what I saw first: the black car turning onto Ocean Avenue from a side street, or my grandma, gaining speed, on the opposite side of the street.

Bizzy was straddling the bottom rails of Dixie, riding her souped-up walker like a skateboard, holding on for dear life. She was wearing a red helmet and her face had a fierceness to it—like her jaw was reinforced with iron.

I spun back around. The black car was headed straight toward Jodi.

Bizzy, riding Dixie, careened out into the intersection.

The black car picked up speed, still gunning right for Jodi.

Bizzy angled toward Jodi, who was turned toward me, waiting for me to explain myself.

Both the black car and my grandma were converging toward one central point: Jodi, still standing in the middle of the street.

"Nooooo!" I shouted, watching the black car as it zoomed within feet of both Bizzy and Jodi.

My arms swung back and forth like two haywire windshield wipers attached to my shoulders.

I screamed at the top of my lungs, trying to get the car to slow down.

But it didn't.

Bizzy cried out as Dixie rammed full speed into Jodi. Both of them went flying back toward the sidewalk. An instant later, I heard the crunch of bone meeting pavement. Bizzy's helmeted head cracked against the concrete. Dixie flew the other direction, slamming into the sidewalk, pieces breaking off as it bounced toward Jodi.

I inhaled deeply.

The black car had missed them by inches.

The car zoomed away and I ran toward the curb, where Jodi groaned in pain. Dixie had rolled on top of her. Bizzy was flat on her back nearby. Her eyes were closed, her face frozen in pain. Jodi moaned as she tried to move the walker. The suffering in her voice made me wince.

"You okay?" I pulled Dixie off Jodi. She opened her eyes and looked at me.

"I'm all right, I think," she said softly, her eyelids fluttering like dancing butterflies. "Your . . . grandma . . . the car . . . she . . . saved . . . me."

I turned to my grandma and took a step toward her. Her eyes were still closed. She was unconscious.

"Bizzy! Can you hear me?" My voice broke.

Jodi slowly rose to her feet and brushed herself off. We both stood over Bizzy's prone body.

"Bizzy?" Jodi said, concerned. "Bizzy, if you can hear me, we're going to call and get you help, okay?"

Nothing.

"Bizzy, hang on!" I insisted.

Still nothing. I began to think it was too much for a seventy-four-year-old to handle. I also started to think the accident was my fault.

"I'll go call an ambulance," Jodi said loudly.

"I'll stay with her. Hurry."

The sound of footsteps drew my eyes away from Bizzy and toward the corner where the black car had first emerged.

A little girl with long straight white hair and a black dress was determinedly skipping down the sidewalk toward my grandma and me. Her expression was as plain as her pale face. I could hear her humming; her small voice was faint in the morning air. Her dress was lined with black ruffles and black lace and there was something unnatural about her joyless face. She looked like a demented doll.

All at once, Bizzy's left eye popped open. She turned her head and eyed the girl.

"The miiiir . . . ," she wheezed, unable to form the word she wanted.

"Bizzy! You're awake! Don't try to talk," I said. "Help is on the way."

"N-ack . . . No! Mirror!" Her eyeballs focused with frantic desperation. She weakly motioned toward one of Dixie's side-view mirrors, partially cracked, lying on the sidewalk a few feet away from her.

"Neeeeooooow! Now!" Bizzy implored, with all of the strength she could muster. I looked at her confused, my pulse still racing, wondering what Bizzy wanted with a mirror, now of all times.

I crawled toward the mirror, grabbed it, and carefully placed it on Bizzy's chest.

Her eyes were focused on something just over my shoulder. I looked up, and the little girl in the black dress was less than a foot away from us, humming softly to herself.

"*You have a date. A date with fate. We shall not be late,*" she sang in an eerie singsong. Her voice was tiny and thin, like a parakeet's, as she repeated it again, in a hypnotic chant. "*The time is here, there's nothing to fear. You have a date. A date with fate. We shall not be late.*"

I stared at the strange little girl in her black dress, completely confused, and then looked back at Bizzy. In her eyes, I saw abject fear.

"What is it, Bizzy? Who is she?"

"*You have a date. A date with fate. We shall not be late,*" the girl continued.

Bizzy groaned as she struggled to lift the mirror with her weak arms. "Show the mirra to the girl," she said, gulping for air and then making a gurgling noise.

I looked back at the sullen girl. She'd stopped singing. She peered at me with her big sand dollar–sized eyes, then at Bizzy. She turned her head and saw Jodi through the plate-glass window, behind the counter, on the phone. I looked at her face and noticed her eyes had become swirling black holes. Suddenly, tears were spilling from them. She opened her mouth and let out a small whimper. The whimper turned into sob.

Then the sob turned into something else entirely.

It sounded like nothing I'd ever heard before, so piercing and loud, I was sure Miss Mora's window would shatter. The shriek was high and deep—it took my breath away.

I crumbled to the ground and covered my ears.

"Stop!" I screamed, looking at the pale-faced, shrieking girl. My brain felt as if someone was pounding it with a rubber mallet. My lungs seemed to be shrinking inside my chest—like two balloons someone had released without remembering to tie them off.

I saw spots and then colors. I rolled toward Bizzy, her face ashen.

If the wailing didn't stop soon, I was certain I wouldn't be able to withstand it. Bizzy grimaced as she pushed the mirror toward me.

I tried to think clearly. Bizzy'd known the girl was trouble even before the wailing—that must've been the reason she was so alarmed. But how did she know?

Show the girl the mirror, she'd said.

I struggled to grasp Dixie's detached mirror in my hands. I lurched to my feet, so dizzy I couldn't see straight. The girl flashed in front of me. Then blackness. Then the girl. The world was dimming around me, my lungs were running out of air.

The mirror weighed heavy in my hands. I could barely lift it. But lift it I did. Right in front of the girl's contorted face so that she was staring directly into it.

I heard an explosive pop, then a rush of air. I winced as the blast of a thousand tiny particles hit my face.

The screeching finally stopped. I dropped to my knees and collapsed next to Bizzy, unconscious.

Miss Mora was standing over me when my eyes fluttered open. Jodi was beside her.

"Lizzy?" she questioned. "Lizzy, are you okay? What on

earth happened? Why is there sand everywhere?" Miss Mora had her arm around Jodi, who was staring at me like I was a stranger.

"She done fainted. Saw me bleedin', poor thing!" Bizzy, still lying on the ground next to me, chuckled. Her voice was weak. I wobbled to my feet and stared at Bizzy, who winked at me.

"Sand's from Dixie," my grandma continued. "I weighed her down with the stuff so she controls speed easier on downhills."

"I'm amazed you're conscious, Bizzy!" Miss Mora said.

"An ox ain't got nothin' on me," Bizzy said. "But criminy, gals. Don't stand there like you're 'bout to put nails in my coffin," she continued, growing quite animated. "Help an ol' lady up, for Pete's sake!"

"We really shouldn't move you in case you have an injury to your spine, Bizzy," Miss Mora said. She then turned to me. "Lizzy, are you sure you're all right?"

"I think I just fainted . . . I'm fine now, I promise," I said, embarrassed.

"You've all had quite a shock, to be sure," Miss Mora said sympathetically. "I think I'll just run in and get you some water. Girls, make sure Bizzy does *not* budge!"

"Okay," I said, catching my breath, my ears still ringing and my brain still throbbing.

Miss Mora's gaze connected with the concerned eyes of her daughter.

"Jodi, honey, Bizzy is going to be fine, okay?"

"Uh-huh," Jodi mumbled.

I dropped to my knees and took off my vest. Then I grabbed Bizzy's head by the back of her cracked helmet and lifted it ever so slightly. I quickly slid the vest underneath.

"That's awful nice of you, Sweet Pea," Bizzy said. Her eyes had a shininess to them that gave her a far-off quality, as if her mind was somewhere else.

"What *was* that? The girl and the mirror and the sand and . . . I thought we were both going to die—"

"Shush up now," Bizzy said softly, shifting her eyes toward Jodi, who was standing a few feet away, still dazed. "Take a look at your hand," she whispered.

I turned my left palm upward. The normal lines and wrinkles were there but nothing else. Jodi Sanchez's name had vanished.

Bizzy's eyes flickered closed. "She's safe," Bizzy said, struggling to form the words, her eyes still closed. "We cheated the death-specter." I surveyed Bizzy's body.

"But what was that *thing*?" I asked, refusing to believe the girl was an actual human being. "That sound—"

"When we're alone!" Bizzy insisted with a whisper.

"You're bleeding," I said, noticing the growing pool of shimmering red on the sidewalk underneath Bizzy's hip. The pool was the size of a paper towel and growing.

"It's nothin' more than an itty-bitty scratch," Bizzy said. "My skin ain't as thick as it used to be, I'm 'fraid."

Jodi knelt next to me. She took off the red apron and tied one of the straps around Bizzy's bleeding elbow.

"Oh my stars," Bizzy said, turning her head toward her elbow and reopening her eyes as Jodi applied the cloth to it. "Why, ain't you as sweet as pie."

"You're supposed to lie still," I chided.

"How did Dixie fare? She in one piece?"

"Dixie is in better shape than you are," I said, looking at Bizzy's fire-engine-colored walker lying on its side a few feet away. The cracked side-view mirror was in the gutter. I'd dropped it there when I blacked out.

Bizzy began blinking more frequently. She was growing more alert.

"Jodi, would you mind runnin' inside and gettin' me a sweater. 'Fraid I'm gonna be spendin' some time at the hospital. It's always as cold as a well digger's heinie in there."

Jodi nodded and headed inside. Once she was gone, Bizzy started speaking quickly. "Lizzy, listen to me: We went to Mora's Market to get you some Pepto. You ran out in front of me," she said, talking quickly, but struggling. "I tried to catch up. That's when the accident happened. Then you fainted when you saw me bleedin'. Simple as that."

"What do you mean?"

"When anybody asks, Sweet Pea, that's what we're gonna tell 'em, okay?"

"But I don't understand, Bizzy," I pleaded. "Why can't we tell anyone what happened?"

"We'll straighten all this out," she said. "But it's important we keep this between you 'n' me."

Miss Mora and Jodi came out of the market with a shawl and some water.

"How are you feeling, Bizzy?"

"Be good as new in a few days!" Bizzy shifted her head slightly so she could look at Jodi directly. "How you doin', Jodi dear?"

"I'm totally fine. Thank you . . . for saving my life," Jodi said, sounding shyer than I'd ever heard her.

Miss Mora looked directly at my grandma. "I . . . I don't know how we'll ever repay you for what you did," she said, growing emotional.

"Oh, it was nothin', Mora," Bizzy responded. "Even a blind hog finds herself an acorn now and again."

In the distance I could hear sirens blaring. The hospital was not far up the road and the ambulance would arrive any minute. But Bizzy's injuries would be only the first in a string of problems.

I suppose I was too focused on the monumental change happening in front of me—that I was a Hand of Fate—to realize everything was connected. Then again, at that point, Bizzy hadn't exactly figured it out either. Now, though, it seems so clear: that the death-specter about Jodi was a part of the larger puzzle that included the murky origins of Crabapple, Agatha Cantare and her horrible sister Vivienne, the shrieking girl, Ambrosius, and Old Arthur himself. Sometimes I blame myself for being unable, at the time, to put more of the pieces together so I could prepare myself.

But that's the thing about fate. It comes at you whether you're ready for it or not. In fact, my next death-specter was only hours away.

Transitions

Transitions assist in the formation of the connections between sentences, paragraphs, and themes of your written work. Without them, readers may have a hard time following your argument.

If you're wondering who wrote that, Mrs. Tweedy . . . you did. It was part of a handout on transition sentences. I remember thinking at the time that it would be pretty handy to have the equivalent of transition sentences in life. Yes, sometimes life moves nicely from one thing to the next: a graduation lets you know you're growing up and school's getting harder; the changing color of the trees from green to red-orange signals that it's about to get colder. A lot of the time, though, there's nothing that glues one thing in your life to the next. You can go from being a normal freshman to a freak of nature in one second, without any signal or reason at all.

Life isn't smooth and flowing, like a well-written essay. It's choppy.

Trust me, I should know. My life started getting choppy the

day I saw Vivienne le Mort in the cemetery. As I watched the ambulance whisk Bizzy away from Miss Mora's Market, I was grateful I don't get seasick, because I knew things were about to get a whole lot choppier.

The paramedics wouldn't let me ride with Bizzy to the hospital, but Miss Mora quickly agreed to take Jodi and me straight there. They loaded Bizzy in the back of the ambulance, strapped to a stretcher. She gave me a thumbs-up because she couldn't talk through the oxygen mask. On the way to the hospital, the avalanche of questions in my brain wouldn't stop.

I wondered if the black car was the one that was supposed to have killed Jodi. Why was Bizzy expecting me to see a death-specter in the paper? What in the heck did I need to do if I didn't want to see any more of them? What about that spooky-repulsive-screaming girl? Where did she go once I flashed the mirror at her? Was I imagining all of it again? I thought about Vivienne and the cemetery, wondering what she meant when she'd said that one of our threads would be cut. Did she mean Jodi?

Because the cell phone reception in Crabapple was sketchy at best (most people blamed the incessant fog), Miss Mora called my parents from the market before we left for the hospital. All she told them was that Bizzy had fallen off Dixie and that she was driving me to the hospital. I was thankful they didn't ask to speak to me. Though I was paying attention when Bizzy outlined our "cover," I wasn't quite performance ready.

The hospital smelled like the inside of our washing

machine—clean and musty at the same time. I sat on a hard vinyl chair next to Jodi in the waiting room while Miss Mora tried to find where they'd taken my grandma. The other waiting room visitors seemed both worried and sad. Jodi was unusually silent. I began to wonder if Bizzy really was going to be okay.

There is a particular word doctors use when describing serious medical stuff. "Sustain." Like, *she* sustained *a near-fatal injury to the head, but after surgery is now in stable condition.* Maybe they use it because it makes an injury sound both serious and fixable all at once.

I wondered how many serious bodily injuries Bizzy had *sustained*.

"Honey?"

Miss Mora was in front of me. I wasn't sure how long she'd been standing there. I blinked a lot of times in a row. Jodi looked up anxiously at her mother.

"Where is she?" I said. Miss Mora looked at me with more sympathy than I deserved. After all, it was my fault Bizzy was here in the first place. If I had just stayed put like she'd told me to.

Wudda, cudda, shudda.

"They are prepping your grandmother for surgery. There's some internal bleeding."

"Internal bleeding?" I repeated. I wasn't positive what that meant, but I was sure that bleeding on the inside was way worse than bleeding on the outside.

"What's wrong with her?" Jodi asked. With one glance

at her guilt-ridden face, I could tell Jodi felt she was to blame, too.

Miss Mora sat down and took my hand and then Jodi's. She must've sensed how awful we both felt.

"Girls . . . she's going to be okay. This was an accident. It's nobody's fault. Bizzy is a tough lady and you'll get to see her when she's out of surgery. I promise."

There was uncertainty in Miss Mora's voice. She rose from her chair and declared she was going to get us bagels from the hospital cafeteria. Jodi leaned over the armrest of my chair and put her arm around me. We sat silently for minutes.

"Lizzy?"

It took me a few seconds to register the face of the tall figure before us. Though I'd seen him at school and, from a distance, outside his house, I could hardly believe Drake Westfall was there, in the hospital.

Drake's icy turquoise eyes were his most striking feature. If you looked closely enough, you could see the dark brown stripe dividing the blue-green of his left eye into two distinct halves. Drake was wearing slacks and a white-collared shirt, which didn't seem to match his bronzed skin and hair or his athletic build. A VOLUNTEER badge dangled from his pocket.

"Lizzy?" he repeated. I couldn't believe he remembered my name.

Maybe you're not aware of what a big deal it was when Drake Westfall returned to Crabapple, Mrs. Tweedy. You know the bad movie cliché where the nice, quiet kid becomes a superstar out of nowhere and suddenly people are asking, "Where has *he* been all this time?" Well, that's the Drake Westfall Story in a nutshell.

See, he disappeared from Crabapple (apparently, his father sent him to an East Coast boarding school to toughen up). In sixth grade he went away scrawny and four years later he came back strapping. When he returned, Drake promptly made the Knights varsity water polo team, was named team captain, and, though he's only a sophomore, started hanging out with the seniors. I'm pretty sure half the girls in Crabapple are in love with him.

Anyway, he was the last person I was expecting to see at the hospital.

I continued to stare at him. He raised his eyebrows expectantly. I couldn't will myself to speak. Finally, Jodi saved me.

"Hey there," she said to Drake. "What's up?"

"Mrs. Mortimer gave me a note. She's headed to the OR but wanted to make sure Lizzy got this beforehand." Drake held a crumpled piece of paper.

Jodi grabbed me and extended my arm out toward him. Drake reached out and pressed the crumpled paper into my hand.

"Sorry about your grandmother. I hope she makes a quick recovery," he said, leaning in. His eyes sought mine like there was something he wanted to communicate.

"Yes," I said, surprised by how soft my own voice sounded. "I appreciate that. Thank you so much."

Drake turned around and began walking down the linoleum hallway.

I held the paper in my hand. Jodi turned to me, shaking her head and laughing quietly.

"You've *got* to be kidding me," she said.

"What?"

"You're better than that, Lizster."

"Better than what?"

"First you turn all dopey when Drake appears and then I have to sit here as your cheeks turn all red and hear, '*I sooo appreciate that, thank you sooooo much,*'" she said, mocking the bashful tone I'd used with Drake, "all while you flutter your eyes at him. Barf."

"Oh, stop it," I said, growing more embarrassed. "That's not true."

"There's no denying that he's nice to look at. It's just so . . . so unoriginal. Though the fact that he volunteers at the hospital *kinda* makes him more interesting."

"I DON'T have a crush on Drake Westfall," I said, focusing on Jodi's implication.

"Yes, you do. You and half the world."

"You're ridiculous," I said, rolling my eyes.

"Ridiculously right," Jodi replied.

I'd almost forgotten Bizzy's note amid Jodi's teasing. I turned away from her, flattening out the paper on my stomach. Bizzy's scrawled handwriting was messier than usual. Jodi took the hint that I wanted to be left alone to read. She picked up a magazine. I began, happy to take my mind off my *alleged* crush on Drake.

Lizzy-Loo,

Looks like they're gonna have to go in and repair some of my parts. I'll be good as new. Better than new. I know you're probably very confused. Don't be. The gift of second sight was entrusted to us long ago by a powerful sorceress. I'll explain all of it to you as soon as I'm up and out of here, but if you have another death-specter, pay close attention. Write it all down. Dates, pictures. Everything. We'll deal with it together. I wish they'd let you in here with me. I've tried everything but all the nurses and doctors get their knickers in a knot about visitors. But there's this great framed poem in my room: Surgeons must be very careful / When they take the knife! / Underneath their fine incisions / Stirs the Culprit - Life!

It's a poem by Emily Dickinson. She knew all about us. Soon, I'll be with you every step of the way.

Love you to pieces and back again,

Bizzy

I was sure if there were any way for me to see her, Bizzy would've found it. When she wanted something, she always played up her age and her accent. Most times, it worked.

"Lizzy! Jodi!"

Dad trotted up to me, wearing his gray trench coat and his newsboy hat. Mom was close behind him. I stuffed Bizzy's letter into my pocket.

Miss Mora entered the waiting room with a bag full of bagels.

"Phillip!" she said, surprised to see Dad. She spotted Mom. "Rita! I'm so glad you're both here."

"Mora," Dad said seriously. "Thanks for bringing the girls. How is everything? What's the latest news?" He was perfectly calm, as always. He probably already had a treatment plan and a backup treatment plan in mind for Bizzy. That was his way.

"Your mother is in surgery, Phillip." Miss Mora put her hand on Dad's trench-coated shoulder.

Mom was at his other side. "What for?" she asked.

"She has some internal bleeding from the fall."

Mom turned to me. "What were you doing out with Bizzy in the first place?"

"We went to get some Pepto for my stomach," I said. That very instant, I felt like I needed Pepto as I remembered the crunch of Bizzy's body hitting the sidewalk.

Mom reached over and felt my forehead. "You feel warm," she said. I'd almost forgotten that I was supposed to be sick.

"How long did they say Bizzy would be in surgery?" Dad asked.

"The nurse said we'd be updated when the surgery was over," Miss Mora answered.

The crease between Dad's eyes deepened. He rubbed one eye with his thumb and the other with his index finger. Without looking, he slumped into one of the hospital chairs.

"She's going to be okay, Phillip," Mom said, sitting next to him. "She's just a little banged up."

Dad didn't respond.

"Excuse me, folks." A man in uniform stood before us. He was wearing a cowboy hat, olive green pants, and jacket with a gold sheriff's star on his lapel. His belt had more attached weapons and gizmos than I could name.

"I'm here to follow up on the accident on the corner of Dolores and Ocean," the star-wearing man said.

"Yes," Dad said, standing up, regaining his composure. Miss Mora stood up as well.

"I was there, Sheriff Schmidt," she said. "As was my daughter."

As soon as I heard his name, I immediately recognized the sheriff. Before his promotion, he used to be just Officer Schmidt. He and Bizzy hadn't gotten along ever since the town meeting held to elect the new sheriff. Bizzy stood up and said that Officer Schmidt was a "boat with only one oar in the water." Most people agreed with Bizzy that Officer Schmidt was useless, but they weren't foolish (or honest) enough to say so out loud. Of course, no one ran against Officer Schmidt, so he won despite Bizzy's objection.

"I've heard Beatrice was involved," the sheriff said. When he said my grandma's name, there was hostility in his voice.

"Yes," Miss Mora said, looking down. Silently, I tried to convince myself I hadn't done anything wrong.

"Bizzy jumped in front of Jodi," Miss Mora continued. Sheriff Schmidt pulled out his small notepad and began writing.

"Was she running?" Sheriff Schmidt questioned.

"Well, no, not exactly. Dixie was doing most of the work."

"Dixie who?"

"Dixie is the name of Bizzy's walker," I interjected. "Sometimes Bizzy coasts down the hills on the wheels of her walker." I wasn't positive because the brim of the sheriff's hat shaded most of his face, but I think his eyes bulged when he heard this.

"She rolled out into the intersection and pushed me toward the curb," Jodi explained. "If she hadn't been there, the car would have hit me. She's a hero."

"Why was Beatrice there?"

"She was there with her granddaughter," Miss Mora said, frowning at the sheriff.

"We were getting some Pepto for my stomach," I offered again, like a broken record. "I ran out in front of Bizzy."

"And *you* are?" The sheriff stared at me, narrowing his eyes.

"Elizabeth Mildred Mortimer," I replied.

"Mmm hmm," the sheriff said, scribbling more notes on his little pad.

Dad put his hand on my shoulder. "I don't understand the purpose of all these questions . . . is my mother in trouble for something?"

"Nothing like that, sir. I'm just writing up an accident report."

"An accident report? Aren't there other things the town sheriff should be doing?" Dad asked.

"We've had a few close calls in the past months with reckless driving. It's a real problem. Beatrice is not under suspicion for anything, but she does seem to find a way to involve herself in a lot of these so-called *accidents*." The sheriff raised an eyebrow at Dad. Dad inched closer to him.

Mom plastered a wide smile on her face. I could tell she was faking it. "Bizzy's had a run of bad luck in terms of being in the wrong place at the wrong time," she said, grabbing Dad's shoulder and pulling him away from the sheriff.

"This time, her being in the wrong place saved Jodi from serious harm!" Miss Mora added supportively. The sheriff ignored them both and turned to me.

"Elizabeth, can you tell me anything else about the make or model of the car? Did you get a good look at it?"

"Uh, no," I said. I wasn't going to tell this man, who seemed to have some sort of grudge against Bizzy, a darn thing.

"There was a large amount of sand at the accident scene. Any idea how it got there?"

"It's from Dix . . . out of Bizzy's walker," I said. "Bizzy weighs it down with sand and when she crashed it spilled all over the place."

"All right, then. Thanks for your time, folks. When Beatrice is feeling better, if you could have her give me a call, I have a few follow-up questions." Sheriff Schmidt pulled a card out of his pocket and handed it to Dad. The sheriff walked away, his leather boots squeaking with every step he took on the white linoleum.

Mom turned to Dad. "Phil, it's probably not a good idea to provoke the sheriff."

"I didn't like the way he was asking his questions," Dad answered gruffly.

We all took seats next to one another. Mom lifted her huge purse from the floor and set it on her lap. She grabbed the reading glasses that always hung around her neck and placed them on the end of her nose. She pulled out a stack of books from her bag, announcing to nobody in particular that "the solution to every one of life's problems can be found within the pages of a good book."

It was something she said at least once a week.

Officially, Mom is the librarian for the middle schoolers at Crabapple Intermediate. Unofficially, she is the librarian for anyone who will listen. Mom figures that if you don't like to read, you simply haven't been directed to the Right Book—the one that makes you realize you love to read just as much as she does. That's why she always carries a dozen books with her, in case she runs into someone in need. There's no doubt about it, she has a knack for finding people's Right Book. Of course, I am her most frustrating case. She has suggested dozens of books. None of them has been my Right Book.

She placed *David Copperfield* on my lap. "People say it's Charles Dickens's most autobiographical work . . . and it's impossible not to adore the hopeful buoyancy of Mr. Micawber, Lizzy," Mom said, with a hopeful uptick of her eyebrows. "Something will turn up!" she added in a bad British accent.

Into my father's lap, she put one of those Master and Commander books by Patrick O'Brian. My father loved adventure stories set on the high seas and had read almost the entire series.

"Miss Mora, would you like something to read?" Mom asked.

"Sure," Miss Mora said. Mom put a slim volume on Miss Mora's lap, *The 13 Clocks* by James Thurber.

"Underrated, whimsical, touching, and you can finish it in one sitting," Mom said, smiling. "I think you'll simply fall in love with it."

"Now, what are you in the mood for, Jodi dear?" Mom questioned, with one eye scanning the books she had left in her large bag.

"Got anything scary?" Jodi asked.

Mom grew excited. She plucked a purple paperback from her bag. In a very deep and dramatic voice she said, "Last night, I dreamt I went to Manderley again." I assumed it was a line from the novel she held out. "*Rebecca*, by Daphne du Maurier. If Mrs. Danvers, the housekeeper, doesn't scare the living daylights out of you, Jodi, nothing will."

"Thanks, Mrs. M.," Jodi said, thumbing through *Rebecca*.

I looked down at *David Copperfield*. The cover didn't even have a picture on it. I didn't have the heart to tell Mom I'd already dismissed Charles Dickens after reading *A Tale of Two Cities* in school this year. No offense, Mrs. Tweedy, but after the first dozen pages, it wasn't hard to tell that the guy was being paid by the word. I wondered how demoralized Mom would be when I didn't make it past the second chapter.

We sat in the waiting room for an hour, without saying much of anything. Mom, Dad, Jodi, and Miss Mora all read their books. I mostly stared off into space.

A tall, gangly woman with long hair pulled up into a ponytail, wearing green medical scrubs, stood in front of us. She held a clipboard.

"Are you the family of Mrs. Mortimer?"

"Yes," Dad said, getting up. "I'm her son, Phillip," he said, holding out his hand.

"I'm the emergency room surgeon on call, Dr. Stuhl," the woman said, without bothering to shake Dad's hand. "Your mother has come out of surgery. We repaired her spleen and kidney. She also broke her tibia in two places."

"But she'll be okay?"

Dr. Stuhl frowned. "It won't be an easy recovery, considering her age. But, yes, I believe she will be fine in time."

"Oh, thank goodness," Dad said, and I could see the worry drain from his face.

"What can you tell me about your mother's history of reckless behavior?"

"Excuse me?" Dad said.

"Mrs. Mortimer's records indicate that this is her third visit here this year. Broken collarbone, sprained wrist, lacerations on her legs."

"Her *third*?" Dad said again.

"There must be some mistake," Mom said, standing next to my father and putting her book on the waiting room chair.

"I only mention it because wandering off in harm's way can be an early sign of dementia."

"Dementia?" Mom asked, with no attempt to hide her distress. Her mouth dropped open and she snatched her glasses off her neck. "Bizzy may be suffering from many things, but I assure you, dementia is not one of them."

Dr. Stuhl hardened her look. "Well, I recommend you keep an eye on her, regardless. It's a wonder she wasn't more seriously injured." Dr. Stuhl began to walk away. She turned back toward us. She looked at me, tapping her pen on her clipboard.

"Oh, and she has asked repeatedly to see someone named Sweet Pea," Dr. Stuhl said. "Any idea who *that* might be?"

"Lizzy," Mom said, pointing to me.

Dr. Stuhl waved me toward her. Dad began to walk to Dr. Stuhl with me. "Only the girl," she snapped. "It was a specific request. So if you'll follow me, Lizzy Sweet Pea, I'll take you to her."

I popped up from my seat, hopeful both answers and a Bizzy-on-the-mend were waiting for me down the long white hallway.

†he Making of an Epiphany

Has something ever happened that made you think about everything else in a new light, Mrs. Tweedy? I know in literature it's called an epiphany—usually this aha moment near the end of a story when the character learns something. It's kind of like the character puts on colored glasses that make everything look completely altered. In books it usually happens all at once.

After I heard Vivienne talk about the Last Descendant in the cemetery and then saw my first death-specter, there's no doubt that I had the different-colored-glasses feeling. But things changed gradually. It was more like a leaky faucet filling up a salad bowl one drip at a time.

The first shift was my perspective on my grandma Bizzy.

When I saw her after her surgery, she looked older. Frail, even. Her arms seemed skinnier and there were tubes coming out of them. One of her legs was in a cast and the other was wrapped in a thin hospital blanket. Her hands were splotchy, black and blue. The worst thing was how pale she was.

But there was this other part of her, something in her face that was transformed. It was like the Emily Dickinson poem Bizzy had quoted. Underneath the wrinkles and bandages, there stirred something else entirely. Maybe it was the defiance that comes with keeping a big secret. Perhaps it was a time-tested toughness shining through. Or it could have been subtle resilience that I'd never noticed before.

She heard me come in. Her eyes snapped open.

"Sweet Pea!" Bizzy exclaimed, sucking in air. "If you aren't a sight for sore eyes!" Her raspy voice sounded as if she'd been yelling all morning.

"How are you feeling?" I asked, venturing gingerly into the room.

"Don't be a dang fool! Come on over here and give your grandmamma a Yankee dime." That was Bizzy's way of asking for a kiss. As she raised her arm to beckon me to her, she winced in pain. She tried to cover it up by smiling widely at me.

"How are they treating you?"

"Here's a pearl a' wisdom for ya: only thing that's a bigger threat to life than death is a hospital."

I grimaced.

"I don't wanna see that forlorn look, Lizzy. 'Fraid my ol' body won't heal up as quick as it used to, but I'll be fine. Ya hear me?"

Bizzy patted the side of the bed, signaling me to climb on the bed with her. I sat down gently.

She put her cold hand over mine and tried to raise herself up.

"We're gonna hafta be quick, Sweet Pea," Bizzy said, breathing more heavily. She looked around the room nervously. "Close the door."

I followed her command and then returned to my place beside her on the bed. Bizzy grabbed the sippy cup from the tray across her bed, took a swallow from its fluorescent plastic straw, then cleared her throat.

"Seen any more death-specters?"

"No," I said, shuddering at the thought of another one. Bizzy studied me. I could hear the clock on the wall ticking the seconds away.

"Was it because of me that Jodi almost got hit by the car?" I asked finally. "She wouldn't have been in the street if I hadn't called out her name."

"You were goin' to warn her about your specter, weren't ya?" Bizzy asked sympathetically.

"I wanted to watch her and make sure she didn't cross the street without looking," I explained. "I wasn't going to tell her anything specific."

"I shudda explained it better. The thing with a specter . . . ," Bizzy said, struggling to find the right words. "The thing with a death-specter is that tellin' the subject of the specter about what'll happen or tryin' to hint they should change somethin' that might kill 'em has the opposite effect you want it to. Try an' tell a person to avoid a place she's s'posed to meet her death and that's exactly where she'll end up."

"Why?" I asked.

"Fate," Bizzy said, "adjusts quicker 'n a hungry dog can lick a dish."

"So why do we see death-specters if we can't do anything about them?"

"There's always somethin' to be done! Think of a death-specter like it's a garden weed. You cut what's above the surface, and it'll grow back in no time, bigger 'n ever. So you gotta get at the root to make sure it's gone for good. When we've got time on our side, the best we can do is figure out the root of why the person ends up in harm's way and fix that." Bizzy took a breath and continued. "I certainly don't have all the answers, Lizzy-Loo. But as far as I can tell, we only see unjust deaths. Deaths that are unnatural. If we figure out the *why*, we can do something about 'em."

It sort of made sense, but the heavy responsibility of it all was overwhelming.

"When will it happen again?" I asked.

"Depends on the person," Bizzy said, shrugging her shoulders.

"How often do you see them?"

"When you get to a certain age, you stop havin' 'em as frequently."

"How did you know that it was going to be my first today?"

"The first is always on a girl's fourteenth Halloween—the day the world of spirits connects with the world of mortals," Bizzy said matter-of-factly.

"So, I'll definitely see more?" I asked, my anxiety growing.

"There will be more names on my hand?" Bizzy looked at me and her eyes shifted back and forth in their sockets. I had never seen her so uncertain.

"There will be more, yes," she said with her head down.

"It can be anyone?"

"I only see the names of those I care about," Bizzy said.

"That little girl from the accident . . . in the black dress. Who was she?" I thought of the tiny girl with the white hair. Her unearthly scream had given me chills down my spine.

"That weren't no girl at all. That was a screamin' banshee."

"A screaming *what*?" I couldn't stomach the thought that there was more to this new life I had to try to understand. It was too much.

"Banshees . . . are creatures from beyond sent to usher souls from this world to the next," Bizzy said.

"So the girl was a spirit? Like the grim reaper or something? Because she sure didn't look like a grim reaper."

Bizzy closed her eyes, sighing. "The thing about banshees is," she began, "they're escorts who come to usher a newly dead soul from this world. Whenever we save someone who was previously scheduled to pass on, a banshee arrives, like usual. Only, because we've saved the life, there is no soul to collect. A banshee is like a petulant child in that way. If it don't get what it was sent after—the soul of the recently departed person—it throws a tantrum. Turns into a fiend. When this happens, banshees let off that piercing scream. But it's not just painful for us, Sweet Pea, it's more than that."

"What do you mean?"

"For Hands a' Fate like you and me, a banshee's scream is deadly," Bizzy said quietly. I let Bizzy's sentence sink in for a few seconds.

"Deadly?" I questioned, shocked by the realization I had another thing to be afraid of. "But it's a small child . . . how is that even possible?"

"Banshees may look like small children to you or me, Lizzy, but I assure you, they ain't of this world and they are very dangerous."

"How do you *know* that the scream is deadly?"

Bizzy looked down for a moment. "Your great-grandmamma, my mama . . . she . . . well, she was killed by the howl of a banshee."

"*What?*" I said, baffled. Life as a Hand of Fate was sounding even more dismaying.

"Saw it with my own two eyes when I was a little older than you. Your father will tell you his grandmamma died of a heart attack. That's what the doctors said. But that weren't it."

"Why didn't you and I die when the banshee started screaming?"

"Takes 'bout a minute. You destroyed it before then," Bizzy said matter-of-factly.

"I did?"

"With the mirra. See, banshees are like ghosts and have no soul themselves, and a mirra reflects a person's soul. If you force a banshee to look at itself in one, it'll be reduced to nothin' more than its most basic element—for the banshees, that's the sands a' time." Bizzy looked at me with concern. "I'm not tellin' you this to scare you, Sweet Pea, but so you'll know to be on the lookout if a situation like that ever arises again. Do ya understand?"

I understood all right: Avoid Banshees at all costs. Still, it seemed like all this was more than a "situation." It was my life from now on. I thought about which question to ask next.

"Bizzy, what does it mean when you cut a person's thread of life?"

All at once, Bizzy's face changed. Her eyes narrowed. "Where did you hear 'bout that?" she asked, her voice cold.

I sensed I had hit on something. I pressed on. "Is Agatha a Hand of Fate, too? Is she the sorceress that gave us this power? Is that why you visit her?"

"Not exactly," Bizzy said. I waited for her to go on, but she didn't.

"There has to be more to all of this than we just have this gift and that's that, right? Do you know her sister, Vivienne? Is she who we got this from?"

Bizzy gasped. She gripped the side rails of her hospital bed. "How did you come by that name, Sweet Pea?"

"Two days ago a woman named Vivienne was visiting Agatha at the cemetery," I said, alarmed at Bizzy's reaction. "Jodi and I overheard them talking about the Last Descendant and Doomsday and then Vivienne came outside and touched our heads. Jodi didn't remember any of it. But I did."

"Though she may be able to control your body, because you are a Hand a' Fate, Vivienne le Mort's powers will never work on your mind." There was something in Bizzy's voice I'd never heard before. It was dread.

"So you know who Vivienne is? You lied to me about why you've been visiting Agatha, didn't you?"

Bizzy deliberated for a few moments. She looked down at her hospital gown.

"Yes, I lied, Sweet Pea," Bizzy said, her voice spiced with regret. The machines behind her continued beeping monotonously. "And I swear I won't ever lie again. I'll tell you everythin' I know." She looked at me with her brimming, moss-colored eyes. "But if you did see Vivienne le Mort here in Crabapple, then we're all in mortal danger. So I need you to think real hard on it and tell me precisely what happened that day in the cemetery."

Fragments

If I had to guess your number-one grammar pet peeve, Mrs. Tweedy, I would say it's sentence fragments. You really dislike it when a sentence lacks a subject, verb, or both. Maybe there's a bright side, though. At least in an English paper, you can go back and edit a fragment to express a complete thought. In life, when a thought is interrupted, there's often not much that can be done to correct it.

I was almost finished explaining what I'd seen in the cemetery, about to launch into a flurry of questions for Bizzy, when the door to the hospital room swung wide open. Mom came in, holding a bouquet of lilies—Bizzy's favorite flower. Dad trailed behind, fiddling with his newsboy hat in his hands.

"We came to check on how you girls were doing," Mom said, sweeping into the room, placing the flowers in a vase by the window.

"Rita, you shouldn't have," Bizzy said. Darn right, Mom shouldn't have. I was right at a crucial point in my conversation with Bizzy. I wanted them to leave immediately.

"It was no trouble at all," Mom said, adjusting Bizzy's movable tray and cleaning it with a sanitary wipe.

"They hire people to do that for me," Bizzy said, frowning at Mom's efforts. "How long am I in for, Phillip?" Bizzy asked.

"They want to keep you overnight."

"For cryin' out loud!"

"Have you read *How Green Was My Valley*?" Mom asked, taking a thick paperback out of her bag and putting it on Bizzy's tray. "You're going to need some entertainment while you're here, I know, and it's such an easy book to get lost in . . . I thought it also might appeal to your Welsh roots."

Bizzy shoved the book off the tray. It hit the floor with a thud. She folded her arms defiantly over her chest. "Rita, I don't want to read, *you hear me*? I want to talk to my grand-daughter. Alone."

Every eye in the room shifted to me. Mom bent over and picked *How Green Was My Valley* off the floor. She gently placed it back on Bizzy's tray, her face shadowed with defeat.

There was a knock at the door. A nurse entered the room.

"I'm afraid that Dr. Stuhl has instructed me to clear the room of visitors. The patient needs her rest."

"I'm no chi-ull!" Bizzy exclaimed.

"It's okay, Mother," Dad said, grabbing her wrist tenderly. "We should be going, anyway. We'll be back later to check on you." He leaned in and kissed Bizzy on the forehead. "Lizzy, too," he added, smiling nervously. "After school."

"A few shackles and bars and this place'd be forced to call

itself a prison!" With that, Bizzy closed her eyes. Dad, Mom, and the nurse filed out of the room.

Soon, I was the only one left with Bizzy.

"No need to fret, Sweet Pea," Bizzy whispered across the room. "Remember what I wrote in my note."

"Okay," I said, unsure of what I was supposed to remember.

Dad poked his head in. "Ready to go?"

"Yeah," I said, garnering a wink from Bizzy as I left the room.

Though Mom wanted me to go to school, I'd had no trouble convincing Dad I was sick. When he dropped me off at home, he said Mom would swing by to check on me during her free period. Despite Bizzy's assurances that there was nothing to worry about, I wasn't convinced. I was convinced, however, that the key to it all was Vivienne le Mort. In my judgment, there was only one person who could tell me exactly who she was: Agatha Cantare. I did the math. I had an hour until Mom would arrive at the house—plenty of time to get to the cemetery and back.

When Drake's black Ford truck pulled up next to me as I made my way to Cemetery Hill, I viewed it as an unwelcome interruption of my quest for information. Of course, back then, I had no way of knowing Drake Westfall was essential to every answer I was seeking.

Drake got his license when he turned sixteen a few weeks before. Since then, I'd seen his shiny black pickup all over town. I stopped jogging as Drake rolled down his window.

"Hey," he said, looking concerned. "Everything okay?"

"I'm fine," I said.

"What about your grandmother? Did everything go all right?"

I felt my cheeks redden. *Of course he meant my grandmother.* "Bizzy's out of surgery and doing well," I explained.

"Good to hear," Drake said. His concern was off-putting. Even in the cloudy morning, his eyes gleamed. I tried not to look at them.

"Do you volunteer every morning at the hospital?" I asked, looking down at the door of his truck. I wasn't any good at chitchat.

"Someone needed to switch with me today. I'm normally there at night, three times a week."

"Oh." I wondered how he managed to squeeze volunteering shifts into his schedule. Between captaining the water polo team and working his way into the heart of every girl at Crabapple High School, Drake Westfall was a very busy guy.

"Do you want a ride to school?" Drake leaned over and used his long, muscular arm to unlock the passenger door.

"It's illegal for you to give anyone under twenty a ride during your first twelve months with a license." I sounded like such a goody-goody referencing the California Vehicle Code, I had the urge to cover my own mouth so I couldn't say anything else. I was glad Jodi wasn't around to give me a hard time.

"I won't tell if you won't," Drake teased, smiling.

"I'm not going to school." I instantly realized how odd it

must've sounded to Drake considering I was headed in the direction of school.

"Well, I can drop you off wherever you're going," Drake offered.

"Thanks, but it's really okay. You're going to be late," I urged.

"Ditching school while following the letter of the law . . . you're not an easy person to figure out, Lizzy."

I had to get out of there before I said another boneheaded thing.

"Yeah, I guess. Later." Without waiting for his response, I cut through the path next to the Ramblings' yard, trying to banish any memory of how idiotic I'd sounded.

When I spotted the row of white fir trees along the border of the cemetery's iron fence, I quickened my pace. I wasn't sure what to expect, only that I had to figure out exactly *who* Agatha and her sister were and what they had to do with Bizzy and me.

Crabapple Cemetery was not a popular place on Halloween. There was no one there. I trudged up the grassy hill, trying to take the straightest path I could between the large tombstones clustered near the top of the hill.

For a moment outside the doorway of Agatha's cottage, I hesitated, gathering the courage to knock.

I heard something. The voice behind the wood door was an eerily familiar one: the harsh tone of Vivienne le Mort. My first instinct was to run, but the thought of missing an information-gathering opportunity kept me on the porch. If Vivienne wanted to hurt me, she could've done so on my last visit to the cemetery.

Trembling, I snuck around to the side window and glanced in. Agatha stood in the middle of the room facing the window, dressed in her white linen shirt and trousers. Vivienne le Mort, in her floor-length black robe, had her back to me. The two women were close enough to touch one another. Vivienne towered over her sister.

I bent down, staying low to the ground. This time, I wasn't taking a chance on being discovered. I could no longer see inside, but I overheard every word.

"The Sanchez girl's thread was cut. She was supposed to die. And yet, she lives."

"Perhaps you made a mistake, Vivienne." Agatha's voice floated out through the open window. I wiggled my toes, making sure I wasn't frozen.

"Mistake!" Vivienne said, angry. I imagined the glow of her flaming eyes. "I have not made one single mistake in *thousands* of years."

"I do not have the answers you seek," Agatha said calmly.

"This is Morgan's doing, I am sure of it!" Vivienne said. "*How* is she doing it? Has she been here in search of the Last Descendant or his Keeper?"

"Our sister has not set foot here, which is more than I can say for you. In fact, if you do not leave right this instant—"

"Fine. You may think me foolish, Agatha. But I will be

watching *very carefully*. If I so much as sense Morgan meddling with my work, mark my words, I shall cut every single thread in this pitiful town first, and ask questions later," Vivienne hissed.

"Do that and you may alter the very fate you have been so desperately waiting for," Agatha said calmly.

"I doubt you will be so smug when Doomsday finally does arrive," Vivienne responded.

When she finished speaking, a small black whirlwind rushed out the window directly above me and up toward the cloudy sky. I blinked my eyes once and the murkiness was gone. Other than the faint rustle of the white firs, my own shallow breathing was the only sound in the cemetery. When I heard Agatha's voice again, I held my breath.

My body still shudders when I recall her saying my name out loud.

"You may come in now if it suits you, Elizabeth Mortimer," she said. "Vivienne has gone."

She must've known I was outside her window the entire time. At that moment, I intended to find out how. I made my way back around the cottage. Turning the knob, I pushed open the door.

The living room was empty. I tiptoed in as if I hadn't been invited.

Agatha's living room didn't have much character. There was the empty rocking chair, a fireplace, and a worn loveseat by the window with a stack of books piled next to it. Most of the books were paperbacks, but at the top of the stack there was a book that was quite different from all the others. It was a thin leather-bound volume that looked very old. Its title and author, *The Last Descendant* by Merlin Ambrosius, were engraved in silver letters across the front. I couldn't stop looking at it. Finally, I willed my gaze away from its cover.

A large gold-framed painting hung on the wall opposite the fireplace. I walked toward it to get a closer look. In the middle of a white-capped ocean, there was an island, covered with huge apple trees.

"It's the Isle of Avalon. Stunning, isn't it?"

I whipped around. Agatha, still barefoot in her white linen, sat in her rocking chair. I had no idea whether she'd come in quietly or just appeared.

She must have recognized the concern on my face.

"There's no need to be alarmed. I mean you no harm," she said. Her gray eyes matched her two neat braids. She motioned to the couch facing the rocking chair with her hand. I sat down on its edge. I didn't plan on staying long enough to get comfortable.

"I don't believe we've officially met," Agatha continued, clearing her throat. "I am Agatha the Enchantress, of the Isle of Avalon."

"Nice to meet you," I said, with more reflex than feeling. Mom would've been pleased to know that, though terrified, I hadn't abandoned my good manners.

"You had your first death-specter, didn't you?" Agatha said. "That's how you saved the girl."

"You mean Jodi?" I asked.

"Yes."

"Are you a Hand of Fate, too?"

"Absolutely not. I am one of the Seven Sisters of Avalon and a Lady of the Lake." Agatha's eyes had a youthful sheen to them. Though she had gray hair, her skin was as smooth and flawless as a freshly painted wall. She seemed as if she'd just awakened from a long, restful nap.

"How do you know about my death-specter?" I asked.

"That is unimportant. What is important, however, is that I am now fairly certain my sister Morgan le Faye is responsible for sending these specters to you." Agatha rocked slightly in her chair.

"Who?"

Agatha looked startled. "Has your grandmother told you *nothing* of the Seven Sisters of Avalon?"

"I only found out I was a Hand of Fate a few hours ago."

Agatha, displeased, shook her head. "You are a direct descendant of Morgan le Faye. Her half-mortal daughter was the first of your kind hundreds upon hundreds of years ago. Whatever gifts you have, you inherited from her."

"What happened to Morgan? Where is she?" I asked. My mind couldn't connect any of the dots Agatha was providing.

Agatha's eyes drifted past my own. I traced her gaze and realized she was staring at the painting on the wall above me. "I imagine Morgan is where she was when I left a very, very long time ago," Agatha said, almost as if talking to herself. "The Isle of Avalon."

"How do I get there?"

"You do not. Even someone like you, a mortal who has the blood of Avalon running through her veins, can only set foot there by invitation, as it is the gateway between this world and the next."

"Well, if this Morgan woman, er, your sister, is the one who's sending the death-specters, I have to find a way to reach her."

"I will repeat what I said to your grandmother when she came here asking for my sister: I cannot summon Morgan, I do not communicate with Morgan, and I have *never* been able to control Morgan." Agatha folded her arms in her lap.

Morgan le Faye was clearly a dead end. I attempted to shift the conversation elsewhere.

"Vivienne le Mort is another of your sisters, then?"

"Yes," Agatha said.

"How old are you all?"

"The Seven Sisters are older than you can possibly fathom." I felt Agatha was being purposefully vague.

"What did Vivienne mean, just now, when she said that she was going to cut every single thread in Crabapple?" Once I asked that question, others followed easily. "And who is this last Pendragon person she seems so obsessed with? Is she fighting with Morgan?"

Agatha's face grew pale. She brought both hands to her face and held her head in them. When she removed them, there were tears in her clear gray eyes. "The dreadful rift between Morgan and Vivienne began the moment I told my sisters of the vision instructing us to find a suitable Keeper to watch over Arthur. My visions have brought me and those I love nothing but agony. Now that Morgan and Vivienne have clashed over the prophecy regarding the Last Descendant, I will not place myself in the middle again." She said it like a declaration and then paused, before adding, "If Doomsday arrives, so be it."

"Okay . . . well then, what *is* Doomsday? If you could just explain what Vivienne le Mort is after, maybe—"

"Enough," Agatha said, putting her hand up. Her voice hardened. "I cannot help you or your grandmother."

"I'm not asking for help, I just want to know what you know."

It turned out to be the absolute wrong thing to say. Agatha's expression changed from sad to angry. "What I *know*? What I know? If you had any idea of the things I know, it would utterly devastate you!" Agatha stood up. Her jaw tightened as her voice rose. "What I *know*, you foolish child, is that if Vivienne does discover your abilities, she will destroy you . . . what I *know* is that you had better think very carefully about the choices that will soon confront you."

"What does that mean?" I said, trying not to cower as Agatha inched closer to me.

"I will not get involved," she said coldly. "You and your grandmother are never to return here." As she finished, white fog seemed to shoot out of every one of Agatha's pores.

Soon, it filled the entire room.

The vapor was so thick, I could barely see my hand when

I held it out in front of me. I stumbled around the cottage, choking on the thick air. When I crashed into the stack of books by the couch, an idea seized me. *The Last Descendant* hadn't left my thoughts completely since I'd seen it a few minutes before. I followed my instincts. After all, Agatha hadn't provided me with any answers, but that didn't mean I had to leave the cottage completely empty-handed. I grabbed the old silver-engraved book, now on the floor, and tucked it under my arm before rushing outside.

I looked at my watch. I had only minutes until Mom would arrive to check on me. Sprinting toward home, clutching *The Last Descendant*, I felt relief with each step distancing me from Agatha's gloom-filled cottage. I hoped (in vain as it turned out) that I would never encounter Vivienne le Mort again.

I was in bed before Mom arrived. Because of the sprint home, I'd managed to heat up my forehead to the point that Mom was sure I had a fever. She tucked me in and placed the book she'd given to me in the waiting room, *David Copperfield*, on my nightstand.

"Books are lighthouses erected in the great sea of time," she said.

"What?"

"It's a famous quote—another way of saying the solution to every one of life's problems can be found within the pages of a good book. Reading might make you feel better and *David Copperfield* was Dickens's favorite of all his books. That must count for something." Mom leaned over and kissed me on the forehead, exactly like she used to do when I was a small child. "Call me if you need anything."

She tiptoed out and shut the door. I had to remind myself I wasn't really sick, because when I thought about the morning's events, I swore the room was spinning—swirling with all the things I'd never heard of before I'd first laid eyes on Vivienne le Mort. Death-specter. Morgan le Faye. The Mark of Arthur. Hand of Fate. Isle of Avalon. Banshees. Doomsday. The Thread of Life.

As soon as I heard Mom's car pull out of our driveway, I took *The Last Descendant* out from under my bed. I cracked open the book. I wasn't expecting Merlin Ambrosius's book to be a lighthouse in the sea of anything, really, but I did harbor the faint hope that it might shed a small lamp's worth of light on my growing pond of questions.

The Last Descendant, as it turned out, played a far simpler yet much more important role: it would be the book that changed everything.

Translations

I've never thanked you properly, Mrs. Tweedy, for letting us read Seamus Heaney's *Beowulf* instead of some Old English version. After all, there have been a lot of major improvements made to the English language in the last thousand years. "Reading is always an act of interpretation," you said when Opal's mother complained that we weren't reading the actual classics, adding that each person's "imagination creates a different translation."

There's no way I could possibly relate every detail of *The Last Descendant*, but maybe you should consider yourself fortunate. I'm not sure exactly what kind of English Merlin Ambrosius wrote it in, but I only understood it by reading very slowly and rereading some parts. I'll admit that some of it sounded familiar from the unit we did on myths and legends, but once I realized that one or more of the characters had some relationship to what's been happening here in Crabapple, it got a lot more interesting.

For better or worse, this is my translation—which is quite a bit shorter than the original. But it's like Bizzy always says: sometimes you gotta skip the salad and go straight for the meat and potatoes.

Around the beginning of time, seven sorceress sisters lived together on an island called Avalon. The Isle of Avalon, sometimes called Glastonbury or Elysium, was the gateway between the mortal world and the world of spirits. It sat in the middle of the sea, surrounded by a bank of clouds, thick with beautiful trees that bore the most delicious apples. Agatha the Enchantress, Vivienne le Mort, Nona, Argante, Morgan le Faye, Cathuba, and Fial all lived happily on the island, laughing, playing, and singing together. Avalon was a joyful, magical place and the sisters were the best of friends.

They also ate a lot of apples.

The Seven Sisters of Avalon, also known as Ladies of the Lake, enjoyed each other's company, but they also had a more serious pursuit. According to the story, they were the gatekeepers between the mortal and spirit worlds, guiding each soul's transition from one world to the next. The one inflexible rule was that the sisters could only leave the island or interact with mortals if they all agreed that destiny required it.

The wisest of the sisters was Agatha the Enchantress, known as the White Lady. She was Avalon's prophetess, who saw visions of the future in the waters of the Sooth Spring, the powerful oracle near the center of Avalon. Agatha advised the sisters, relying on her visions to settle the rare disputes between them.

The second sister, Nona, watched over the creation of life. As a gifted cook and farmer, she naturally controlled the fertility of the world and all creatures in it. Argante, the strongest of the sisters and a fierce warrior, was entrusted with watching over the vitality and vigor of the human body. Fial, responsible for the intellect and passion of mortals, was learned in all areas of knowledge and possessed impressive artistic talents. Cathuba was the most empathetic of the sisters, and her talents lay in her ability to communicate with every type of living creature—she concerned herself with mortals' interaction with the world around them.

The two most notorious sisters were Vivienne le Mort and Morgan le Faye. These two were entrusted with each mortal's thread of life. Every mortal's life—the amount of time and unique fate granted to each person from birth to death—was measured by his or her thread. Morgan le Faye was tasked with measuring each life and Vivienne with cutting it.

The two sisters worked together. Morgan would have a death-specter and Vivienne's cut would send a banshee to usher the mortal's soul through Avalon to its proper resting place. Quite simply, Morgan knew the *why* and the *when* of a death and Vivienne was responsible for the *how*.

The sisters were as beautiful as they were notorious. Morgan had waves of long black hair and piercing sea-foam eyes and wore a long red-hooded cloak and sandals made of gold. She had a reputation for being cold and calculating, preferring logic above all else.

Vivienne le Mort was the exact opposite of Morgan le

Faye in both temperament and appearance. The youngest of the sisters, Vivienne had flaxen hair and magenta eyes that clouded over when she grew angry. She wore a dark robe that set off her lovely golden hair and was known for her hair-trigger temper. She could go from calm to cruel in a matter of moments.

The Last Descendant explains that for many years, the sisters lived peacefully, never leaving Avalon. One day, Agatha the Enchantress had a vision that the mortal world's delicate balance between life and death, hope and despair, was in great danger. Agatha's vision required the sisters ensure that the mortal Arthur Pendragon become king. Among other things, they were to find a suitable Keeper for Arthur—a trustworthy and perceptive mortal who would alert the sisters to all potential dangers Arthur might encounter. Arthur, according to Avalon's oracle, was to guide civilization out of the Dark Ages. The righteousness of the selfless Arthur Pendragon, paired with Avalon's power over fate, would restore balance to the mortal world.

Vivienne and Morgan watched carefully over Arthur from his birth forward. Fial recruited one of the most powerful sorcerers in the land, Merlin the Magnificent, to be Arthur's tutor and advisor. Argante forged a sword for him called the Excaliber and trained him to use it to defeat men stronger than himself. Cathuba taught him of the world's natural order and how to tame every kind of beast.

Vivienne and Morgan oversaw his thread of life, ensuring he was protected as he grew and matured. After careful consideration, the sisters decided that Guinevere, the daughter of the dutiful King Leodengrance, should be appointed the mortal Keeper for Arthur. Guinevere was unusually intelligent, trustworthy, and altruistic. Her intelligence was matched only by her beauty, which caused people to confide in her and tell her all sorts of useful information.

The sisters permitted Fial and Morgan to travel from Avalon to convince Guinevere to accept this vital role as Arthur's Keeper. Arthur prospered as a knight, then as king, and brought peace and balance back to the land. He also fell deeply in love with Guinevere and made her his queen. Camelot, the castle and court of Arthur's empire, became a symbol of beauty and enlightenment.

Not too long after the establishment of Camelot, a deep schism developed between Morgan and Fial. The cause was a common one—familiar to spirits, gatekeepers, and mortals alike.

It was love, plain and simple.

Watching over Arthur necessitated journeys by the sisters from Avalon to this world. During these visits, though she knew it was forbidden, Morgan le Faye fell deeply in love with a mortal—a knight from King Arthur's Round Table. The knight had never met anyone as captivating as Morgan. Her trips became more frequent until she was spending very little time on Avalon. It was Fial who first discovered Morgan was having an affair with Sir Lancelot, by then the most famous knight of King Arthur's Round Table. Soon rumors spread that Sir Lancelot was having a relationship with someone in King Arthur's court. Many assumed that Lancelot was involved with Queen

Guinevere herself, which began to poison Arthur's trust in his queen and weaken her ability to protect him.

Fial tried to reason with Morgan, reminding her that the Seven Sisters of Avalon were only to visit the mortal world when a prophecy bid them to do so. But the change in Morgan had already taken hold. She complained about life on Avalon. She became restless and temperamental—quite unlike the logical, reasoned sorceress her sisters had known. She longed for Sir Lancelot and began to think the rumors about Lancelot and Guinevere were true. Finally, she fled Avalon permanently.

When the remaining sisters learned of Morgan's departure, they were concerned that the precise order they'd so carefully maintained was in extraordinary danger. With no one left to measure the threads of life, no one died at his or her proper time and the world's delicate balance was turned upside down. Arthur's kingdom fell into disarray, as wars raged with the Saxons to the north and the Romans to the south. The six remaining sisters decided that they would wait until Agatha received a vision in the Sooth Spring advising what course they should follow.

Vivienne, furious that Morgan had broken the vow between the sisters by leaving the island without consent, took matters into her own hands. She lured Merlin away from Arthur's side through trickery. And though it was not his time, she cut Sir Lancelot's thread in a fit of anger. Lancelot died shortly after, in a brutal battle on the Fields of Camlann. King Arthur, without his most powerful knight by his side or his sorcerer to safeguard him, struggled mightily on the battlefield. Meanwhile, a few villainous members of Arthur's court, convinced that Guinevere had committed adultery with Lancelot, made it known that they intended to punish the queen for her alleged misdeeds. As her final act as Arthur's Keeper before she fled Camelot in fear for her own life, Guinevere sent word to Avalon that the king was near death. Soon after, Agatha and Fial swooped in to take the injured king to Avalon. Arthur begged Fial and Agatha to find Guinevere and protect her, but Agatha explained that Guinevere was gone, and Arthur would never see her again.

When Fial and Agatha arrived back at Avalon with King Arthur, the other sisters were furious. Arthur was a mortal and did not belong on the island. Agatha explained that she was simply trying to fulfill the prophecy—Arthur needed to be safeguarded and bringing him to Avalon was the only way to heal him. Meanwhile, Morgan returned to the island after Lancelot's death, revealing to her sisters that she was now carrying Lancelot's child.

"We should cut the thread of Morgan's unborn as punishment for her actions," Vivienne said, seething.

The other sisters objected to such a severe punishment.

"Children have no place on the Isle of Avalon," Vivienne argued.

The disagreement caused a permanent rift between Morgan and Vivienne. Despite their initial misgivings, the other sisters knew that Vivienne was right—a half-mortal child had no place on Avalon.

In the end, the Seven Sisters agreed to a compromise called the Great Truce. Because no one else could do the work of Morgan and Vivienne, each would resume her job measuring and cutting the threads of mortals. Neither was ever to return to the mortal world. Morgan and Vivienne consented, but decided to inhabit different parts of the island, each viewing the other with contempt bordering on hatred.

As part of the Great Truce, once King Arthur had fully recovered and Morgan had the baby, all agreed that Arthur, his entourage, and the child were to set sail for the edge of the known world. They would start new lives in this unknown land.

Morgan, as punishment for disobeying the laws of Avalon, would only see her child in the brief moments after the baby was born, and then, never again. Agatha would sail with King Arthur to the new world, where she would remain to ensure neither Vivienne nor Morgan left Avalon and broke the terms of the Great Truce. If either sister ever set foot in the mortal world, Agatha would be able to sense a sister's presence and would travel immediately to Avalon and inform the other sisters.

The sisters decided it was the only way.

Several months later, when the mortal and spiritual worlds united during the Feast of Samhain, King Arthur and his court, along with Morgan's only child and Agatha the Enchantress, set out from Avalon for new lands.

Now, Mrs. Tweedy, that's as far as I got into the story. But it's not because I was bored. In fact, I gobbled up *The Last Descendant*, anxious to find out everything I could about King Arthur,

Agatha, and all the rest. Although it was difficult reading at first, it got easier as I went along. But when I got to the part about Arthur sailing away from Avalon, something happened. I couldn't read anymore.

I had my second death-specter.

But it wasn't simply my second death-specter. It was the particular death-specter that one resident of Avalon had been anticipating for many years. It was also the reason Merlin Ambrosius had written *The Last Descendant* in the first place.

Redundancy and Repetition

Maybe I'm way off base to keep comparing life and literature, but each is supposed to resemble and inform the other, right? I know redundancy is high on most teachers' What-Not-to-Do List, Mrs. Tweedy. In fact, I think you said that it's the sign of an "undisciplined" writer. But the fact of the matter is, life is pretty redundant. Even when the facts change, some experiences feel so much like other stuff that's happened, it's hard to tell everything apart. Things repeat. Then they repeat again. People try to convince themselves that things won't repeat yet again, but they often do.

There are the obvious things in life that always feel the same—sunrises, trips to the dentist, the piercing sound of an alarm clock in the morning, stubbing a toe. You'll have to take my word for it when I tell you that death-specters are the same way. When I had my second death-specter, the beginning of it felt almost exactly the same as the first.

Then it got much worse.

I remember the sentence I was reading when the page went blank: *King Arthur and his passengers sailed from Avalon on the eve of the Feast of Samhain.*

At first, I thought the bulb in my bedside lamp blew out.

I blinked hard and refocused on the page.

The letters had disappeared completely.

I gasped.

I slammed the book shut.

I closed my eyes as thoughts raced around and crashed against the inside of my skull. Beads of sweat formed on my forehead and I went into all-out-panic mode. I stared at the plain leather cover of the book.

I pressed my elbows to my chest, wishing that this was a dream. My arm settled on my collarbone and I heard the soft crinkle of Bizzy's note in the pocket of my shirt.

I pulled it out.

Write it all down. Dates, pictures. Everything. We'll deal with it together.

I knew exactly what Bizzy wanted me to do. *We'll deal with it together,* she'd written. After what Agatha had told me, I wasn't sure if I wanted to deal with it at all . . . but I'd decide on all that later.

I opened up the book to the page I'd been reading. This time, there was no normal book print. There was large, bold print at the very top of the first page.

DRAKE WESTFALL'S BODY DISCOVERED AT CANNERY

The entirety of Crabapple was stunned Monday by the loss of Drake Westfall, honor student and captain of the Crabapple Knights water polo team. At four in the afternoon on Tuesday, officials announced that Westfall's body had been discovered among the rubble of the burned-down Del Monte Cannery. Investigators have not yet determined the cause of the fire, though some locals reported hearing a large explosion in the early morning. An autoposy will be performed. Local authorities have not ruled out foul play, though the preliminary cause of death is believed to be smoke inhalation. Westfall was beloved by many and is survived by his parents, Mark and Melody, and his older brother, Damon. Memorial services will be held this Friday, December 18. The family has requested that, in lieu of flowers, donations be made to the Westfall Memorial Scholarship Fund.

I squeezed my eyes shut once again. I counted to ten, hoping I could write all of it off as a very bad dream.

When I opened them again, the letters were still there, floating in the middle of the blank page, reporting the death of Drake Westfall. Then I saw something gradually appearing on the other side.

A faded color photograph.

Of Drake Westfall.

It was his water polo picture. He looked tan. His hair was dark, with a golden shine to it from a constant barrage of chlorine and sun. Drake was smiling his perfect white smile. He

looked very alive. I tried to swallow but found my throat closing up. I remembered the look in Drake's eyes when he handed
me Bizzy's note. My eyeballs bounced from the words in the
book to the note. Without thinking, I rushed to my desk and
grabbed the first thing I could—my copy of the *Crabapple
Intermediate Yearbook*. Frantic, I flipped to a blank page in the
back and began jotting down notes.

·Drake Westfall, Del Monte Cannery—body found
·Explosion?—Early morning on Tuesday
·Official announcement, 4 p.m., body discovered
·Authorities think foul play???
·December 18—Funeral

As I read the words about Drake Westfall again, making
sure I didn't miss anything, they faded away.

"Come back!" I shouted, as if the words could hear me.
Within a few seconds, they were gone completely. I shut *The
Last Descendant* again and then opened it slowly, peeking in at
the pages as if I was spying on them.

The headline had disappeared. In plain text, there it was
again: *King Arthur and his passengers sailed from Avalon on the eve
of the Feast of Samhain.*

The first sentence of the page I'd been reading reappeared.
In fact, all the words, the regular words from the book, were
back. I flipped through every page. All were intact. The image
had come and gone in a matter of minutes.

I'm not sure how long I lay there on the bed, *The Last*

Descendant in one arm, my *Crabapple Intermediate Yearbook* in the other, in a complete daze. My mind had blown a fuse. I needed to reboot. It was all too much.

My head felt like a hot air balloon that was about to lift off and separate from my body. I tried to calm down.

I felt a slight tingle at the base of my left palm. I remembered the Hands of Fate and slowly lifted my hand within view.

The crimson letters were back. The same as before. Bright as day. Like someone had taken a tiny hot poker and branded a name there.

Drake Westfall. *The* Drake Westfall.

If someone saw Drake's name on my hand, I'd never hear the end of it. Instantly, what Bizzy had said about death-specters came to mind. *A Hand of Fate only has death-specters about people she cares about*, she'd said. Sure, I had a few conversations with him, but I didn't really even *know* Drake Westfall, yet alone *care* about him.

Or did I?

Had Jodi's teasing in the hospital been closer to the truth than I wanted to admit? Though I was alone, I became self-conscious, covering up Drake's name with my other hand. I had no way of knowing then that my death-specter about Drake had nothing to do with our immediate pasts and everything to do with our futures.

So I continued to rack my brain for possible reasons why I might have had a death-specter about Drake. When we were little, before he left for boarding school, Drake and I used to play together. But that was only because he lived across the street and Mom wanted to make sure I was properly socialized since I was an only child.

Restless, I went to my window overlooking Earle Avenue. Directly across the street stood the Steins' house, named Let the Good Chimes Roll because of the forty or so wind chimes that hung from the porch and two large elm trees in the front yard. Drake's old stone house, Happy Landing, was next to it on the south side, opposite The House of Six Gables. I pressed my face to the windowpane, peering across at the window on the second floor that I knew was Drake's.

That's when I spotted her in the middle of the street, standing there, motionless.

Though I couldn't see her bloodred eyes, her long flaxen hair and dark robe identified her immediately. I was beginning to think Vivienne le Mort was following me. Or was I following her? Vivienne seemed focused on the same point I'd been staring at moments ago—the window of Drake's room. I ran downstairs, unsure of what I was going to say to Vivienne le Mort once I met her in the street.

†HE ARCHE†YPE

When I finally reached the street, out of breath, nobody was in sight. Vivienne le Mort was gone and I wondered if I'd really seen her at all. My eyes turned upward to Drake's window. I raised my hand to my face. The name was still there, in red letters.

DRAKE WESTFALL

I ran my index finger over each of the bumpy letters, trying to rub them off. But it was useless. I pulled the sleeve of my hoodie over my palm as I thought about what I knew about Drake and what it meant that his name was now on my hand.

Let's just say that if an archetype of "popular" exists in Crabapple, Mrs. Tweedy, it's Drake Westfall. Everyone likes Drake. Seniors, teachers, Mayor Gilroy, Kenny the Quack (Crabapple's eccentric cafeteria worker). Other people's mothers fawn over him. He has dimples and a perfectly symmetric smile. He was recently elected sophomore class president. It's sickening, really.

Most people who have that much success turn into total

jerks—but not Drake. He isn't just a jock. See, Mrs. Tweedy, I have a theory about Drake I started developing the day I saw him in the park with Roger Riley.

I'm sure you know who Roger is. Everyone knows him. He's undersized with straggly shoulder-length hair and is, by most accounts, a little odd. Not like I'm one to talk, but Mom says a lot of Roger's oddities are a result of his Asperger's. Mom says Roger's brain isn't wired like yours or mine. When he talks, his words come out in this strange syncopated rhythm.

Roger loves trees more than anyone I know—to the point that he'll stop in the middle of the sidewalk on his way to class and point at a tree and rattle on about it.

"The *Acacia pendula* or weeping acacia," Roger said on the first day of school this past September, looking up at one of the newly planted trees in the quad, "requires clay, loam, or sand as soil, grows at an average rate of twenty-four inches per season, and is not native to California."

You can never be sure who he's talking to, but behind his quizzical brown eyes, Roger's harboring a tree encyclopedia. It's pretty amazing. Still, high school can be a cruel place for someone like Roger, because although he's a lot smarter than most of the people here, he's also a very easy target. A couple of times, I've seen Drake stick up for Roger when Garrett Edmonds (who is, by all accounts, a bully of the worst order) was taunting him.

When we don't want to go straight home after school, Jodi and I head to Cedar Tree Park, named after the grove of cedar trees at the top of the largest hill there. Early in the year, when everyone was still buzzing about Drake's return to Crabapple, we saw Drake and Roger at the park.

The strange thing was that they were flying kites. Or one kite, to be exact. Jodi and I were sitting on a bench on the hill overlooking the grassy field below, the ocean at our backs, when we spotted Drake. He was walking away from Roger with a large, multicolored triangle kite in his hands. Roger held onto two spools of string that were attached on both sides of the kite Drake held. After putting thirty feet between himself and Roger, Drake tossed the kite up in the air. It took off, climbing higher as it danced in the wind. Drake ran back to Roger and carefully showed him how to manipulate the two strings to keep the kite flying. Soon Roger had his arms extended straight out, flailing as they gripped the two kite strings, while he shuffled his feet back and forth in an odd dance. The rainbow-colored kite cut across the sky, flipping over, diving, and then rising once more. Drake clapped enthusiastically with each trick Roger pulled off. Roger grinned in response.

"Drake Westfall *flies kites*?" Jodi said, her voice disbelieving as she sat next to me on the bench.

"What's wrong with that?" I asked.

"Other than the fact that the last time I flew a kite, I was about five . . . nothing, I guess," Jodi added sarcastically.

"For someone who prides herself on thinking the uncool is cool, you seem kind of judgmental about kite flyers."

Jodi arched an eyebrow and considered my argument.

"You know what?" She paused. "You're right. And bonus points go to Drake for hanging out with Roger. He's definitely a lot more interesting than the meatheads Drake hangs out with at school."

Jodi and I must've watched Drake and Roger fly that kite for at least forty-five minutes. The push and pull of the strings, the slashing angles of the kite, the way the kite would get so small that it looked like nothing more than a discolored pixel on the blue display of sky—it was transfixing.

My theory even before I knew what I know now, I guess, was that although Drake was the prototype of the popular jock, he was also more than that.

Drake Westfall was capable of totally surprising you.

I doubt I would've been able to ignore any death-specter, and I was absolutely certain I couldn't ignore one about Drake.

Once I was back in the house after I couldn't find Vivienne le Mort in the street, I crammed the *Crabapple Intermediate Yearbook* in my backpack, then headed out into the backyard. My old fifteen-speed rested against the back wood fence. The bottom bracket clicked as I wheeled it through the back gate. I figured I'd better put on the helmet hanging from the handlebars. I always hated wearing it, but I'd be much less conspicuous that way. Or, at the very least, I'd be law abiding (consistency has to count for something, right?). I headed down to Ocean Boulevard toward the hospital and Bizzy.

Normally, I loved bike riding. The feeling I always got

when I was riding with the wind whipping around me was pure happiness. Though most of my friends had stopped riding their bikes to school, walking or getting a ride instead, I couldn't give it up.

It was one of the things that Jodi and I bonded over. She's even more into bikes than I am. In fact, she has her own "fixie," which is a lightweight single-gear bike that lacks the ability to coast. The pedals go as fast as you're going. There are no brakes on it, either, which means it's superdangerous. Which is just fine by Jodi. Her fixie is painted hot pink and the wheel rims are bright white.

Some afternoons, if we don't go to Cedar Tree Park or the cemetery, Jodi and I ride our bikes to the beach and lie on the sand for a little while before heading home. Most mornings, I ride solo. I usually put in my headphones and play Jodi's latest mix while coasting down Delores Avenue. It's my favorite part of the day. If I pick up enough speed, I feel like I might E.T. it right off the ground.

I estimated it would only take about seven minutes to arrive at the hospital. My estimate may have been dead on, but it seemed like twenty.

It was the middle of the school day and I was obviously not in school. So I kept my head down and pedaled on the uneven sidewalk through town—past the Rip Tide Inn, past Miss Mora's Market, through the town square, and toward the hospital. As I zipped past Crabapple Lens & Camera and the Camelot Theater, I tried to keep breathing.

Each time I heard a car approaching, my heart felt like it might try to save itself by tearing through my rib cage, sprouting legs of its own, and running for safety.

As soon as I saw the first sign for St. Joseph's, I pedaled faster. The small hospital rested on top of one of Crabapple's many hills. There was barely any breath left in me when I reached the top of Ocean Drive. Through the fog, I could make out the sparkling whitecaps of the Pacific in the distance. I hopped off my bike and searched for a suitable hiding place for it and my helmet. I shoved them under the hedges that lined the parking lot and ran to the emergency entrance.

Fortunately, I'd memorized Bizzy's floor and room number the last time I was at the hospital. No one gave me so much as a curious glance as I strolled into the elevator and pushed the "four" button several times. Without bothering to stop at the nurse's station, I followed the path through the maze of white hallways and double doors that led to Bizzy's room.

The door was cracked open when I arrived. I pushed gently, in case my grandma was sleeping.

Bizzy's eyes popped open as if she'd suddenly been possessed. She rasped and wheezed and she tried to speak. I stepped toward her bedside tray and held the sippy cup of water to her lips. She gulped three times and then nodded for me to set it down.

Bizzy clutched my wrist with her hand. She pulled it closer to her eyes.

"You seen another, haven't ya?"

Oral Tradition

During our unit on folklore, Mrs. Tweedy, you made a big deal about oral tradition. You said it included the messages, morals, and tales that aren't written down but instead are passed from one generation to another through songs, stories, and chants. I assumed the tradition was long gone. It wasn't until I talked to Bizzy at the hospital that I realized I was way off.

Bizzy was fully alert in a few seconds. The sun streamed in through large panes of the fourth-floor hospital window. The wrinkled flesh of her face drooped from the stress of the day.

"Where'd you see it, Sweet Pea?"

"A book I was reading." I wasn't ready to tell Bizzy the specifics about my visit with Agatha or pocketing *The Last Descendant*.

"You write down everything like I told you?"

"Yes," I said. "It's in my backpack."

"Good girl! Let's give your grandmamma a gander, then." Bizzy held out the hand that wasn't hitched to her IV. "Pull up a chair," she said, "we ain't got time to fritter away." Bizzy grew more excited as I fished through my backpack for the Crabapple yearbook.

"I wrote it all on the back page."

She clutched the book expectantly and flipped to the last page, honing in on the few details I'd written down.

"There was nothin' else?" Bizzy said once she'd completed reading the list.

"That was it. It was written like a newspaper article."

"The Tuesday before December 18. Well, we got a little time, then," Bizzy said. She fooled with the remote attached to the side of the bed. The head of the bed elevated with a jerk. When Bizzy was almost sitting upright, she dropped the remote and the bed clanked to a halt. "Much better," she said. "Now I can lay eyes on you."

I had a million questions I wanted to ask. The problem was picking the one to ask first. I started from the beginning.

"Bizzy, when did you see your first death-specter?"

"Remember it clear as day. It was Halloween and I was walkin' through town on my way home from school. In the middle of West Monroe, there's this fountain, spews water all day long in purty patterns. As I passed the fountain, my cousin Jimmy, a famous rodeo cowboy from Monroe, appeared in it, right in front of me, in the water. I was right fond of Jimmy, too. He'd been like a big brother to me after Henry's passin'."

"You saw Jimmy in the water?"

"That's my channel."

"Channel?"

"Where you see your visions . . . your death-specters. Your channel depends on how you first learn about death. Most everyone learns about death in a different way."

"Yours is water? Why?"

Bizzy looked at me, and filled her lungs with air. She released the air in one large gush and sighed all at once. She began speaking, but without her usual zest. "Every summer, Henry would take me to the swimmin' hole off the Ouachita. One day, when I was four years old and our parents were away, Henry took a big dive off the tree swing," Bizzy said, her voice rattling in her chest. She paused for a moment to catch her breath. "Only he slipped and knocked his head on a rock and fell in the swimmin' hole. I tried and tried to drag him out. I screamed and screamed," she said, as her voice broke. She forced herself to continue. "When the men finally came and pulled him onto the shore, I ran to him. Threw myself on his body. It was as cold as the water was. He couldn't wake up. One of the men explained that the water had filled his lungs and killed him." A tear had formed at the tip of Bizzy's eyelash. She blinked and it slid down her sun-wrinkled cheek.

We were both silent for a minute.

"Was a long time ago. But it sealed my fate. I'd have my visions in water. For the first few months, I would look the other way when I saw water in the distance. I was scared to swim."

"How'd you get over it?"

"My mama and I figured out how to control it. If I took a swim every mornin', and I was gonna have a vision, she figured I'd probably have it durin' my swims. I don't like being taken unawares."

"And it works?" I asked.

"Surely. When I was floatin' underwater, the death-specters would come easier, playin' in front of me like a television show. My mama always told me that clear eyes and a clear mind allowed for some control. In time, I learned it was true. So will you."

My thoughts darted through my oldest memories. When did the concept of death creep into my consciousness?

I pulled up the memory of my own first time.

I was little.

Joltin' Joe DiMaggio's picture stared out at me from the morning paper. I couldn't read many words yet, but I knew that face anywhere. DiMaggio was simply referred to as "Joe" in our house. Along with a framed *Sports Illustrated* cover of him, Dad had an autographed photo of DiMaggio in his office. Joe had signed it for him after he'd been elected to the Hall of Fame in 1955. The story went that Joe told Dad he'd grow up to be a great baseball player. I think from that point on, Joe was Dad's favorite hero. To hear my dad tell it, baseball hadn't had a hero like him since. Or America, for that matter. While I didn't understand most of the article, I could pick out the headline:

JOE DIMAGGIO GONE FOR GOOD

"Where did Joe go, Dad?" I remember asking Dad. "On vacation?"

Dad looked at me and that crease between his eyebrows appeared. He got this strange look on his face and left the table in a hurry for the bathroom. Mom came up behind me and whispered something in my ear. I can't remember what exactly. Something about Joe having lived a long and happy life and being up in heaven. Bizzy explained that heaven was a beautiful garden where you could have all the food and Konriko Creole Seasoning you wanted.

When Dad came back, his eyes were red rimmed and I knew he'd been crying. Mom had put the front page of the newspaper in the trash.

Bizzy was watching me intently.

"Joe DiMaggio, right?" she asked, without missing a beat. "I remember. Beatrice Mildred Mortimer's been watchin' over you a very long time now, Sweet Pea."

"So my channel is the newspaper?"

"Or some kind a' typewriter words, I s'pose," Bizzy said, grabbing the sippy cup with her hand, pulling the IV tubes along with it. I pictured the cover of *The Last Descendant* and it hit me. Sure, I wasn't reading's biggest fan, but would I ever open a book again without trembling?

"You're lucky in many ways." Bizzy became more animated and continued, completely in her element. "Simply learnin' about death by hearing a story the first time is the worst. Then, the channel will be either voices in your head or dreams. Voices and dreams have driven more 'n a few Hands a' Fate plum crazy." Bizzy shook her head as if remembering a Thanksgiving where someone accidentally set the turkey on fire but things worked out fine. She smiled again.

"How do you know all this, Bizzy?"

"My mama told me and helped me with it all. Been passed down from one generation to the next. Normally a girl hears it from her mama, but I'm 'fraid since it skipped a generation, your daddy bein' an only chile an' all, you got stuck with me, Sweet Pea."

"Doesn't there have to be more to it than one person passing it down to another? Haven't you ever wondered how it all began?"

"A' course I have. But life never gives a person all the answers."

"But why, in all the time you've lived with us, didn't you tell me about being a Hand of Fate? You could've warned me . . ."

I was surprised by the resentment in my voice.

Bizzy shook her head. "If I had told ya, would you have believed a single bit of it?" I thought about her question. I didn't know the answer. "I sure wouldn't a' believed before I saw my first."

"Well, when did you start believing?"

Bizzy laughed. "Mama took me along on one of her errands. That's what she called it when she set out to change the course a' fate—an 'errand.' Anyhow, according to her latest death-specter, a dear neighbor of ours was set to be killed in a robbery

119

gone wrong at the local Savings 'n' Loan. First Mama showed me her hand and then we watched outside the bank as Mama summoned the police right before the robbers set foot in the bank. The police caught the whole lot of 'em waitin' outside in a truck with weapons and masks. Prevented the whole grisly thing. Our neighbor came out of the bank unharmed. The neighbor's name disappeared from Mama's hand." Bizzy studied my face for a moment. "I'm so sorry I didn't tell ya sooner, but I just didn't think there was any way you'd believe me."

After reading *The Last Descendant* and witnessing Jodi's near death, I was inclined to believe all of it. But I wanted to find out for certain what Bizzy knew. So I limited my questions to what she'd told me so far.

"Who is the sorceress you said gave us this gift?" I asked, referring to the letter Bizzy had written me in the hospital.

Bizzy sighed and closed her eyes for a few seconds.

"Oh, Lizzy-Loo," she began, almost sadly. "What if I told ya that your great-great-grandmamma, many times over, a woman named Morgan le Faye, was a sorceress who lived on a magical island with her enchanted sisters, around the time of King Arthur . . . and that her other sister is Agatha from the cemetery. I'm mighty sorry I don't have all the answers, but I only know what my mama told me, which was passed down to her, and so on. The gist of it is this: we inherited our gift from Morgan le Faye and now every Hand a' Fate needs to watch out for the nastiest of Morgan's sisters, the tall woman with red eyes and a black robe, Vivienne le Mort. See, *that's* why I was so scared when you said you saw her visiting Agatha." Bizzy's face was lined with anxiety.

My mind raced, trying to reconcile this new information with what I had read in Ambrosius's book. "You don't know anything about what Vivienne was talking about . . . like Doomsday or the Last Descendant?"

Bizzy looked confused. "I ain't never heard those terms before in my life."

"Well, why do you think we inherited this gift from Morgan? Why is Vivienne after us?"

"My mama put it this way: we see death-specters to correct the fundamental balance in the world—it's our job to prevent the deaths that aren't s'posed to happen. Vivienne le Mort doesn't like what we're up to, I'm afraid. My understandin', too, is that Vivienne and Morgan have been fightin' for so many years, there's nothin' left but bad blood between 'em. Mama said some Hands of Fate have guessed that it started over a man. You know how sisters can be . . . no one's sure."

"I know about the Seven Sisters of Avalon and Morgan le Faye," I said calmly.

"You do?" Bizzy's eyes opened wide.

"Agatha explained it to me . . . when I visited her earlier today." I'm not sure why I omitted the part about reading *The Last Descendant*. Maybe I wanted to keep a secret of my own, at least for the moment. Though I'm not proud to admit it, I guess I liked the feeling that I might know more about the Hands of Fate than Bizzy did.

"You visited her!" Bizzy said, lifting her body slightly more upright.

"Before I came here. I wanted to find out what she knew. She told me about Avalon and her sisters, right before she threw me out and told me that you and I were never to visit her again."

"Lizzy," Bizzy said, growing insistent, "you gotta understand that I was in Crabapple for years watching over you before I realized that Agatha might be one of the Seven Sisters. And once I suspected who Agatha was, I did start visiting her. But it was only to find out if there was any way to contact Morgan to see if you could avoid becomin' a Hand a' Fate."

"You wanted to *prevent* me from seeing death-specters?" It's hard to explain, but after hearing that Bizzy was trying to prevent me from becoming a Hand of Fate, I felt as if I was serving someone else's prison sentence for a crime I didn't commit or really even understand.

"From the moment you were born, Lizzy, you were this lovely and carin' creature. Truth be told, I wouldn't a' wished this on any of my kin . . . most of all you." She tried to shift again in bed, but grimaced when she attempted to move her broken leg. "But what's done is done. And even if a person's got no choice in somethin', she's always got a choice about how she reacts to that somethin'."

"What do you mean?"

"I'm sayin' when life gives you a lemon . . . throw it at the fella who's in your way. That's one of Bizzy's pearls a' wisdom, free a' charge."

I admired Bizzy's strange brand of spunk. But it wasn't making me feel a whole lot better.

"I was tryin' to protect you from this, like any grandmamma worth her salt would, but you musn't view it as some kind of curse. It's not about seein' death, Sweet Pea. It's about savin' lives. You'll get older and you'll realize that every dang day we have on this earth is a blessin'. If we can help a person get a few more circles 'round the sun—why there ain't no better gift to give 'em than that."

"So it's like we're giving people life extensions?"

"Why, that's perfect! Think of it that way." Bizzy paused. Her face darkened as she looked at my puzzled expression. But then she perked up again. "A new name can do a world of good. I reckon 'Hands a' Fate' is a bit outdated . . . it's too gloomy and lacks color, don't you think?" Bizzy put her free hand on her chin and squinted her eyes.

"How 'bout we call ourselves Preservation Fairies?"

"No way."

Bizzy and I thought in silence for a few more moments.

"What 'bout Life Leprechauns?" she offered.

"That's heinous," I said, unable to keep my half smile at bay. Bizzy let a smile go as well.

"Pixies of Passings?" she suggested.

"Um, no. That sounds like it relates to the bathroom somehow."

"Well, let's see now. There's simply gotta be somethin' . . . ," Bizzy said, staring out the window.

"The Death Catchers?" I offered timidly.

Bizzy raised her bare arm in the air triumphantly. She knocked the IV fluid bag off the hook and onto the floor. I rushed off my chair and picked it up, rehooking it.

"By gum, that's brilliant, Sweet Pea!" Before I could sit back down, Bizzy grabbed my wrist, pulling me toward her. She pulled so hard, I fell into her. Now, I was inches away from her face. Her eyes were clear and bright in the afternoon light.

"Tomorrow, soon as they let me out of this jailhouse, we're gonna get started on your Drake Westfall specter," Bizzy said, refusing to release my arm, growing more insistent. "It's not your burden to carry alone, you hear me?"

"Okay," I said, almost startled. Bizzy released me and I stumbled back into the chair.

"In the meantime, start gatherin' every shred of information ya possibly can on that boy, pronto, okay? Nothin' is too insignificant. Talk to people. Feel 'em out. You never can predict what turns out to be important in the end."

Truer words had never been spoken.

"Okay." I grabbed the Crabapple yearbook off her lap. Once I was packed up, I said good-bye.

"All this excitement's made me tired," she said, adjusting the bed with her remote so that it was flat again. She closed her eyes. I was about to leave when she spoke.

"Bizzy and Lizzy! The Die-namic Duo! Death Catchers till the end!" I looked back at her. My grandma still had her eyes closed. I chuckled a little. I still felt uneasy about it all, but one thing was certain: only Beatrice Mildred Mortimer could make me laugh at a time like this.

I pushed the hospital room door open. My hand came away from the door handle and I glimpsed Drake Westfall's name inscribed on my wrist. I thought of the way he looked at me with his puzzled blue eyes from his truck, as I declined a ride to school. What did it mean that the death-specter I'd seen was about him?

The awful responsibility of carrying around someone's life in the palm of my hand hit me head-on with the force of his shiny black pickup, driving full speed.

Would it ever be less overwhelming?

Irony

Normally, if Jodi accused me of having a crush on someone, I would probably go out of my way to prove I didn't by ignoring that person. Now, I couldn't ignore Drake. In fact, if I wanted to save his life, I'd have to do just the opposite. You'd probably call the whole situation ironic, Mrs. Tweedy. If you did, I think you'd be right.

Jodi and I had different class schedules, so I didn't see her until lunch. We usually ate lunch behind the outdoor stage on a grassy area, enjoying the sun on days when it managed to conquer the fog. After the close call outside Miss Mora's Market, I was anxious to talk with my best friend. I spotted her coming out of her history class. She was wearing a sparkling green headband, a pocket T-shirt, seersucker shorts, fishnets, and red Converse high-tops decorated with her own drawings.

As soon as we sat down, though, I started feeling guilty. Bizzy was insistent that I start gathering information on Drake as soon as possible. What if I had already missed seeing something critical? From behind the outdoor stage, I had no view of him.

"Mind if we eat over there today?" I pointed to the planter near the cluster of picnic tables, which was where most of the athletes sat. "It's kind of hot. I think I need some shade." For emphasis, I pulled up the sleeves of my hoodie to my elbows.

"Super idea. After my NDE," Jodi said dramatically, "I've been having the urge to change things up."

"Your *NDE*?"

"Near-death experience," Jodi said, as if a *duh* was implied at the end. She laughed.

"Of course," I said, rolling my eyes.

"Speaking of NDEs, when does Bizzy get out of the hospital?"

"This afternoon," I said.

We settled on the edge of the planter. I spotted Drake across the quad. He was eating a brown-bag lunch with the other boys from the water polo team. As I watched him, the first thing I noticed was that he didn't seem to be enjoying himself. He laughed along with the rest of the boys, but he didn't seem to be talking much or telling any jokes of his own.

It was as if he was sad about something.

As I watched him, another thing occurred to me. Garrett Edmonds and Drake didn't like one another. Garrett Edmonds was a senior and was captain last year before Drake returned. I'd heard Garrett had to change positions on the team to make room for Drake. They sat on opposite ends of the lunch table and never once looked each other in the eye.

"Earth to Lizzy . . ."

First I thought Jodi's voice was just inside my head. The

image of Jodi waving her hand in front of my face came into view. I'd completely zoned out.

"Um, do you have anything you'd like to share with me, Lizster?" Jodi smirked.

"What do you mean?" I asked.

"Oh, I don't know . . . maybe you'd like to confess to me that the real reason we moved over here was so that you can drool over Drake while he eats his ham sandwich."

My face flushed.

One of the things I like best about Jodi is that she pays attention. I wanted to tell her everything, but how could I? As she took a peanut butter and banana sandwich out of her bag, Jodi eyed me curiously.

"What is it?"

Suddenly, Jodi dropped her sandwich right into the planter. Then, she grabbed my left hand. As soon as she did, I realized the huge mistake I'd made rolling up my sleeves earlier. Jodi had my wrist clamped between her fingers and she pulled it toward her eyes. There it was. DRAKE WESTFALL in tiny red letters on my wrist, as bright as ever.

Jodi dropped my hand.

"Mmmkay . . . ," Jodi said, lowering her voice. "I think it's time to have an intervention." Her eyebrows came together.

"It's not what you think!" I sounded desperate. There was no way I could explain the actual truth to Jodi.

"Take a breath," Jodi said.

"What?" I searched for a way to explain why Drake's name was on my hand.

"It's what my mom tells me to do when I'm about to flip out," Jodi said sympathetically. "So take a breath and calm down. I'm not going to go blab to a million people about the fact that you're carving Drake's name on your hand—"

"I'm *not* carving his name on my hand."

"Okaaay . . . *writing* his name in red ink on your hand. Whatever. People do all sorts of crazy stuff when they're in love—"

"In *what*?" I interrupted.

This was not going well.

"Fine, fine, fine. I get it. You're sensitive. You're just 'in *like*' with Drake . . . you pretend you're immune to human emotion and you can keep pretending like it's some big secret that only you know, but I'm your best friend, Lizzy. If you don't talk to me, who are you going to talk to?"

I didn't say anything. So Jodi continued.

"First things first . . . a little friendly advice . . . you need to stop writing his name on your hand. It's just a *little* bit freaky, you know? If someone-who's-not-me sees that, you'll never hear the end of it. You might as well write in the sky that you're obsessed."

Jodi had a point. I needed to come up with a foolproof method like Bizzy's pearls to hide my hand. I vowed to buy a watch with a thick leather band. I would slide it over my wrist so that it would cover the writing. "Okay. I'm sorry." I considered arguing that I wasn't obsessed with Drake, but there was no other explanation that made sense—especially not the truth.

"You don't have to say sorry to me," Jodi said. She paused,

pondering something. "I know no one ever believes it when someone says this . . . but you know you're worth two Drake Westfalls combined, right?"

I didn't believe her. But it was nice to hear.

"Thanks," I said.

"Anyway," Jodi continued, "the other day I was reading *Dating for Dummies*—"

"*Dating for Dummies?*" I interrupted, raising my eyebrows.

"It's my mom's," Jodi explained. "Don't you dare judge her for it. You try being a thirty-five-year-old single woman in Crabapple sometime. There are about two and a half eligible men here, so, yeah, she needs all the help she can get."

"No judgment here," I said, with a half smile.

"Anyway, it says the way to form a connection with someone you're attracted to is to strike up a conversation about shared interests." Jodi looked at me, expecting me to react.

"Where are you going with all this?"

"I want to *help*, see?" Jodi explained. "We just need to find out what Drake's interested in and maybe follow him around to see where he hangs out and then—"

"So, basically, you want to help me *stalk* Drake?"

Jodi began to laugh. "It's not stalking if you have a good reason," she defended.

"That's the thing about stalking," I said. "A stalker always *thinks* she has a good reason."

"All right, then. Think of it as 'researching' Drake." She stopped for a moment and grinned at me. "Look, Lizster . . .

I'll probably always think you're better than Drake Westfall, but that doesn't mean I'm not going to help you get what you want. I mean, who doesn't love a project!"

I shook my head, unable to refrain from laughing and marveling at the complete wonder that was Jodi Sanchez. Ironically (take note, Mrs. Tweedy), what I was so desperate to deny—that I was in love with Drake Westfall—was exactly what I needed to cop to in order to have a partner in crime. It was the kind of boost I needed to save Drake.

"Well, okay," I said. "Thank you, Jodi."

"No prob," Jodi said. "But I'm only going to help you if you promise me something."

"Name it."

"When we finally do make Drake fall madly in love with you, you have to swear you won't turn into a whiny, lovesick girl and completely ditch me. I don't want to have to go to the trouble of finding a new best friend." Jodi stuck out her hand, wanting to shake on it. "Deal?'

"Deal," I said.

Knowing full well there was no chance Drake was going to fall for a law-abiding truant he barely knew, I figured it was one of the few promises I could be sure I wouldn't have to keep.

"Good. We're all set," Jodi said as the lunch bell rang. "Let the stalking begin!"

Alliteration

Jodi informed me that the first stop on the quest for Drake "research" was Mickey's Music. Mickey's Music is right next to Billy's Books on Ocean Avenue. Both are owned by Mickey himself, who didn't want to name the bookstore part of his retail empire Mickey's Books because he has a thing for alliteration, just like you, Mrs. Tweedy (how many handouts have you made with the title *Tweedy's Tips* or *Tweedy's Tidbits*, after all?). Needless to say, Mickey is very envious of Miss Mora's Market.

A large open doorway unites the two stores. The bookstore side has books crammed in holes, shelves, nooks, and crannies up to the ceiling. The books are sorted, not according to title or author or even subject, but according to mood. If you go to the "Restless" section of the bookstore, you'll find a variety of travel books along with other books like *Roughing It*, by Mark Twain, and the self-help book *Who Moved My Cheese?* Needless to say, it is Mom's absolute favorite store in Crabapple.

Most everyone else complains that there is neither rhyme nor reason to how anything in the store is arranged, but Mom has declared it to be a "lovely" way of organizing a bookstore.

Fortunately, Mickey knows where everything is, so all you have to do is ask him. Mickey is an older guy, about forty, with thick-rimmed glasses and straggly hair down to his shoulders. He usually wears a white shirt and khaki pants. He surfs every morning. Also, I think he may be secretly in love with Mom. Or at least, he and Mom flirt with each other shamelessly, bonding over things like which volume of Marcel Proust's *In Search of Lost Time* is best. They do have a special connection—Mom is the only person in Crabapple who knows more about books than Mickey does.

"Hey, girls," Mickey greeted us. "How's it going?" Most other people in Crabapple would've asked Jodi and me why we weren't in school, but Mickey didn't care about those things. In truth, he was almost as big a fan of Jodi as he was of Mom. Mickey's two loves were music and books; and Jodi, a music nut herself, would get in long debates with Mickey about things like the evolution of shoegaze pop into nu-gaze pop. Half the time, I had no idea what they were talking about.

"Everything's good," I responded, smiling at Mickey.

"Looking for anything in particular today?" he asked, pushing his glasses up the bridge of his nose.

"Do you know Drake Westfall?" Jodi said. I tried not to let any surprise show on my face. Clearly Jodi's detective style was not going to be subtle.

"Crabapple's all-American water polo star? Sure," Mickey said, smiling. "He comes in here a decent amount."

"What do you think of him?" I asked, before realizing what a clumsy question it was.

"Drake's a good kid. His dad's a real jerk, though."

"No kidding," Jodi said, pushing me behind her so I couldn't ask any more questions. Apparently she wasn't a fan of my detective style, either.

"Yeah, one day he found Drake in here and pulled him out by the ear, yelling at him about wasting his time."

"Total jerk," Jodi repeated, nodding her head in enthusiastic agreement. I thought she was overdoing it, but Mickey seemed to be buying it. "Well, Drake's a good friend of ours and his birthday is coming up . . . so we were kind of wondering if you could clue us in as to what he's been buying lately. You know, so we could surprise him with something he'll like."

"Ahhh," Mickey said, smiling impishly at us. He put his index finger to his unshaven chin. "Let's see now . . . if I'm remembering correctly, I think Drake picked up a copy of Irving Stone's *The Agony and the Ecstasy* the last time he was in here."

"What is that?" Jodi asked.

"It's a biographical novel of Michelangelo. A great one. For something in that vein, I'd go check out the 'Tortured and/or Brooding' section . . . third shelf up from the bottom on the far wall."

"Cool, thanks," Jodi replied. "What about music?"

"Hmmm," Mickey said, visibly thinking. "Oh yeah! Drake's been into Op Ivy, Sublime, the Slackers, and that kind of stuff lately." Mickey paused thoughtfully. "*Remain in Light* by the Talking Heads is something I bet he would like if he doesn't already have it. That record still blows me away."

"Perfect, thanks so much, Mickey," Jodi said. "We owe you one. I'm going to go find *Remain in Light* . . . why don't you pick out a book for Drake and then we'll be set."

"All right," I said, agreeing to Jodi's division of labor. Jodi turned away and headed into Mickey's Music. I was moving toward the "Tortured and/or Brooding" section of Billy's when I had a thought.

"Hey, Mickey," I said, "do you have anything here about King Arthur?"

Mickey raised his eyebrows. "On an Arthurian kick, huh? What have you read so far?"

"Ever heard of *The Last Descendant*?" I asked.

Mickey paused for a moment and brought his finger to his chin once again. "I'm not familiar with that one. Who wrote it?"

"Merlin Ambrosius," I said, unsure of myself.

"I don't think I know it. But if you're just starting out, you can't go wrong with Thomas Malory's *Le Morte d'Arthur*, which is a definitive version of the story. Or more currently, T. H. White's *The Once and Future King* is as solid as they come."

"I'll take both those, please," I said.

"All right, but I've got to warn you. It's not a happy story.

And the person who you think is the heroine of the story, Guinevere, kinda turns out to be a villain in the end. Her betrayal of Arthur ends up bringing down his whole kingdom."

I had to stop myself from telling him he had it all wrong. But I only responded, "I consider myself warned."

"I'm also looking for anything you have by Emily Dickinson," I said.

"Ahhh," Mickey said. "Beginning to ponder death and immortality?"

"It's for school," I lied.

"Well, either way, there's no better source of poetry for those deep life questions," Mickey said. "You should probably start with *The Complete Poems of Emily Dickinson* in the 'Reclusive' section. Wait, it'll be faster if I just go grab it for you."

"Thanks, Mickey," I said.

I bought it without so much as leafing through it.

Mickey ended up picking out another book for me as Drake's "present"—Irving Stone's *Lust for Life* about Vincent van Gogh. After he helped Jodi with her purchase, he rang up the four books. We thanked Mickey for all his help.

"My pleasure," he said, placing *Le Morte d'Arthur* and *The Once and Future King* in a bag with the novel and the book of poems. "Oh, and tell your mom that I know she thinks it's juvenile, but she needs to give *Catch-22* another chance. It's a comic masterpiece."

"I'll deliver the message." Mickey waved good-bye to us as we headed out the door.

Jodi waited till we were outside Mickey's before she spoke. We were climbing up Delores Avenue, me on my fifteen-speed and Jodi on her fixie.

"Since when are you interested in King Arthur?" she asked curiously as she labored up the hill.

"I don't know," I said.

"And Emily Dickinson?" she asked. "Since when are you interested in poetry?"

"Since now." The truth was that ever since Bizzy had written that Emily had known about "us" in her hospital note, I had developed a deep curiosity about her. For some reason, I thought there must be secrets in her poems that would help me understand being a Hand of Fate.

"You're kind of strange," Jodi said, grinning.

"Oh, and you're not?"

Jodi charged up the hill, past Almost There, where the Coles lived, pedaling faster and faster, almost daring me to catch her. I threw more gears on my bike and gave it everything I had left. Jodi turned her head and laughed as she saw me struggle. When the hill leveled off, Jodi had enough air in her lungs to speak again.

"Well, I'd say that was a very successful mission."

"Yeah, but you might want to be a little subtler about investigating Drake."

"We don't have time for subtlety. Also, we're in luck. My mom lived in the East Bay in the late eighties," Jodi said. "She went to a lot of those bands' concerts Mickey mentioned."

"Miss Mora?"

"Yup. She used to be a total musichead," Jodi proclaimed, proudly. "Her record collection is how I got my start."

"You kind of lucked out with your mom, you know."

Jodi looked straight ahead. "She has her moments, I guess . . . but my point is, I think we found your shared interest. I can teach you everything you need to know to bond with Drake. It'll be a POC."

"What?"

"Piece of cake."

I could tell Jodi was thoroughly enjoying herself with this new project. Though Jodi thought the project had a different goal, she would be a huge help as I tried to figure how Drake ended up in the cannery. We split off when she got to Miss Mora's Market and I thanked her for all that she'd done.

When I was nearly home, I removed the heavy Billy's Books bag swinging from my handlebars. It was going to be a late night. After all, I had a lot of King Arthur and Emily Dickinson to catch up on.

Personification

When considering which of my parents I'm most like, or which of their characteristics I most personify, I used to believe I'd grow up to be just like Dad. Mom is all that is warm, messy, and sentimental. I don't mean that in a bad way. I realize she's also the rubber band that keeps everything together. It's just that everything brews right beneath the surface with Mom. It's never hard to tell where you stand in her eyes at any given moment—which is a very good thing most of the time.

Dad, on the other hand is calm, calculating, and introspective. When he gets somewhere, not only does he arrive on time, he is totally prepared. I relate to this side of him. I don't like surprises. Mom always says that I'm "levelheaded" like Dad is, but I've recently realized that I'm not an exact replica of either of my parents.

Seeing Dad fret over Bizzy underscored all this. For the first time, he seemed a little unhinged, like he couldn't possibly be ready for whatever might happen next with her. He was so calm most of the time, I think, because he was usually prepared. Bizzy wasn't exactly the kind of person you could anticipate, though.

When I got home from Mickey's, Dad let me go with him to the hospital to pick up Bizzy. He wheeled her out the automatic sliding doors in her spanking new wheelchair. She had a bright blue cast that went all the way up to her midthigh. Her broken leg stuck straight out in front of her, parallel to the ground. After she'd cleared the hospital, Bizzy lifted up her hospital gown, peeled back a bandage, and showed me the new stitches across her abdomen.

"Makes me look pretty tough, eh?" she said, smiling. Her wild white hair hadn't been brushed this morning and she looked a bit like Medusa's jovial grandma.

"Mother, please," Dad said, partly shocked by Bizzy's behavior, partly amused.

It took a lot of fancy maneuvering to get Bizzy into Dad's Volvo. Every time Dad made a turn, he checked his rearview mirror to make sure Bizzy was doing okay. We were silent until we got to the corner of Delores and Ocean, the scene of the accident. I could see Miss Mora through the large pane window, waiting on a customer. Jodi must've been upstairs, probably listening to *Remain in Light* or some of her mom's ska albums as she began her "Drake research."

"Can't wait to use Dixie again. Bet she misses me," Bizzy said, looking out the window wistfully.

"I'm not so sure *that's* a good idea," Dad said, raising his eyes to the rearview mirror once again.

"Good idea?" Bizzy replied.

"Your doctor thinks that if you keep carrying on like you have been, you'll become a danger to yourself and others."

Bizzy adjusted her position in the back, sitting up straight.

"Me? Carryin' on? You're gonna wear me to a frazzle, Phillip." Bizzy tapped her cast angrily with two of her fingers. "Tell you one thing, sonny, I haven't made it seventy-four years on this earth by accident."

Once we were home, Dad fussed over Bizzy, making sure that she had everything she could possibly need. Fortunately, Bizzy's room was on the first floor—she wouldn't be climbing stairs for some time. The walls of her room looked like one large bulletin board. Pictures, articles, cartoons, random cards, and thank-you notes covered every inch of blank wall space—a mosaic dedicated to memories. Mostly, Bizzy used duct tape to attach things. Mom had groused about Bizzy's odd mode of interior decorating initially, but finally realized it was a losing battle.

Bizzy was crankier than usual.

"Okay, then," Dad said, putting his hands on his hips and looking around Bizzy's room. "Lizzy," he said, turning toward me, "I'm heading back to work. If your grandma has any trouble with anything, call me immediately."

"I will," I said. Dad took one last look at Bizzy and me and turned to leave.

Bizzy didn't say a word until she was sure that Dad's car had pulled away.

"I thought he'd never skedaddle!" she said, slowly wheeling

herself away from the kitchen window. "How I raised a naggin' worrywart sure does confound me."

"Dad doesn't want you to hurt yourself again."

Since she didn't yet have the mobility to get pants over her bulky cast, Bizzy had changed into her favorite old purple nightgown. She'd found a wool hat with a large orange pom-pom on the top and pulled it over her ears.

Of course, she still managed to put on her pearls so the end of her palm was covered with her customary bracelet.

As soon as she had put the pearls on her wrist, she looked at me.

"We're gonna have to do somethin' about coverin' your wrist—if someone sees it, they'll ask all sorts a' questions you don't wanna answer." Bizzy wheeled over to her dresser and began tossing garments all over the room. I didn't want to tell her that it was too late for that.

"Aha! Here it is!" Bizzy rolled back to me and grabbed my wrist.

She slid a purple sweatband over my hand.

"It's a lot lighter than it was at school today," I said, staring at Drake's name. At school, it looked like a dark tattoo. Now, it was faint enough to almost blend in with my skin.

"The closer you are to the person whose name is on your hand, Sweet Pea, the darker it gets."

"Really?"

"For better or worse, you're bound to whomever you have a specter 'bout."

I blushed at the thought of being bound to Drake in any capacity. Bizzy adjusted the purple sweatband so it covered the bottom of my hand.

"There!"

I looked at it. It was from a different time and place, clearly. It smelled musty and had JAZZERCIZE in large white letters on the top.

"Won't this just call more attention to my wrist?"

"Maybe. But no one'll bother lookin' underneath."

"Okay," I said, planning to wear it until I found the right kind of watch.

"Now quick, quick!" Bizzy said, growing excited, clapping her hands once. "Wheel Dixie over here where I can reach her!"

Dixie sat in the corner, in front of a collage of pictures of Mom, Dad, and me.

"Push a little closer," Bizzy beckoned. She reached around the back of her neck and unwrapped a chain. Fumbling with it, she reached its end and held it in her hand.

"'Fraid with all these bandages, I can't seem to bend low enough. You mind doin' the honors?" Bizzy asked me.

She held a key in her hand and motioned at the bottom of Dixie. I looked down and saw the box that rested on the bottom racks was locked. Taking the key from Bizzy, I thrust it into the keyhole. It was an exact fit. "This is for you," Bizzy said, reaching into the box herself and pulling out a pocket-sized mirror. "In case you have any surprise encounters with a banshee."

I shuddered at the thought of such an occurrence.

"So what do we do now?" I asked, feeling overwhelmed.

Bizzy seemed to be gaining strength just as I was losing it. The soft wrinkled flesh below her chin was now stretched tightly as she reviewed our situation. "We know Drake Westfall is set to pass on Tuesday the fifteenth of December. We know that authorities will immediately suspect foul play and we know that his body'll be burned and found among the ruins of a fire at the cannery. Don't know much else, do we?"

I told Bizzy what I'd learned about Drake that afternoon.

"That's a great start!" Bizzy said, adjusting her purple night-gown so that it covered the gauze and medical tape underneath her collarbone. "The Miss Mora specter was open-and-shut so quickly. But this one's a lot more complicated. We're gonna have to throw everything we've got at this thing. I got another pearl for ya—brains in the head saves blisters on the feet. We need to know everythin' about him. For instance, what does Drake eat for supper? What gets him goin'? Where's he spend his time? Who's he tell his secrets to? Who tells their secrets to him? Most importantly, who in the world would want him dead?"

A frown formed on my face. Though I knew more than I had yesterday, the details of Drake's life were a mystery to me.

"We've got ourselves plenty of ways to find everythin' we need to know about Drake Westfall."

"Like spying on him?" I stopped short of telling Bizzy that if she wanted to spy on Drake, she was going to have some company in Jodi Sanchez.

"That's only the half of it. We'll come up with a plan afore you know it, Sweet Pea."

"What kind of plan?"

"I think a little visit to the scene is our best first step," Bizzy said.

"The cannery?"

"You betcha!" Bizzy cried. "Hopefully, seein' the place'll open things right up for us. Near as I can tell, we'll need a lucky break or two. After all, we're fightin' the most terrible enemy of 'em all."

"Who's that?" I asked.

My grandma looked at me as she wheeled inches closer to me.

"Fate," she said, clenching her jaw shut.

Aphorisms—Bizzy's Best Pearls

Bizzy's habit of dropping unsolicited pearls of wisdom is very annoying to most people, especially Mom.

The pearl Mom particularly dislikes is the one Bizzy says the most: "If the cat gets caught in the blender, best get yourself a new blender . . . and a new cat." I think it's Bizzy's way of saying that you shouldn't cry over spilled milk. Anyhow, before your class, Mrs. Tweedy, I would've never known the fancy name for Bizzy's pearls of wisdom: aphorisms.

Bizzy loves aphorisms.

I bring up all this because as we were planning our expedition to the cannery, Bizzy spouted an aphorism I'll never forget. She was trying to convince me to drive us there, though I didn't even have my learner's permit yet.

"We'll take my car. I'll instruct ya the whole way. It'll take no more'n a few minutes," Bizzy said.

"Sheriff Schmidt is already after you. If he sees me driving you around, he'll arrest us," I countered.

"That ain't gonna happen. Even if it does, I can talk circles around that fella usin' only half my mouth," Bizzy said, letting out a *parumph*.

"I'm not so sure, Bizzy . . . it just seems like a bad ide—"

"Listen here, Sweet Pea. In this world, everybody's gotta make the same choice: it's either the lice or the hedgehog. That's one of Bizzy's pearls, free a' charge."

"What?" I asked impatiently.

"I'm sayin' a person has to choose to be the hedgehog or the lice."

"I'm not sure I under—"

"The hedgehog makes his own way in this here world. The lice on the hedgehog don't. Now, there ain't no shame in the lice choosin' to get a free ride on that hedgehog. But there ain't no guarantees that the lice gets a say in where it's goin'. Catch my drift?"

Honestly, I wasn't sure I did.

"If I drive us to the cannery, am I the hedgehog?"

"One step closer to choosin' your own way, that's for dog-gone sure."

On the one hand, I did think I was *capable* of driving to the cannery. But on the other, if we were to get caught, I was sure I'd be grounded until I was Bizzy's age. Not to mention that Mom might try to ground Bizzy, too. And what was the use of deciding to be the hedgehog if you were confined to your room for the next five years?

"I'm not sure I can get you into the car by myself," I said, trying to think of a bulletproof excuse.

"We ain't got time for you to wheel me and walk," Bizzy

insisted. "Drivin' is the only way. Whaddaya say?" Her algae eyes shone like laser beams that penetrated into my skull. I got the uncanny sense that she could tell what I was thinking. Bizzy's reasons for wanting to go to the cannery were selfless—to help Drake. She wanted to scope it out, gather information, and see if there was anything that jumped out at us.

"The cannery is only about three miles, right? What if I pull you along in your wheelchair behind my bike?" I asked, wondering whether I was being licelike or hedgehoglike. Bizzy reached up and slapped me on the shoulder. She beamed, like a child does when she gets her way. I couldn't help but smile back.

"Ain't you just as handy as a pocket in a shirt!" she exclaimed. Bizzy began wheeling herself toward the front door. "Gonna be a workout, for sure."

"I can handle it," I said. Other than the beginning, the ride was mostly flat.

First, I tied rope to both handles of Bizzy's wheelchair. I tied the other ends to the rack over the back wheel of my bike so that the rope formed a triangle around Bizzy, with my bike at the front tip.

I tested the contraption out in the driveway. I double-checked the knots, making certain they were tight enough. Though it was a beast to get going, once I had some momentum, towing Bizzy behind me wasn't all that difficult.

"You're going to wear the helmet," I said, taking charge by removing Bizzy's snow hat and putting it on my own head. "Because you can't afford another injury."

Bizzy held a stick in each hand—they were to act as make-shift emergency brakes in case we needed to stop in a hurry.

I nervously edged down the hill, braking every couple of feet, as I heard the wheels of Bizzy's chair rattle from the cracks in the sidewalk.

"Not so herky-jerky," Bizzy said calmly, as I jutted out into the intersection toward Ocean Avenue. I released the brakes and looked back toward Bizzy. She gave me a thumbs-up and tapped the red bike helmet I'd put on her head.

We began to gather speed, barreling down the hill.

It was exhilarating.

"Woooooweeeee!" Bizzy yelled gleefully. "Brakin's for sissies!" Bizzy shouted at the top of her lungs. Trees whizzed by. The wind whipped through the strands of my hair which stuck out of Bizzy's snow hat. I laughed as I cut right through the grassy town square and headed for Mission Street.

"Ben-Hur ain't got nothin' on us, Sweet Pea!"

Bizzy and I were slicing through the thick, damp air like a knife.

I looked around, glad the streets of Crabapple were empty. I couldn't imagine what an random pedestrian would think.

Soon, the large square brick frame of the cannery was in sight. I braked slightly, preparing for our landing. I looked back as Bizzy began pressing the sticks to each wheel. She cackled as sparks flew off the wheels.

"Chariot of fire!" she yelled to me, laughing. We skidded to a stop, both of us breathless.

We examined the large abandoned building in front of us. Bizzy guessed that it had been vacant for at least a dozen years. On one side of the crumbling brick building, I could still make out the Del Monte emblem, and THE CANNERY in huge painted block letters underneath. The first-floor windows were boarded up and those above were either broken or missing completely. Brown weeds filled the spaces between the building and the wood-planked fence out back.

"Our best bet'll be goin' around back," Bizzy said.

She was right. If we wanted to find a way in, we weren't going to have much luck with the front of the building. The entrance door had a large combination padlock on it and the boards on the front windows had dozens of nails in them.

Bizzy signaled for me to untie the ropes from her wheelchair. Still breathless, I undid the double knots and leaned my bike against the side of the fence. I pushed Bizzy through the gravelly side yard. Her chair shook. I tried to go slowly, concerned that the rattling must be hurting Bizzy's still-mending leg. Bizzy gripped both armrests of her wheelchair and urged me on.

The back of the cannery was in an even worse state of repair than the front. Abandoned tires, toilet seats, and burned-out couches were piled high in each corner of the back lot. Plastic bags and soda cans decorated the broken asphalt. I struggled to weave Bizzy through the piles of junk.

"There!" Bizzy said, raising her arm so that it was parallel with her broken leg. She pointed at a first-floor window on the left side of the building. The board covering it had been dislodged from the upper left corner and hung diagonally, revealing a person-sized hole at the bottom right side.

"See that wood crate?" Bizzy pointed. "If we push it up against the wall, you can climb right in."

I eyeballed the window. It was eight feet off the ground. It was doable, depending on what waited for me on the other side, inside the cannery.

"What are you going to do?"

"I'll be your eyes and ears here on the ground," Bizzy said, grinning.

The crate wobbled below me as I grabbed the ledge of the window with both hands. Bending my knees, I jumped off the crate. It tipped over. My feet dangled against the bricks of the building.

"Pull yourself up, Sweet Pea!" Bizzy yelled from the ground. "Pull! Pull! Pull!"

I pulled, pulled, pulled. Finally, I swung my legs up over the ledge. I grabbed the wood board partially covering the window and tugged on it. It didn't take much force to yank it completely off.

"Watch out!" I shouted at Bizzy, who was directly below the window. She wheeled over a couple of soda cans as the board clanged to the ground on her left.

I crouched on the ledge, my body half-in and half-out of the cannery. I caught a whiff of the air—it smelled a little like a porta potty.

"What do you see?" Bizzy yelled.

The inside of the cannery looked like a large, empty warehouse, about the size of a baseball field. Slices of white light beamed in from cracks in the bricks. A large gaping hole in the ceiling provided most of the light. Cobwebs as thick as phone wires hung from the rafters. In one corner, there was a hulking metal machine that had a huge cylinder in the middle and large rusted metal arms jutting out. Underneath it, there was a grate that was emitting sewerlike fumes. I moved quickly to cover my nose.

I jumped down, landing on a pile of empty cans and beer bottles. Cigarette butts littered the floor. My eyes were immediately drawn to a small structure in the far corner. To the left of it was a manhole that was uncovered. I peered down into the hole, but couldn't see where it ended.

"Anythin' of interest?" Bizzy shouted from outside.

"It looks like there's a tunnel or something that leads down beneath the cannery."

"Don't go in there!"

"Wasn't planning on it," I said.

"It's probably just a basement or somethin'. Anythin' else?"

"Maybe," I said, creeping toward the corner, trying to avoid stepping on a nail or glass from a broken bottle.

Bizzy's voice drifted into the vacant building and echoed off the walls.

"Pay particular attention to any signs a' life. Or anythin' that might cause an explosion in the future—candles, exposed pipes, remnants of homemade fire."

The sound of an aluminum can banging on a brick wall stopped me dead in my tracks. A small squirrel squeaked and darted across the warehouse floor, toward a dark hallway on one side. I took a deep breath.

When I was within twenty feet of the structure I'd spotted, I could see it was a tent made from wood beams with blankets draped over them. It looked like the blanket forts I made in my bedroom when I was little, with a baseball bat acting as the tent pole. I would crawl in and pretend I was no longer in my bedroom, but braving the elements in some faraway forest.

There were a couple of empty pizza boxes and some old water-damaged *Hot Wheels* magazines strewn around the makeshift tent. Pulling back the blanket flap, I found more blankets and a flashlight. I clicked it on and off. It didn't work.

Hesitating for a moment, I grabbed one of the magazines, shoving it under my arm. I had no idea what good it might do, but Bizzy had said any detail could be important.

An animal had chewed the edges of the blankets, and the inside of the tent smelled faintly of mildew. The cannery was probably a haven for rats and all sorts of other vermin.

Still, there were no candles or any dead-giveaway clues (personally, I was hoping I'd find a piece of paper with the name of the person who'd stayed there written on it). It was hard to tell if someone had been there yesterday or six months ago.

According to the specter, the cannery was supposed to be Drake's final resting place. My imagination began to work in fast-forward as bits and pieces of scenes flashed in front of my eyes: *Drake in the tent. A red-orange explosion. Drake's yells echoing*

*off the burning walls. A dark figure running away from the cannery.
Billows of smoke. The wail of sirens. Fire trucks and hoses of water.
Drake, motionless, his face covered with soot. Drake being carried out
on a stretcher in a black body bag.*

Sadness overcame me. I retreated from the tent, shuddering,
and made my way toward the machine on the opposite side of
the cannery.

"What else do you see?" Bizzy's voice echoed.

"There are some blankets and a flashlight in one corner—
someone stayed here, but it looks like it was a couple of months
ago," I said. It was impossible to determine the function of the
machine, but there were all kinds of grooves and perforations
in the arms. From a distance, it looked like a metallic monster.
The shafts of light cast menacing shadows on the machine itself.
On one side there was a hallway. I poked my head into it, as
glass crunched under my feet. With no visible windows or
cracks, the corridor was pitch-black.

"There's a hallway," I said, my voice echoing, "but it's completely dark."

"I think we got enough of an idea," Bizzy said. "Come on
out!"

I used a rickety crate to hop back onto the ledge of the
window and swing my legs to the outside. I hung on the ledge as
if I was about to perform a high-bar gymnastics routine, then
let go and landed in the weeds with a thud.

"We may have to work a teensy bit on your breakin' and
enterin' skills, but not bad for your first time," Bizzy said,
extending her arm.

"I took this from the tent. I thought we might be able to use it to figure out who stayed here," I said, thrusting the issue of *Hot Wheels* into my grandma's hands.

Bizzy looked at it for a moment and shoved it in the pouch of her wheelchair. "Interesting. We best get on outta here before someone sees us snoopin'," she said, glancing around.

I hooked Bizzy's wheelchair to my bike once more. This time, already exhausted from my journey into the cannery, I did not look forward to the climb from Ocean Avenue to Beside the Point. We crossed from Mission Avenue to Ocean and I rode up onto the sidewalk as I heard the sound of a car approaching.

Turning to look, I saw the flashing red lights of a Crabapple patrol car. My head suddenly felt exposed, as I remembered that I was not wearing a helmet.

The sirens flashed as the horn sounded. I heard "Stop your vehicle" echo from a bullhorn. I hit the bicycle brakes and Bizzy and I jolted to an abrupt halt. Afraid to look back, I heard a car door open and close.

We were completely busted.

Brainstorming

"Let me do the talkin'," Bizzy said softly.

I looked up. Sheriff Schmidt was in front of us, whistling while skeptically shaking his head. He wore his cowboy hat, green and yellow uniform, and boots. This time, he was also wearing sunglasses. He smirked.

"Well, ladies," he said, taking his time as he examined our bike-wheelchair contraption, "this is a first."

"You ain't never seen a girl and her grandmamma out for a bicycle ride?" Bizzy snarled.

"Not when the girl in question is towing her grandmother like a rickshaw driver," Sheriff Schmidt said, raising his voice to match Bizzy's.

"Dixie's in the shop, Sheriff. What else am I s'posed to do?"

"Where were you two coming from?" the sheriff asked, looking directly at me.

"I convinced Lizzy to take me out for a spin," Bizzy said, not altering her tone one bit.

"That's funny . . . because I've been tailing you two since you left the cannery. Now why would a girl and her elderly grandma be at a place like that, do ya think?" Sheriff Schmidt said, mocking Bizzy's accent.

"I don't have to put up with your ageist slurs. The cannery's a Crabapple historical landmark. Sure, we stopped there. *S'pose* you never seen a grandma explainin' town history to her granddaughter, neither?"

Sheriff Schmidt squinted at Bizzy as he removed his hat.

"You haven't *taken* anything from the premises?"

"Stealin'? From the cannery? Are you plain outta your mind, Sheriff? What would we be stealin' from there?"

"These are routine questions," Sheriff Schmidt said defensively.

"Aren't *routine* questions usually tied to reality?"

That's when Sheriff Schmidt got really furious. His left eyebrow crept clear up to the middle of his forehead. He leaned in closer. Then closer. He put his index finger inches from Bizzy's face.

"Listen, Beatrice. I could arrest you for trespassing if I wanted to. But how's it gonna look if I lock up a recuperating old lady? I get it. You're trying to incite me. But I'm not an idiot. People may think you're harmless, but I know better. There have been several reports of strange noises coming from within the cannery and now I *know* it's you," he said, jabbing his finger in Bizzy's face. Bizzy's hard expression remained unchanged. "I'm not going to arrest you . . . THIS TIME. Instead I'm going to get back into my car and pretend I didn't see you. I don't know what you're up to, but I suggest you not go anywhere near the cannery again. Are we clear?"

The sheriff was nearly quaking with anger by the end of his speech. He lowered his hand and stared at Bizzy. Bizzy pursed her lips. Her jaw jutted out and for a moment I thought she might take a swing at the sheriff. Instead, she nodded her head once, slightly.

Sheriff Schmidt put on his hat and stormed back to his squad car. When he'd cleared the area, I looked at Bizzy, expecting her to say something.

"That man sure is unpleasant." It was as if the whole incident amused her. "And I don't think he's playin' with a full deck. He cudda dragged us down to the station on account a' you not wearing a helmet and me endangerin' you with this makeshift rickyshaw. But he couldn't think a' that. Had to make up some dang theory about us stealin' from the cannery."

"But we did steal from the cannery . . . ," I said, waving the *Hot Wheels* magazine in front of us.

"We only collected some trash. He was actin' like it was somethin' much bigger that he was concerned about. Tell you one thing, we know *someone's* been hangin' 'round the cannery."

"Yeah," I said.

"You better step on it," Bizzy said, making a mushlike movement with her hands. She gave me a smile that urged me on. I straightened up and pushed off the ground with my heels. Before long, we were chugging up the hill toward the house.

When I got home, I ran upstairs, telling Bizzy I had to use

the bathroom. My face was flushed from the strain of the bike ride home. Bizzy said she would wait for me downstairs—anxious to reveal the next step of her plan.

To be completely honest, Mrs. Tweedy, I was concerned about Bizzy. At first, she'd wowed me with her supreme confidence in all things death-specter related, but I was visibly shaken after Sheriff Schmidt's sidewalk warning.

The sheriff had treated Bizzy as if she was a bad person—as if he was sure she was hiding something. Did he know something I didn't?

I turned on the faucet and splashed water on my face.

My confusion morphed into anger at Sheriff Schmidt. He'd made me doubt Bizzy, but she was only trying to do what she could to stop Drake's death. To accomplish that, I realized, she was going to need my help without me second-guessing her.

I thundered down the stairs and hallway into Bizzy's room. She was in her wheelchair with the Crabapple yearbook in her lap.

"What I can't figure," Bizzy said, without looking up as she studied my notes in the back of the yearbook, "is what's gonna be the cause of the cannery burnin' up. Unless someone torches it on purpose."

"What do you mean?" I sunk down on Bizzy's bed. For the first time since I'd entered her room, I faced the photo-covered wall opposite her bed.

"Holy . . . ," I said, trailing off. The duct-taped wall of photos had been peeled away completely, resting in a roll in the corner. Behind the rolled-up mural of pictures and notes was an erasable white wall with Bizzy's writing all over it. In the corner where the wall of photos had once begun, I noticed a strip of Velcro. It must have held the pictures in place and allowed Bizzy to roll them back whenever she pleased.

"It ain't permanent marker or anythin'—I just like to sketch out ideas and such," Bizzy said matter-of-factly.

"It's a brainstorm," I said, scanning a few of the interconnected phrases. In almost every language arts class, we'd had to brainstorm before we wrote. You called it prewriting, Mrs. Tweedy. No offense, but whatever it's called, I don't like it.

This brainstorm was different.

On one side, there was a numbered list printed in large purple letters with a box drawn around it:

Accidental Causes of Death
 1. *Motor vehicle crashes*
 2. *Falls*
 3. *Poisoning (solids/liquids)*
 4. *Drowning*
 5. *Fires and burns*
 6. *Suffocation*
 7. *Firearms*
 8. *Poisoning by gases*
 9. *Medical and surgical complications*
 10. *Misadventures and machinery*

Next to the numbered list, more malevolent causes of death had been scribbled in—like murder and various diseases.

Bizzy saw me studying the list.

"Helps me visualize so I don't overlook anythin'," Bizzy said. "Almost fifteen thousand people in the US die from accidental falls a year. Only thing that trumps it is, a' course, auto accidents. A car's nothin' more than a two-ton killin' machine."

Bewildered, I nodded my head.

"You'd probably also be fascinated to know that plenty more people die after an earthquake due to structural uncertainties and explosions from gas leaks than from the quake itself."

I moved to the other side of the uncovered section of wall. It was blank except for two words and a few numbers written at the top in purple marker: "Jodi Sanchez" and yesterday's date—the date I'd seen my first death-specter. There were dozens of purple smudges on that half of the wall, evidence of many names and facts that had been written and erased.

"Be a doll and get a wet cloth to wipe the wall."

"When did you write Jodi up there?"

"As soon as you had your first specter. In fact, I was staring at it when I realized you might try to look for her right then and there. When you weren't in the livin' room, I knew that's where you'd gone. So I got there as fast as I could."

I had to hand it to Bizzy . . . her system may have seemed unorthodox, but her instincts were pretty impressive.

She picked up a small red book from her lap and handed it to me. I opened it. All the pages were blank.

"What's this?"

"A notebook. I want you to write down every single thing

you learn about Drake. We'll chart everythin' here eventually." She handed me a marker.

I stood on my tiptoes and wrote Drake's name on the top of the wall, then a dash, then December 15. I stepped back and Bizzy grabbed the marker from my hand and wheeled herself to the wall. About halfway up, she wrote "The Cannery" in large letters and "Who's living there?" beneath it. The marker squeaked as she moved it against the wall. "Connection to Drake?" she wrote, then wheeled backward so that she was next to me.

We both stared at the wall. I turned to Bizzy, who looked lost in her own thoughts.

"Hmmm," she said aloud.

"What are you thinking about?" I asked.

"I'm thinkin' we need a whole lot of information if we're gonna solve this before our deadline," she said. Her choice of words forced me to think about what would happen if we failed—if Drake actually, well . . . if he actually ended up all alone, in that warehouse, crying out for help.

"Sweet Pea, are you cryin'?"

I put my open palms over my face. I could feel the hot tears streaming from my eyes. I was embarrassed, but once the tears started falling, I was incapable of stopping them. I was getting to know Drake. Drake was nice. As far as I could tell, he was perfect. I thought about how close Jodi had come to fulfilling the death-specter. It scared the living daylights out of me. Drake didn't deserve what fate had planned for him.

"What is it?" Bizzy questioned, pushing her chair back so that she could get a better look at me.

"What if all this doesn't work?" I asked.

"All what doesn't work?"

"What if we fail and Drake dies?"

"Come now! What's brought all this on? We ain't gonna fail!"

"It seems like all Emily Dickinson writes about is dying . . . she was obsessed with it and sad and it's probably because once she found out about us, she couldn't make sense of any of it or get over how quickly a life can disappear."

Even now, I don't know what possessed me to blurt out my theories about the cause of Emily Dickinson's depression. But ever since I'd bought the volume of her poems at Mickey's bookstore, I'd become fixated on her, staying up late into the night reading her poems. I think I was secretly hoping that I'd find a way to escape my fate as a Death Catcher. Instead, I found grim depictions like *"Because I could not stop for Death, / He kindly stopped for me; / The carriage held but just ourselves / And Immortality."* The idea of riding anywhere in a carriage with death made me want to vomit.

"You just ain't been readin' the *right* ones of Emily's poems," Bizzy said, interrupting my thoughts. *"If I can stop one heart from breakin', / I shall not live in vain; / If I can ease one life the achin', / Or cool one pain, / Or help one fainting robin / Unto his nest again, / I shall not live in vain."*

"You've read Emily Dickinson?"

"A' course I have, Sweet Pea. Your great-great-great-grandmother saved her life and Emily, who was smart as a whip, caught wind of our talents. Emily became your great-great-great-grandmother's confidante. And in return, Emily was like our own poet laureate—I think it changed the way she thought 'bout the world. Since then, every Death Catcher has known 'bout Emily. I had to find out for myself what all the fuss was over."

I can't exactly explain it, but the revelation made me feel closer to Bizzy. She, too, had also looked up Emily Dickinson, hoping to unlock some of the mysteries of the Death Catchers.

"Now, I know dear ole Emily had a habit a' writin' a depressin' rhymin' couplet or two, but it ain't all bad," Bizzy said, craning her neck toward me. "No mistakin' it, the job we got handed is no easy task." Emotion was gathering in Bizzy's voice. Her eyes misted over. "What you must realize, honeychile, is that death is a part of life . . . and sometimes there ain't nothin' we can do about it. No use lyin' to you: I've lost a couple a' tough ones in my day." Bizzy paused for a few seconds. "But there ain't no way I'm gonna let one of your first specters slip through our fingers." She clamped her jaw shut and sniffed. The sentiment in her voice had all but drained away. She blinked many times in a row until her eyes returned to normal. "You hear me?"

I heard her, and I wanted desperately to believe her. My grandma was a force, a dynamo, a woman not to be trifled with. But she was also newly out of the hospital, wheelchair bound, a public menace, and over seven decades old. I turned back to the wall.

"What now?" I asked.

"Well, first thing we gotta do is gather more information," she said. "The cannery was a start, but I'm talkin' some ole-fashion observation. A person's death is most often intimately tied to his life. Which means, for a spell at least, you're gonna have to be on Drake like white on rice."

I nodded. I clutched the small journal Bizzy had given me.

"Things aren't as clear when they're inside your head as they are when you write 'em on a piece of paper. So, when you learn somethin' 'bout Drake, it's real important that you write it down right away."

That I could do. As long as it didn't mean I'd have to talk to him.

The Analysis

Mrs. Tweedy, you know how you told us that with any good story, there's always more going on than just the words on the page? How if we take the time to analyze and question what the author means and how it affects us, we'll begin to understand on a deeper level? "Our impression of the words matters more than the words themselves," was how you put it.

Anyhow, I'm pretty sure all that applies to people, too.

Watching what someone does or says is the first step to knowing a person. When you start thinking about why someone says or does something—that's when things really get interesting.

The first few weeks Jodi and I tailed Drake Westfall, we only observed him. We learned that Drake always parked in the same spot in the lot. He had a postcard of a Salvador Dali painting hanging in his locker. He liked graphic novels and had a different one in his backpack every week. As part of Jodi's plan, after school we went to her apartment and we would play her mom's punk and ska albums, as Jodi carefully instructed me on the details.

After a week of careful monitoring, Jodi decided that I was ready for some "forced serendipity." Basically, I was supposed to purposefully bump into Drake when he was alone and pretend it was an accident.

We decided my best chance was recess. Drake's recess behavior was very unusual. As soon as the dismissal bell rang, Drake would get in the cafeteria line and buy a Dr Pepper. Then he would walk out to the edge of the grass, beyond the soccer fields, and stand near the fence of the high school. He'd check to make sure no one else was around. He would take out a small slim notebook and write in it, sipping his Dr Pepper. Sometimes, he'd stare off into space and not write anything at all.

Jodi named the red journal that Bizzy had given me the DWOR, which stood for Drake Westfall Observational Research. In it, we'd sketched out Drake's exact location during recess and the path for my approach. We considered it an airtight plan.

There was a cluster of trees in the corner of the field near where Drake liked to stand. There was a bench in front of the cluster. If I arrived there and hid behind the trees while Drake was waiting in line to buy his Dr Pepper, I'd have the perfect lookout point. Once Drake was standing near the fence, I would slip out of the trees and sit on the bench. I could then start a conversation and pretend I'd been there the whole time and he hadn't noticed me.

Once the bell rang, Jodi wished me luck and I sprinted toward the trees. I thought about Bizzy's latest advice.

"No one finds anythin' out by bein' shy," she'd said one morning, trying to encourage me. "Ain't nothin' wrong with bein' bold and brazen."

I arrived at the cluster of trees and I stood behind one, testing how much I could see of Drake's usual spot. I had a perfect view, about ten feet away. I didn't have to wait long until Drake came striding up. The crack of the Dr Pepper can opening echoed through the field. Everything was still, though I could feel my pulse quicken. I tried to breathe quietly. Drake rustled through his backpack ten feet in front of me. I was sure he was pulling out his notebook. I closed my eyes. Swallowing hard, I resolved that in four seconds, I would take my first glimpse from behind the tree. Four . . . three . . . two . . .

"Lizzy?"

Startled, I let out a little yelp and jumped to my feet.

I was standing eye to eye with Drake. He was in front of the bench and I was behind it.

He scrunched his eyebrows together and looked at me curiously. "Are you hiding out?"

"Maybe," I said. My stomach burned, an inferno of ignited nerves. It felt like someone was holding a hot poker to my left hand. Drake's name was on fire. I slid the new wide-band watch I had bought down my wrist, making sure it covered my brightly glowing palm. Then I looked down at Drake's hands—he was clutching the slim notebook in one and a pencil in the other.

He sat down and motioned for me to sit next to him. I walked around the bench and sat, leaving less than a foot between us. I couldn't believe I was so close to Drake Westfall.

"What are you hiding from?" he asked. His eyes gleamed even though it wasn't sunny out. He tightened his grip on the notebook.

"Everything, I guess," I finally answered. "If I sit in the middle of the trees, I can pretend I'm somewhere else, put my headphones in, and zone out to Operation Ivy."

"*You* listen to Op Ivy?" Drake questioned.

"Is that so shocking?" I asked.

"Well, it's not exactly normal for someone like you . . ."

"Someone like *me*?"

"I just mean that I'd never expect law-abiding Lizzy Mortimer to listen to Op Ivy."

"Well, if we're talking about the East Bay ska scene, the Dance Hall Crashers are a little more my style. I like the female vocals and they don't scream as much."

As soon as I brought my eyes up to Drake's, he looked down and dug one foot into the ground, as if he were trying to make a small hole. His tan skin and gold-flecked hair were as perfect as I remembered them. He looked at me again. This time he smiled widely. At me. I could hardly believe it.

"Apparently, you're just full of surprises," he said.

"If you say so," I said. I still couldn't believe I was talking to Drake alone like this. "Hey, why are *you* out here?"

"I'm always here at this time," he said.

"That's not answering the question," I said, emboldened by Drake's teasing. "What's in the notebook?"

"Nothing," he responded, clutching the journal to his chest.

"If it's nothing, then can I look at it?"

"No," he said, laughing as he held the notebook closer to his chest.

We stared at each other. It was one of those stares where you start wondering if the other person is thinking the same things you are. As I was thinking how completely handsome Drake was when he smiled, his dimples and turquoise eyes flashed all at once. Without saying anything, Drake held the journal out in front of him. The gesture confused me at first. I soon realized that he was holding it there for me.

I carefully took it from him as he watched, his eyes wide like an owl's. Our index fingers touched as I grabbed it. I felt something less than a shock but more than a tingle pass from his finger through mine. The red letters of Drake's name began to throb on my palm. I looked down, almost ashamed, though I knew Drake couldn't see them.

I flipped to a random page. It was a sketch of Breeze in the Trees, my favorite house in Crabapple. Breeze in the Trees is a giant tree house, complete with rope ladders and circular windows. The wood shingles blend in with the knotted trees that grow out of every corner of the lawn. It looks as if elves live there. The penciled-in detail of Drake's sketch was astonishing. I flipped to another page. It was a sketch of Mrs. Bowman. Mrs. Bowman taught European History and had tormented Jodi for much of the year. (Maybe since she's a coworker of yours, Mrs. Tweedy, you think she's nice. But you should know that most of her students can't stand her.) Drake had made Mrs. Bowman's head too big and her eyes too small—but entirely realistic. I began flipping faster. It seemed Drake had sketched almost every noteworthy location in town, along with a few of Crabapple's best-known teachers. I was astonished by both the number of drawings and their quality. The drawings had an exaggerated character that brought them to life.

"What is all this, Drake?"

Drake shrugged his shoulders. "I'm out here because it's the only time I have a couple of minutes to myself to draw," he said.

He slid toward me on the bench and gently took the journal out of my hands. He lowered his head and began tracing the spine with his finger. When he spoke again, it was in a lower tone.

"I read that when Michelangelo was young," Drake said, looking out at the ocean beyond the school yard's fence, "his dad was a banker and then worked for the government. He sent Michelangelo to school where it was assumed he would learn to do something practical. But he was constantly sneaking into churches—he didn't seem that interested in his school classes. He would plant himself in the pews and sit there for hours, trying to create exact copies of the masterworks that hung on the walls. I like to think church was the one place he could practice without anyone bothering him."

"Have you read *The Agony and the Ecstasy*?" I asked. Mickey had told us the Michelangelo book was Drake's most recent book purchase. I remembered it because Jodi had written it down in the DWOR and quizzed me on it at lunch.

Drake was astonished. "You listen to Op Ivy and you've read *The Agony and the Ecstasy*?"

"No, no . . . I haven't read it," I said, thinking quickly. "My mom's talked about it, though. She's kind of a book nut."

"Oh yeah, I knew that," Drake said, sticking one of his long arms out behind me, resting it on the top of the bench. I pretended not to notice. "The last time I ran into her outside my house, she pulled a book called *Fever Pitch* out of this huge bag and handed it to me. She said I would like it because it's about sports."

I put my hand over my face to indicate my mortification. "Did she also tell you that the solution to every one of life's problems can be found within the pages of a good book?"

"Yeah, I think she did," Drake said.

"I'm so sorry. It's like her personal mantra. She's obsessed. It's her goal in life to find every person in Crabapple a book they love."

"It's fine," Drake said, his arm hovering above my shoulders. "The book's actually really funny. I liked it."

"That would probably make her month."

"I'll have to let her know the next time I see her, then," Drake said.

"Please don't. She doesn't need any encouragement. It's not healthy, trust me."

Drake let out a laugh.

I knew it was stupid, but I wished that the tardy bells would stop working. I wanted to stay out there, talking with Drake. I looked through the chain-link fence and saw the ocean, a strip of dark blue against the light blue sky.

"So, this is your church?" I asked, motioning to the area around the benches and then the notebook.

"Something like that," he said.

"Your sketches are really good." I knew I should have said something deeper or more meaningful, but it was all I could think of. They were.

"Not really," he said. "But I think it'd be cool to be an artist for graphic novels."

"They really *are* good. In fact," I said, letting out a small laugh, "the one of Mrs. Bowman looks so real, when I first saw it, I honestly thought the drawing was going to start yelling at me."

"You're a good liar," Drake said, smiling at me again, without any restraint.

"If by 'liar' you mean 'truth teller,' then yes," I said, mocking him. Without thinking, I reached out and pushed Drake's shoulder playfully. Our eyes locked.

Drake was still smiling. He let his arm slip off the top of the bench. It was warm against the bare skin of my neck.

I was so lost in my own pool of nervous thoughts that I didn't notice when she appeared.

Her dark black robe swished as she stalked across the grass soccer field with her hood up. She marched right for us. I squeezed my eyes as tightly as I could. I opened them once more.

She was closer still. Vivienne le Mort was so close, in fact, I could make out the bloody color of her eyes.

"Drake," I said, the fear embedded in my voice. "Do you see that woman?"

I tried to turn toward him. But I couldn't.

I was frozen and so was he.

†HE A∏†AGO∏IS†

When it comes to antagonists or villains, Mrs. Tweedy, I think the most chilling ones are those with seemingly no motivation at all. I'm sure there are more horrific things than finding yourself unable to move while a paralysis-inducing sorceress responsible for "cutting the threads of mortals" approaches, but at the moment it happened, I couldn't think of one. It wasn't merely her imposing height, her yellow teeth, or the fact that she'd managed to freeze Drake, too. Vivienne le Mort terrified me, in large part, because I had no idea what she was after.

I also seemed to be the only one who could see her.

Drake was as still as a stone next to me on the bench. Vivienne approached slowly. With her long robe dragging on the ground, she floated above the Crabapple High School soccer field. I halfheartedly tried to scream, but knew it was no use. She was less than a foot away when she stopped in front of us. Vivienne scrutinized me for a brief second before taking a large step to the side.

She bent down in front of Drake, until she was eye level with him. Though I couldn't turn my head to look at her, out of the corner of my eye I watched Vivienne take her bony hands and place them on each side of Drake's face. She tilted up his head, staring into his eyes as if she might be brainwashing him.

I would never have guessed that she was only trying to identify him.

Then, as suddenly as she appeared, she vanished, leaving behind a rising whirlwind of black smoke in her wake.

"Then what?" Jodi asked.

The day after Vivienne le Mort's visit, Jodi and I were at our familiar spot at Cedar Tree Park. I'd already told her the whole story of what happened between Drake and me (with a few necessary omissions) at lunch the day before, but Jodi wanted to write it down. She had the red DWOR journal in her lap and was taking detailed notes. For the second time, I recounted my conversation with Drake during recess the day before.

Even then, I recognized how strange it was that both my grandmother and my best friend were so intent on gathering information about Drake, but for very different purposes: Jodi to make him fall in love with me and Bizzy to prevent his death. I couldn't quite pinpoint what my interest in Drake was, other than that it was more than just saving his life—I was beginning to feel like our fates were intertwined somehow.

"Then the bell rang and we went to class," I said, keeping quiet about Vivienne le Mort. When Drake and I could finally move, he reacted the way Jodi had when Vivienne touched her. He didn't mention seeing anything or feeling frozen and I began to wonder if I had a brain tumor all over again.

"Things are moving along," Jodi said. "At this rate, you two'll be married by June."

"Oh, stop it," I said.

The truth was, if I didn't have feelings for Drake before, I did now. At the time, I would've denied it. Looking back on it, though, I started to fall for Drake Westfall when I saw him in the park with Roger. It wasn't just that he was the best-looking guy at Crabapple, or that he was a water polo star—he was kind and funny and smart. He may have been a celebrated jock, but there was so much more to him. I felt like I was one of the only people in Crabapple who knew he was also part geek.

All this explains why, when his black Ford truck screeched to a stop in front of Jodi and me as we biked home from school, my heart fluttered. My Hand of Fate burned once more.

"Hey," Drake said, leaning out the window when we caught up to him.

"Hi," Jodi said first, grinning.

"Do you girls want a ride home?" He was wearing sunglasses.

"We have our bikes," I objected.

"You can just throw them in the back of the truck," Drake said.

"This is where Lizzy and I separate," Jodi said. "But thanks for offering! See you tomorrow, Lizzy." Jodi didn't wait for me or Drake to respond. She took off pedaling down Dolores Avenue toward Miss Mora's Market.

Drake bounded out of his truck and with one swift movement put his hands on my hips and hoisted me right off my bike. It was as if I weighed nothing at all in his strong arms. He set me down on the sidewalk and put my bike in the back of his truck. Drake grinned at me as he climbed back in the truck.

"Well?" he asked.

I couldn't even pretend to resist. I ran around the front of the truck and jumped in on the passenger side. Drake accelerated down Delores Avenue.

"Do you feel different?" Drake asked, his sturdy hands on the wheel. I thought about how they felt on my waist.

"Different?" I repeated.

"Now that you're a confirmed law-breaker," Drake said. "It really didn't take all that long to corrupt you."

"Oh, don't worry. I have a plan. If we do get pulled over," I said, smiling as I glanced at him, "I'm going to explain that you stole my bike and the only way I could pursue you was by getting in the truck. I'm sure the police will understand."

Drake grinned, taking his eyes off the road and fixing them on me. "I can't believe you'd turn on me so quickly. Especially when a pretty girl like you could bat your eyes at the cops and get us both off, no problem." Drake snapped his fingers.

Was it my imagination or had Drake Westfall just called me pretty? I almost asked him to say it again, but stopped myself in time. He continued to tease me for being a turncoat until the moment he pulled into my driveway. He got out and lifted my bike out of the bed of the truck.

"You could have just let me off at your house," I said. "It's only about twenty feet away."

"Oh no, no. I offered you a ride home. Not partway home."

"Well, thank you," I said.

"Of course," he said.

I stood there with my fifteen-speed as Drake pulled out of the driveway. Before he put the truck into drive, he poked his head out the window once more.

"I almost forgot . . . I've got something for you at my house. What are you doing later?" Drake asked, as casually as someone might ask a stranger for the time.

"Later?" *Studying you*, I thought. What I said, though, was "homework."

"Do you want to come by around five? I'll be back from practice by then."

"My mom won't let me do anything until I've proven to her that I've finished my homework." I immediately thought about what a dork I sounded like.

"Bring your backpack and say you're getting help on an assignment," Drake advised, as if he'd done this before.

"Okay." I tried to remain calm until Drake was a safe distance away. As soon as he pulled into his garage, though I'm embarrassed to admit it, I jumped off the ground and ran into the house.

"You win the lottery or somethin'?"

I looked up, startled. Bizzy had wheeled close to me and was studying my face.

"What?" I asked.

"I haven't seen ya smile like that in a while, Sweet Pea."

"Oh," I said. "I found out some things about Drake. And I'm going over to his house later. He invited me." Because Mom had been hovering more than usual for the past day, I hadn't had a chance to talk with Bizzy since I'd last seen Vivienne le Mort. With both Mom and Dad still at work, now was the perfect time.

"Let's go into my room and see if we can't make somethin' out of it."

Bizzy began pressing me on what I'd learned about Drake.

"So he loves to draw?" she questioned. "And he doesn't want anyone to know?" She wheeled to the wall and with the purple marker, she put a bullet point and then the word "artist" under Drake's name.

"Not quite sure how it fits, Lizzy-Loo, but I got this feelin' it's important somehow."

"I don't know," I said. We stared at the wall. December 15 was less than two weeks away and we didn't seem to have the right clues.

"How come only I can see Vivienne, Bizzy?"

"I'm sure Vivienne doesn't know you can see her," Bizzy

offered. "You've got to remember that us Hands a' Fate have the blood of Avalon runnin' through our veins. It must make you able to see her even when she doesn't want to be seen. Just like we got that particular weakness with regard to the scream of the banshee."

"What was Vivienne le Mort doing to him when she touched Drake?" I asked.

"I'm still not sure what she's after," Bizzy said. "But I think it's high time we found out for certain, don't you?"

"What do you mean?"

"For now," Bizzy said, "you just concentrate on gettin' ready for your date with Drake . . . I'll fill you in later once I figger out exactly what we're gonna do."

"It's *not* a date," I argued. "He just has to give me something."

"You say potato, I say french fries," Bizzy said, winking in my direction. She paused one moment before she let out a string of laughs, one right after the other.

Drake hadn't meant it as a date, I was sure of it. But that didn't mean that I wasn't secretly hoping Bizzy was right.

Dialogue

Maybe I shouldn't admit this, Mrs. Tweedy, but whenever I have a reading assignment, I secretly cheer when there's a lot of dialogue because I know it'll be a faster read. I'm not alone on that front, I bet.

One thing about real-life dialogue I don't like is that when it starts, sometimes you can't stop it. Some conversations are kind of like a big, round boulder on the top of a huge hill. As soon as you nudge the boulder a little, it gets going down the hill with so much momentum that there's nothing you can do except get out of the way. I guess, when you're mid-dialogue and you don't want to be anymore, you can get up and walk away, but that's pretty rude. I'll tell you one thing, Mrs. Tweedy: when I was at Drake's house, I've never wanted to run away from dialogue more in my life.

The whole thing started out okay. But if I'd known how it was going to end, I would've, to use one of Bizzy's expressions, "packed up the pets 'n' particulars and headed for the hills."

I felt anxious all afternoon as I thought about going over to Drake's. I actually went to the pharmacy and picked up some lipstick and mascara. Though I had no idea what I was doing (for the first time, I wished I had an older sister) as I fumbled with the tubes, I covered my lips with goop and wanded my eyelashes until they looked good and crusty. I don't know if I looked any better, but I certainly looked older.

Drake's house was a large stone building with a pointed roof and two pine trees growing in the front yard. I had slipped the mascara and lipstick into my backpack in case I needed a touch-up. It and the impending visit weighed heavily on my shoulders as I stood on the Westfall porch and knocked. Mrs. Westfall answered. "Lizzy Mortimer! It's so nice to see you," she said, wiping her hands on the front of her red-checkered apron. "Drake said you'd be dropping by this evening. Go on up to his room," Mrs. Westfall said, ushering me in.

I took the stairs one at a time.

The farther I climbed, the closer I got to Drake, and the more the fateful writing on my hand burned.

Drake's room was different from what I expected. Though his water polo team pictures hung above his bed, he didn't have much else in the way of sports memorabilia. In the opposite corner rested a red and white Fender guitar and the multicolored kite Jodi and I'd seen him flying at Cedar Tree Park.

There were two large posters hanging on his walls. One pictured the members of the Clash, in yellow and black tones, announcing the band's concert at the Palladium in 1979. On the wall next to Drake's window, there was a print of a painting that looked like it was from the Renaissance with a gathering of men in bright togas in a large domed cathedral. Drake had his back to me, wearing his headphones and staring at his computer.

"Hey," I said.

Drake spun around and followed my eyes to the poster. He removed his headphones and got up. I set my backpack down by the doorway.

"Do you know that painting?" he asked.

"No," I said as I stepped toward it.

"It's called *The School of Athens*. Most of the famous Greek philosophers are pictured in it," Drake said, moving to the wall. "That's Socrates, I think, and there's Plato." Drake had pointed at two of the bearded men in the center of the painting.

"Lizzard-Breath! Long time no see."

Drake and I both turned in the direction of the voice. Drake's older half brother, Damon, stood in the doorway, smirking. Damon was bigger and thicker than Drake. His left arm was covered with tattoos. He always wore an off-kilter Oregon State hat over his bushy black hair.

"Hey, Damon," I said, trying not to show my annoyance.

"It's been too long. No, wait . . . it hasn't," Damon said, smiling obnoxiously.

"Go away," Drake said.

Damon looked at both of us as if he were watching a very amusing scene from a movie. It took all the self-control I had not to reach over and slap him in the face. I'm not one of those people who spends a lot of time disliking others, but I don't mind admitting that I've spent some time hating Damon.

I have my reasons.

First of all, there is his nickname for me, "Lizzard-Breath," which actually may be too unimaginative to be truly hate worthy. Though I hadn't really been at Drake's house in a long time, when we were little I would come over and Damon would always call me by that nickname.

Worse than that, Damon had a cruel streak. At the last birthday party I attended for Drake years ago, Damon came into the living room, reeking of cigarettes. He plopped on the couch right in the middle of the party. In front of everyone, he asked me if they'd let me out of the kennel especially for Drake's birthday.

Some of Drake's other friends laughed. Drake just looked embarrassed and told Damon to shut up. I was pretty young at the time and had no idea what kennel meant until I looked it up in the dictionary that night: "a small shelter for a dog." When I read the definition, I felt tears swelling, ready to well up into my eyes and spill out.

I know it was a long time ago, but let's just say that if I ever have a death-specter about Damon Westfall, I'd have to think twice about saving him. Of course since I couldn't care less about him, that probably would never happen.

We all stood in Drake's room. Drake glanced at his brother, then at me, then walked over to the door and pushed it shut right in Damon's face.

"Sure. You two probably want a little privacy," Damon

shouted through the closed door. "But remember that Mom could walk in any minute, lover boy."

I knew I was turning red. Drake just rolled his eyes and sat back down in his chair. He swiveled in it so that he was facing me. His hair was still wet from water polo practice and he smelled like soap and chlorine.

"Don't pay any attention to him," Drake said without looking at me.

"Sorry for sneaking up on you, but your mom let me in."

"You can sneak up on me anytime, Lizzy," Drake said. The warmth Damon had sucked out of Drake's voice was back.

I grew nervous. "So, are you a big kite flyer?" I asked, trying not to show it as I pointed to the triangular kite in the corner.

Drake picked up the kite. He sat on the bed next to it. He nudged the rolling chair toward me. I sat down. Drake's eyes were brilliant blue in the dim light of his room.

"Have you ever flown a kite?"

"No," I said. "But you have. Jodi and I saw you flying that kite at the park with Roger Riley."

"You were *spying* on me?" Drake asked. Quaking, I honestly thought we'd been discovered. But then Drake laughed, displaying his dimples, and I realized he wasn't serious.

"The park's a pretty public place," I fired back.

"I'm kidding," Drake said. "Roger wanted me to teach him. Do you know Roger at all?"

"Only what other people say about him."

"Everyone gives him a hard time, but he's a good kid."

"Well, you must be a decent teacher. By the end of your lesson, we saw Roger doing some pretty fancy tricks."

The side of Drake's mouth crept up his face. "Maybe it's a pretty lame thing to do."

"It's just different."

"Well, it reminds me of fishing, except it's more collaborative. At the end of the day, you're not trying to kill the kite like you are the fish. Once you get the kite flying, you feel its pull on the other end of the line and all you have to do is pay attention and react and the kite should theoretically stay up until there isn't any wind left to carry it. It's peaceful, if that makes any sense at all."

"It does," I said. Drake looked at me like he was memorizing my face. I grew self-conscious, but I also felt strangely at ease with Drake. It was like we'd known each other really well in the past and were getting reacquainted after a long time apart. Drake grabbed a small black rectangular object off his desk and held it in his palm. He flipped it open with his thumb. A flame ignited from within the small box.

"Is that a lighter?"

"Yeah," Drake said.

"You smoke?" I questioned.

"No. It's an antique. It belonged to my grandfather during World War II. See?" Drake held out the lighter for me to inspect. It was covered in a rough black material. At the bottom of it, someone had carved in the letters *WAW*. "Those are his initials," Drake explained.

"It's neat," I said.

"My grandfather was a war hero. He said this lighter was responsible for keeping him alive during the Battle of the Bulge. He gave it to me a few years ago, before he passed away. I carry it around with me for luck . . . it makes me feel better somehow."

"People say death is a part of life, but I think it makes a lot of sense to have something to remind you of all the memories you have of a person who's gone." Drake flipped the cover of the lighter up and then flicked his wrist and it clacked shut. "Do you miss him?"

"Yeah. You're really close with your grandmother, aren't you?"

"Definitely. Bizzy's a bit of a kook, but she's got this perspective on things that makes you think and laugh all at the same time," I said. Drake continued lifting the cover of the lighter and closing it.

"So that's where you get it from," Drake said. "Does your grandmother ask as many questions as you do?"

"What do you mean?" I asked, wondering if Drake was insulting me.

"I've just never met anyone who asks so many questions," he said.

"Well, it's amazing what you can find out about a person if you ask the right things," I said. "People are pretty interesting if you take the time to figure them out."

I thought about how much I'd learned about other people by paying attention in the past few days. For instance, I'd learned that Dad always put two heaping spoonfuls of sugar in his coffee at home, but when we were at restaurants, he ordered it black. I now knew that Mom put her hand on Dad's shoulder when she wanted him to do something in the yard. I noticed that Jodi always played with the left side of her hair when she was nervous, and the right side when she was excited about something. I'd realized Mrs. Bowman never talked about Mr. Bowman and would change the subject if you brought him up and instead talk about her two pugs, Bert and Ernie.

"Oh? And what have you figured out about me, Lizzy?"

"For one, you're a lot different than people think you are," I said, afraid to look at him.

"So are you." Drake put his long legs on the ground and leaned closer to me, his torso bridging the distance between us. I gripped the arms of the rolling chair, willing myself to sit still.

"Are you wearing makeup?" Drake asked.

"No," I said defensively, startled.

"I wasn't criticizing. It looks nice," Drake said, pulling his body back. "You look good without it, too." Embarrassed, I racked my brain for a new subject.

"Why is Damon home?"

Drake's half brother had packed up to begin his junior year at Oregon State last summer. Watching from our driveway, I, of course, was delighted to see him go. But it was still a little early for him to be home for winter break.

"He got kicked out of school," Drake said. Perhaps I hadn't picked the best subject change.

"I'm sorry," I said. Part of me wanted to reach out and grab his hand. Maybe all of me did.

"There's nothing to be sorry about," Drake said, raising his voice a little. "Damon's always been a screwup. Now that he's home all the time, my parents are crazier than ever," he said.

"Has *your* mom handed out any books to strangers lately?" I asked. "Trust me, your parents aren't any weirder than anyone else's—even with Damon home."

Knock. Knock.

Drake's mouth was half-open when the knock came at the door, but he closed it as soon as he heard the noise. Mrs. Westfall poked her head in the room.

"Your grandma just called," she said. Her smile was disarmingly wide and bright, just like Drake's. "She has to run and help a friend tonight . . . so I told her we'd have you stay for dinner. Sound okay?"

"Oh . . . okay," I said. "Thank you."

"I figured you were too smart to pass up my meat loaf," Mrs. Westfall responded. "We'll eat in about twenty minutes." She left the door a crack open.

Bizzy had struck again. She'd obviously wanted me to spend more time inside the Westfall household. She really was a master at manipulation.

"Before I forget," Drake said. He got up from his bed and picked up a CD off his desk. He handed it to me. "I figured if you like the Dance Hall Crashers, then you need to go back to where it all started with the Selecter. I put some other 2 Tone stuff on there. Mostly British second wave . . . what inspired things over here."

I stared at the CD in my hands. Drake had written "Songs for Lizzy" in large letters and then under that "From Drake."

"Thank you," I said. No one had ever made a mix for me before. Or anything else, really.

"I hope you like it."

As we headed down the stairs to the dining room, I told Drake I needed to wash up before dinner. Once I was back upstairs, I closed the door to the bathroom that Drake and Damon shared. It smelled like boy and it was not very clean. I was washing my hands when I noticed a stack of magazines in the corner by the shower. Almost as if Bizzy was whispering in my ear to investigate further, I picked one up.

Hot Wheels. The same magazine as the one I'd taken from the tent in the cannery. I dropped it quickly and straightened the stack. Bizzy had told me to write any important discoveries down, but I was sure I'd remember this one.

I bolted downstairs for dinner, my mind racing.

Cacophony

Anyone who knows me will tell you that I'm never going to win an award based on my dazzling memory. Things like vocab quizzes and geography tests aren't, as Bizzy would say, my "strong suit." Maybe you already know all this, Mrs. Tweedy. But one thing I really liked about this past semester is that you always gave examples for the words we were going to be tested on. It helped my memory lapses tremendously. That's why I'll always remember "cacophony." You said that it was two sounds that didn't go together at all—like the *caw* of a crow and the *meow* of a cat.

After about five minutes at dinner with Drake and his family, the one word that came to mind was *cacophony*. That's what it was. Sheer and utter cacophony. None of the Westfalls seemed to go together. They were pieces to four different puzzles.

Dinner started out normally. Damon was to my left at the round table, then Mrs. Westfall, Mr. Westfall, and then Drake on my right. I would have chosen a chair that wasn't next to

Drake, but only two chairs remained empty by the time we sat down.

Within minutes, everything turned nasty.

Mostly, it was my fault.

Maybe you've met Mr. Westfall at a parent-teacher night or something, Mrs. Tweedy. I'm sure you'd remember him if you did—he's tall and lanky like Drake. At six and a half feet tall, with his sandy blond hair cropped close to the scalp, Mark Westfall is hard to miss. He's unnaturally tan and his face is all angles and wrinkles. His chin looks like it is made of Legos. When I was at Drake's house as a kid, Mr. Westfall never paid much attention to me. For that I was grateful. He spoke gruffly to Drake, usually about something water polo related. Drake always replied, "Yes, sir." Mr. Westfall would then march out of the room with a frown on his face. He never struck me as a particularly happy person. But he was certainly an involved father—he attended every one of Drake's water polo matches, as well as many of his practices.

The sour of Mr. Westfall was only matched by the sweetness of Mrs. Westfall.

She always concerned herself with the comfort of other people. As I piled mashed potatoes beside a large slab of meat loaf, Mrs. Westfall tried to draw me into the conversation.

"So, Lizzy, did you end up sticking with the flute? You had so much natural talent." She gave me a warm look as she scooped some mashed potatoes onto her plate. She wore a collared shirt. Her hair hung in shiny loose brown curls around her face. Mrs. Westfall was very pretty, but it never looked like she was trying that hard.

"I'm taking orchestra zero period this year, but I'm not sure I'm going to do it next year," I said.

"Oh, you should! I remember your solo in the spring recital a few years back . . . you were wonderful!" Mrs. Westfall exclaimed.

"Ma, if she doesn't want to be tormented, Lizzard-Breath is gonna have to ditch the dorkestra," Damon said, shoveling potatoes in his mouth at a ferocious rate.

"Damon, please! Lizzy, I think it would be such a *shame* if you gave up on your extraordinary talent," Mrs. Westfall said kindly.

"Oh, I'm not really talented . . . not like Drake is, anyway." I was embarrassed the moment I said it.

"True, Drake is a very good water polo player," she said, "but having a—"

"I'm not talking about water polo, Mrs. Westfall, I'm talking about Drake's art," I blurted. "You should see some of the stuff he's done lately!"

All four Westfall jaws dropped simultaneously. Mr. Westfall's fork clanged to his plate. The color drained from Mrs. Westfall's face as she stole a glance at her husband. I focused on Mr. Westfall. His face had turned the color of cranberry sauce. He stopped cutting his meat loaf and squeezed his knife until his knuckles turned white.

"Drake," he said, inhaling deeply as he looked down at his

plate. He pursed his lips and gnashed his teeth. "Have you been wasting time with all that again?"

"No, sir," Drake said.

"Because you know that state finals are coming in a few short weeks," Mr. Westfall said, "and we've talked about how *foolish* it would be to spend *any* time—"

"Now, Mark," Mrs. Westfall said, directing all her attention toward Mr. Westfall, "Drake said he wasn't, and I think it's best we take him at his word."

"I was only talking about a few sketches I saw in his notebook," I said, hoping to ease the situation. "Just doodles, really."

Mr. Westfall zeroed in on Drake, who was expressionless. He raised his knife and pointed it directly at his son.

"Are you goofing around in class, young man?" he questioned, jabbing the knife in the air with every word.

"No, sir," Drake answered quietly.

"If there's one thing I've told you over and over, it's that now is the most critical time in your life. School and water polo. Water polo and school. That's all you should be thinking about. Focus, son. You must FOCUS," Mr. Westfall continued, waving his hands wildly, growing more agitated. "You're competing with a thousand other athletes across the country. Athletes that are bigger than you! Faster than you. Working harder than you. Practicing harder than you. You want a scholarship? You want the glory that comes with being an elite athlete? Then you don't have time to MESS AROUND with a bunch of girls and crayons in ART class! We've worked *too* hard to get here. You'll be able to pick any school you choose if you stick with our plan. Do you hear me? Drake? You'll regret it for the rest of your life if you lose sight of the prize now! Are you even *listening* to me?"

Mr. Westfall was now the color of a stop sign.

"Mark, please," Mrs. Westfall begged.

"Maybe I'll get an art scholarship instead," Drake replied.

"Oh, you think this is all *funny*, do you?" Mr. Westfall was yelling now. "Do you want to become a complete loser like Damon here?"

"Mark!" Mrs. Westfall yelled. "Calm down!"

Damon, who had been delighting in the confrontation between his younger brother and his father, suddenly looked wounded. I always assumed Damon felt less-than because his father had divorced Damon's mom when he was very young. I'd never seen Mrs. Westfall treat him differently from Drake, but he had a chip on his shoulder about it. His pain transformed into anger.

"I don't have to put up with this," Damon said, muttering expletives under his breath as he pushed back his chair and stormed away from the table.

"I'm not hungry anymore," Mr. Westfall said, throwing his cloth napkin down onto his plate. He glowered at Drake, narrowing his eyes and tightening his square chin before plowing down the hallway. First Damon's upstairs bedroom door slammed, then the door of Mr. Westfall's study followed.

The three of us—Drake, Mrs. Westfall, and I—were left

sitting at the table. Silence permeated the air. Drake refused to look up from his plate but I could tell he was fuming.

Mrs. Westfall adjusted the collar of her shirt. Without looking at either Drake or me, she picked up her fork and began moving the mashed potatoes in circles around her plate. I could see her chest heave as she breathed in deeply. She looked up. I couldn't tell if she was smiling or grimacing.

"Sorry for the commotion, Lizzy," she said. "You know how families are."

I did know how families were. They were full of buried resentments and confidences ready to boil over at any moment. I thought about Bizzy and my mother, at each other's throats last Thanksgiving after an argument over how much flour to put in the gravy.

The three of us finished our meat loaf and mashed potatoes in silence.

"Do you need any help cleaning up, Mom?" Drake asked. Even after his father had chewed him out, he still managed to be a considerate son.

"No, dear. I can manage. Lizzy, if I don't see you before you go, it was wonderful having you," Mrs. Westfall said as she cleared off the table.

"Thank you very much for dinner," I replied, hardly able to control my confusion.

"I'm going to walk Lizzy out, Mom," Drake said as he headed toward the entryway of the Westfall house.

I followed him out into the hallway. Drake's face said it

all. He wore an expression of absolute disgust. He had confided in me and I had betrayed him to the person he least wanted to know.

Drake opened the door.

"I forgot my backpack," I said.

"I'll go get it," Drake said, his voice devoid of emotion. "You can wait on the porch." Drake was in a hurry to get me out of his house, not that I blamed him.

I opened the front door of the Westfall house and plunged into the cold night. I watched as a pair of headlights grew brighter from the south. The car pulled in front of Let the Good Chimes Roll, the house next door to the Westfalls'.

I squinted through the darkness and felt a strange familiarity overcome me as I eyed the black sedan. After a moment, I was sure I recognized it. The car was identical to the one that had tried to run down Jodi.

Wordy

Last year, my language arts teacher told me that my "wordiness and run-ons gave her migraines more painful than the birth of Willie." Willie is her second child, and that is a direct quote. I think I've made improvements on that front, using your "when in doubt, take it out" mantra, Mrs. Tweedy, but clearly wordiness had gotten the best of me at the Westfall dinner table. As I waited for Drake to get my backpack, I still couldn't believe I'd blurted out something about Drake's art.

I didn't hear Drake approach. He spun me around. His eyes were wide and he put his index finger to his mouth, signaling for me to remain quiet.

"Follow me," he whispered.

He began to walk around the side of his house. He reached up and unlatched the wood-planked side gate. We passed through it to the backyard. December crispness ruled the air. Minus the chirping of a few crickets, it was quiet in the Westfalls' backyard. In the distance, I could hear the roar of the surf. Drake and I made our way around the pool. He opened the door to the pool house and then closed it behind us.

I was shivering from the cold night air. It was nearly dark but there was enough light coming in through the two square front windows of the pool house for me to make out the clutter inside. There were boxes piled high all around us with junk randomly thrown in corners. Drake moved quickly through the jumble of covered furniture and boxes. Soon he was in the far corner. I didn't move from my position near the door, afraid that if I did, I would stumble and fall.

"Drake?" I whispered. "Drake, what are we doing in here?"

Drake shifted items in the corner. Something scraped against the wall as Drake grunted under the weight of a large box. I heard Drake's lighter open and then clamp closed. Drake's face was now bright with orange flickering light. Holding a candle, he walked over to me, slipping between boxes. Once he was in front of me, he stared at me.

I gulped. My hands were shaking. I was more confused than ever before. What was Drake doing? Had he brought me here to yell at me?

He moved closer. I had to resist the urge to throw my arms around him in a heartfelt apology. My senses were at their sharpest. I was recording each detail in case this would be one of those moments I'd replay a thousand times in my mind.

"I'm so sorry that I said anything, Drake," I stammered. "I didn't realize it was such a sore subject and I can't imagine why someone wouldn't be proud of how talented you are and—"

"Lizzy, it's okay. You didn't know how crazy my dad is. Now you do."

The shimmering candle flame reflection danced in both of Drake's blue eyes. Our faces were inches from one another. As much as I wanted to linger in the moment, the scratched-in letters now throbbing on my wrist would not let me forget my task.

"Do you read the magazine *Hot Wheels*?" I blurted.

Drake gave me a strange look. "Um, no. Do you?"

"No . . . I was just wondering," I said, trying not to look embarrassed. Bizzy had made fact collecting sound so easy. In truth, it involved so many awkward questions.

"I'm sorry you had to witness all that," Drake said softly.

"It's okay. I'm sorry that I said anything . . . I really didn't know . . . I feel awful."

"Can I ask you a favor?" Drake leaned in closer to me. I could feel the warmth of his breath on my nose.

"Okay," I said, barely able to hear myself.

Drake turned away from me and edged toward the rear of the pool house. Not knowing what else to do, I followed him, carefully stepping around the boxes and abandoned electronics that littered the path. The candlelight cast winking shadows across the walls.

Drake walked down a hallway and entered a bathroom. As we crammed into the small room, Drake closed the lid of the toilet and set the candle down on it. The room reeked of mildew and another even less pleasant odor I couldn't identify.

"What is that smell?" I asked.

"I can't really smell anything anymore. To me, after spending years in the pool, everything smells like chlorine," he replied. "It's probably just the paint."

It was hard to see much in the dim candlelight, but I noticed a few oddities about the bathroom. The sink was covered in paint goops and splotches. On a chest opposite the toilet, there was a slab of glass with different globs of paint colors. Bottles of paint lined the baseboard. Drake turned toward the toilet and stared at the wall behind it.

"I started sneaking out here a few months ago in the early morning . . . and I just sort of painted this."

I squinted at the wall behind the toilet. I stepped closer to it. The entire wall—or at least a four-feet-by-four-feet square of it—was covered with a large canvas painting. It was mostly blues, greens, and yellows. I peered at it more closely.

"It's the view from the Point," I said, leaning in toward it. I could make out the cypress trees that lined the beach and the thick gray mist hovering over the jutting rocks of the cove. The crest of a wave was painted perfectly as it approached the cream-colored beach.

"Drake, it's beautiful," I said. It was, even in the dimness of a single candle's light. I could imagine how stunning it would be in the brilliance of day. He shuffled aside so I could turn toward him.

"My parents haven't been out here in about a decade, so I figured it was a safe place to keep it."

"Sure," I said, looking back at the painting. I knew that if

I told anyone at school that Drake Westfall snuck into his pool house in the early morning and painted, they would have laughed at me in disbelief.

"But with my dad obsessing about my painting again, I'm afraid he might stumble out here and find it," Drake said earnestly. "If he does, he'll burn it."

"There's no way he'd do that," I responded.

"You haven't seen him when he really gets angry," Drake said.

"Like tonight?"

"Tonight, he was in front of company," Drake said, putting his hand on my shoulder so that he could scoot past me. "That was nothing." He began unhooking the canvas from the wall. Taking one end in his hands, he rolled it up carefully, so that it was perfectly even. "I thought maybe you could keep it until I figure out a place to finish working on it," Drake said.

"Of course," I answered. "I'll put it in the storage closet out back. It's unlocked, so whenever you want it back, you can just go get it."

He laid the roll in my arms like he was passing a newborn to me.

Crrrrreeeeeeeaak.

Drake and I both heard it at once. We froze. Someone had entered the pool house. Drake leaned down and blew out the candle. There were no windows in the bathroom, and only a small amount of light from windows in the rest of the pool house filtered in.

I heard muffled voices. Drake pulled on my sleeve. He was so strong and did it with such force that I stumbled into him. My backpack crashed to the floor. Our knees knocked together. He nearly fell over backward. But he braced himself with one arm against the wall. I regained my balance. We crouched, in the dim light, like two frogs facing each other, balancing on an unsteady lily pad.

Voices carried into the bathroom. The first one I recognized was Damon's.

"We'll do it on Christmas Eve. People don't pay attention around the holidays," Damon grunted.

"How much cash can we pull out of there?" a second voice asked.

"At least a couple grand apiece, I think . . . but I'm not sure how reliable our entrance and exit plan is," Damon added.

"No need to freak out, man. We've got the blueprint. We've got the combo to the safe. We'll be in and out before anyone realizes we were even there. In and out in under ten minutes," the second guy said.

"With enough cash to leave and never look back," Damon said.

My legs cramped. Drake, who was quite a bit taller than I was, shifted positions slightly. But when he did, he moved his arm and bumped the toilet lid. The candle toppled over, rolling off the lid and thumping to the floor. It wasn't a large thump, but as soon as it hit, the voices stopped.

After a few seconds, I heard the second guy again.

"What was *that?*"

Feet shuffled toward us from the other room. The footsteps came closer. Then closer. Beams of light flashed down the hallway. Then closer still.

Drake put his hands around each one of my elbows. He leaned against the wall and pulled me so close to him that not even a piece of paper could fit between us. I could hear and feel his breathing.

In the murky light I could see that Drake had closed his eyes. As I was still trying to focus on him, my eyes wide, his face darted forward. His lips found mine like a missile. He pressed them against mine. I had to stop myself from pulling back. His lips were soft, and a little slippery, like rose petals. My whole body seized up and I could feel the warmth of his face and his body as we embraced. I didn't have time to think *Drake Westfall is kissing me in his pool house!* But I would think it many times after that. Instead, I closed my eyes, too.

I pressed back, not wanting the moment to end.

Soon, I felt intense light beaming through my eyelids. I opened them. Two bright flashlights were focused on Drake and me, huddled in the corner of the bathroom. Drake released me as we squinted in the light. Damon was there with another large guy. They both looked angry.

Damon's accomplice, a guy I recognized from the neighborhood named Randy Maroy, took two big strides toward Drake. Randy growled as he shoved his forearm into Drake's throat. The force of it slammed Drake against the wall. Before I could let out a cry of protest, Drake pushed Randy backward, smashing him into the opposite wall. Veins protruded from Drake's arms and neck. Randy raised his flashlight above him, and swung it hard downward, aiming for Drake's head. Drake grabbed Randy's shoulder with one hand and raised his other to block the blow of the metal flashlight, knocking it to the ground. Drake's quick reactions and timing were clearly giving him the upper hand.

"Whoa, calm down," Damon said. "Let's not get carried away, bro." Drake released Randy, whose look had changed from hostility to one bordering on fear. Drake moved toward me and put his hand protectively on my shoulder, squeezing it once as if to tell me things were going to be okay.

"What are you two doing in here?" Damon asked. I got a better look at Randy. He wore an oversized sweatshirt with the hood up and had mean eyes and greasy hair.

"Hey, I know her," Randy said, stepping toward me. He turned to Damon. "This is the girl who was running toward me that morning I was casing—"

"Shut up," Damon growled.

"What if they've been following us?" Randy inched forward. Drake stepped in front of me, glowering back at Randy, looking ready to tear into Randy at a moment's notice.

"You're being paranoid," Damon said, pulling Randy back.

"What did you two hear?" Randy asked, glaring at Drake

and me. I stood immobilized with fear. It was as spine chilling as when I was actually frozen by Vivienne le Mort.

"Hear?" Drake asked dumbly. "I didn't know you guys were even here. I don't know if you noticed, but I was kind of in the middle of something when you two came in and killed the mood."

"You better not be lying, you—"

Drake lunged at Randy again, but this time Damon intercepted him and got between his younger brother and his friend.

"Lay off, man," Damon said, pushing Randy back. "He didn't hear anything. He was too busy making out with his lame girlfriend."

Randy Maroy stepped forward, and turned his flashlight upward at his own face. It shone up his nose and eyes, giving them a reddish, demonic quality.

"Just remember, ladies," Randy said. He looked at Drake, and then me. "If you *did* hear something," he said, before turning to me, "or *see* something, and you happen to tell anyone, we'll find you. And when we do . . ."

He clicked off his flashlight.

"It'll be lights out," he finished, laughing.

"I'd like to see you try," Drake snarled, unmoved by Randy's threat. "You want to finish this right now?"

"That's enough," Damon said before turning to Randy. "Let's go."

Damon and Randy walked back through the hallway to

the door, pointedly kicking boxes out of their way. They didn't seem to care if they disturbed the whole neighborhood. Soon Drake and I were left standing on the cold tile of the bathroom, together in the dark. Drake got on his hands and knees and began combing the floor. With another flip, he used his lighter to relight the candle.

Drake held it to my face. He examined me. Reeling from what had just happened, I put my finger to my lips. I could still taste the kiss.

"Are you okay?" he asked, near a whisper.

"Are *you*?" I asked back. Drake's throat was red and puffy where Randy had first planted his elbow.

"I'm sorry for pretending we were . . . you know. I wanted to make it seem like we weren't listening." I looked at Drake. I couldn't believe how quickly he'd gone from ferocious to shy.

"I didn't mind it," I said.

Drake smiled. "Neither did I."

We slumped against opposite walls of the pool house bathroom for a minute, silent.

"Does Damon's friend drive a black four-door car?" I blurted, unable to stop thinking about the black car parked out front the Westfall house.

"Randy? I think so . . . why?"

"What do you think they were planning?" I asked.

"They were just talking," Drake said. He folded his arms across his chest. "Please don't worry about it, okay?" Drake used his most comforting tone. But I was worried about it. A lot. Drake must have known.

"Damon is messed up right now," Drake continued. "He's not thinking straight, but he's not a bad person. I'll talk some sense into him. And as far as Randy Maroy is concerned, he's all bark, no bite."

"Okay," I said.

Drake moved toward me. He put one hand on each shoulder and looked at me.

"I will not let anything happen to you," he said fiercely. "I promise. Do you trust me?"

"Yes," I said. I did trust him. As I peered into his eyes, I felt the same fated connection I'd felt in his room earlier. At that moment, I thought I'd always trust him. The feeling was thrilling and frightening all at once.

"You'd better get out of here before my mom or dad gets suspicious that I'm gone."

I found my backpack upside down, textbooks falling out of it, and carefully put Drake's rolled-up canvas under my arm.

"I'll take good care of it."

"I'm sure you will."

Before I left, Drake wrapped me up in a long hug on the porch. I scanned the street for the black car. It was no longer there.

I turned my thoughts to Drake and our first kiss. I walked home, but I honestly felt like I could've floated there.

Of course, as I crossed Earle Avenue, I didn't yet know about the one thing that would ruin it all—the red journal, with the initials DWOR scrawled on the cover, lay forgotten in the corner of the Westfalls' pool house bathroom.

Proofreading

I worry a lot, Mrs. Tweedy. For instance, before I leave for school in the morning, I'm constantly double-checking to make sure I have keys to the house and my homework. But worrying makes me pretty good at proofreading. I usually double- and triple-check to make sure I've spelled something correctly. Also, because Mom is such a syntax stickler ("You didn't go quick, Lizzy, you went quick*ly*," she's always sure to point out), I'm much better at grammar than most people my age. Proofreading is really about being careful. And I am careful.

At least, I thought I was.

I now know when the red DWOR journal slipped out of my bag, but I'm still not sure how I failed to notice it on the floor as I was packing up my things. I blame the commotion in the pool house—and that kiss. It made me careless.

As soon as I arrived on my porch, I sat down on the steps. I wanted to make note of everything I'd learned at Drake's house: about Damon and his mysterious plans, Drake's father, the magazine I'd found in the bathroom, and the mysterious black car. When I couldn't find the red journal, I flipped out. I dumped everything out and unrolled Drake's canvas. The DWOR wasn't there.

When I replayed the day's events, I remembered the back-pack turned upside down in the corner of the pool house bath-room. It was the only possibility. I knew what I had to do.

Scampering back across Earle Avenue, I made my way to the side of the Westfall yard and shoved the gate open. With a single deep breath, I plunged into the backyard, trying to remain calm.

Drake was still there, standing outside the entrance to the pool house. I froze, considering whether I should hide or announce my presence. He held something in his hands . . . something red. I wanted to scream. It was the DWOR.

I was too late.

I turned around, heading back to the side gate.

"Lizzy?"

I stopped moving, my back now to Drake. I could hear his footsteps behind me.

"Lizzy," he said again. I had no choice but to turn around. If I ran away now, it would only make things worse.

Drake held the red journal out to me. "What *is* this?"

I wondered how far he'd read. Had he seen page after page of detailed descriptions about what he did, what he ate at lunch, and what he bought from Mickey's Music? Had he read the page devoted to charting his location during recess when he sketched?

There was no way I could explain it. "I came back because I think I left my math book."

"No . . . you came back because you left this. What is it?"

I felt a lump rising in my throat. "I . . . I . . . I'm not sure."

"How long have you been following me?"

"Well . . . ," I stammered.

"Do you even like Operation Ivy? Was any of it real?" Though I wanted to, I knew telling Drake everything, including how he was supposed to die, would only make it certain to happen.

"Do you have anything to say?" Drake looked wounded. He held out the journal for me to take. I could feel my eyelids puff out. Tears would follow in minutes, maybe seconds.

I took the journal from Drake and put my head down as I sprinted to the gate. I ran past the jasmine hedge lining the path, catching my leg on a jasmine bush, crashing into it. I fell to the ground, banging into a low light fixture with my head, crushing the bush under the weight of my body.

"You okay?" I heard Drake question. He didn't move to help me.

"I'm fine," I said. But I wasn't. Drake had *liked* me—he'd made me a mix and he'd *kissed* me. More importantly, he'd understood me. But it was over before it got off the ground. He would never like me again. I couldn't blame him.

I stumbled around like a dazed bull, careening from the hedges to the side wall of the house until I finally reached the gate. Once in the street, hot tears surged from my eyes down my cheeks. I gulped the cold night air and continued running, gasping, as I retreated to Beside the Point.

I didn't bother opening the door to my house quietly, thinking no one would be in the living room when I arrived. Mom usually went upstairs to the den to read, but there she was, in the living room, sitting on the couch by herself, reading the *New Yorker*. She was wearing a big furry turtleneck and had her hair up in a bun—looking like the quintessential librarian. I was a jumbled mess of tears and blood.

"What on earth is the matter?"

Mom rushed over to me. She put her thumb and index finger under my chin and raised it so she could get a better look. As she did, I could see my reflection in the large hallway mirror. Bizzy probably would have told me that I looked like something the cat brought in. Actually, no self-respecting cat would have gone anywhere near me.

My face was puffy and I had a cut above my left eyebrow that was bleeding from my encounter with the Westfall backyard light. Along with my face being tear streaked, my jeans were splattered with yellow paint. At first I wondered how it could've happened. But then I realized I'd been huddled in the bathroom with all those bottles of paint nearby. I could've easily knocked one over. Right before Drake kissed me.

I tried to stop crying. Mom looked at me, a combination of sympathy and concern. I sniffed all the snot running out my nose back into my sinuses. I dried my eyes with the back of my hand.

"Honey, what happened?"

"Nothing," I said.

"How did you get that cut?"

"I fell," I said. My brain was already overloaded with all the details of the past hour. It was hard to come up with a story that Mom would buy. "I was running from Drake's house because I was cold and I tripped in the street and hit the curb."

Mom slipped on her reading glasses to examine the cut.

"Well, it's a pretty good gash," she said. "You might need stitches."

"No, please—I'll be fine," I said.

Mom frowned at me. She put her hands on her hips. "Well, at least let me clean it for you." We went into the kitchen together. I sat down as Mom took a warm, wet cloth and mopped the area around my cut. She wiped away all remnants of my tears. The Bactine stung sharply when she dabbed it on my forehead, but at least it distracted me from thinking about Drake.

"Bizzy said that you had dinner over at Drake's tonight."

"I did," I replied.

"How is he?" Mom asked as she applied some additional ointment.

"Fine," I said, hoping she would get the message that I didn't want to talk about it. Mom rummaged through the pantry for a Band-Aid.

"Did something happen between the two of you tonight?" Mom looked at me with knitted eyebrows. I wanted to say something to lessen her worries . . . to let her know that I was fine, but that I didn't want to talk about it. Yet as I thought of Drake—how elated I'd been when I thought he'd kissed me for real and how miserable I was now that everything had come crashing down—I felt an avalanche of tears reforming. Despite everything, I still hadn't made enough progress in my information gathering. I'd never felt so much pressure.

"No," I said.

"Does it have anything to do with whatever you were discussing earlier today with Bizzy?" The idea that I was confiding in Bizzy and not her was clearly upsetting Mom. I wanted to explain that it wasn't like that—that she wouldn't understand—but I knew I'd be wasting my breath and might hurt her even more.

"It's nothing . . . just stupid school stuff." It was so much more than that, but it was the best I could do.

"All right," Mom said, forcing a halfhearted smile. "But if you do need some advice, I *was* a teenager—"

"It's okay, I promise," I said, cutting her off.

Mom studied my injured face for a moment. "Okay." She continued to stare at me, and as she did her eyes took on a sad resignation. Mom would do anything to help me, but there were limits to what a mother could do for her daughter. She handed me the tube of ointment. "Put this on your cut before you go to bed, okay? I don't want any scar mucking up that beautiful face of yours."

Mom reached out and hugged me. "I love you," she said, squeezing tightly. She stepped back from me.

"Thank you," I said.

"Just doing my job," she responded, taking off her reading glasses so they dangled from her neck again. She peered at me like she was studying a painting in a museum she was seeing for the first time. "Did you start reading *David Copperfield*?" she asked. I hadn't even cracked the spine.

"I'm not sure it's my kind of book," I said.

"Then the search for your Right Book continues!" Mom challenged. "Headed to bed?"

"I'm going to go say good night to Bizzy first," I said. Mom's face blanched.

"Oh," she said quietly. "Okay." I knew she was trying desperately to hide her disapproval and pain. But it was dawning on me that I'd ruined any chance I'd had of saving Drake's life. Mom turned around and wandered out of the kitchen without another word.

Mom had worried about me before, but it was different this time. Especially now that Bizzy and I were spending so much time together—planning, discussing . . . bonding. She felt left out. I wished I could run after Mom and tell her that there was no way she could understand what had been going on with me lately. That I would talk to her if I could. But even saying that would be too much. I vowed I'd straighten it all out after we'd figured out a way to save Drake.

Once Mom was upstairs, I knocked softly on Bizzy's door.

"Come on in," Bizzy said.

Bizzy was sitting in her wheelchair with a crocheted blanket over her legs. She was reading a book titled *1,001 Deaths, 1,001 Ways to Die*. She was staring at a picture of a woman with a headdress made entirely of fruit.

"You aware that though there ain't one documented case of someone dyin' of stage fright, Carmen Miranda went and had a heart attack while she was dancin' onstage?" Bizzy looked up at me excitedly. She closed the book when she saw my face.

"What in the world happened to ya, Sweet Pea?"

My despair had become anger. "Why did you call the Westfalls and force me to have dinner there, Bizzy?"

"I thought it was a perfect opportunity to gather more information," she answered, startled by my tone.

"Well, after dinner, Drake found the journal you gave me—with everything I'd written about him in it."

"Oh my! What did he say?"

"He didn't have to *say* anything. He doesn't want anything to do with me now."

"It takes two to tango, but only one misplaced foot to ruin the dance."

"What?" I asked, furious that Bizzy would offer up one of her ridiculous phrases at a time like this.

"Listen to me, Sweet Pea. Nothin' can't be undone. We got ten days to go and I promise we'll figger how to straighten out all this Drake mess."

"We're no closer than we were a month ago!" I argued. "We don't even know how Drake dies or why Vivienne le Mort keeps showing up or what she is after."

"But we *will*," Bizzy said, remaining calm. "Patience's the name a' the game."

"I don't want to do this anymore. I'm just going to tell Drake."

"You *can't* do that, Lizzy. Under any circumstances. You'd be puttin' Drake in mortal danger."

"He's already in mortal danger. Vivienne le Mort is involved somehow, I know it. But I've been thinking about it, and listening to you hasn't really gotten me anywhere. So maybe it's time I stopped."

I turned around and began walking out the door.

"I'm beggin' ya. Sleep on it. Don't do anythin' rash or you'll surely regret it." For the first time since I'd found out I was a Hand of Fate, I turned my back on Bizzy. I could hear my grandma wheeling after me, so I climbed the stairs back up to my room quickly, knowing even Bizzy couldn't follow me there in a wheelchair.

I was about to flop down on my bed when I noticed that Mom had left a book and a note on my pillow. I picked up the book. It was her old hardcover copy of *Pride and Prejudice*. I examined the note.

Lizzy—

I was surprised to see The Collected Works of Emily Dickinson on your nightstand. I didn't realize you liked poetry. I also couldn't help but notice Le Morte d'Arthur (I wasn't snooping, I promise . . . it was in plain sight). I'm all for the classics, but that's an old book! I would have never guessed that would be something you're interested in . . . but it just goes to show you that there's no predicting taste. It's a timeless legend, that's for sure. If you like that, you might try <u>The Winter King</u> or <u>The Mists of Avalon</u> for a more feminist take. Either way, I figure it might be high time you read my favorite classic. I know this might not be your Right Book—but I thought maybe it was the perfect Right Now Book. Sometimes, after all, Right Now Books are just as important.

    I'm also writing this because I have to confess something to you. I know you think that I named you after your great-aunt Elizabeth. I told your father that in order to placate him, because he loved his Aunt Elizabeth. I think he was the only one. I actually couldn't stand the woman. She was bossy and mean-spirited—qualities that seemed to sharpen with age. In truth, I named you after the heroine of <u>Pride and Prejudice</u>, Elizabeth Bennet. You do the name proud! In your story, there is much yet to be written, but as with your namesake, I know all will end well. You'll see. Keep your head up, okay?

    I'm always here to talk to you if you feel like it.

XOXO,
Mom

    P.S. Remember to put medicine on your cut before you go to sleep so it doesn't scar!

I folded the note inside the book and placed the book next to the growing stack on my nightstand. Through my distress, I was touched that Mom went to all the trouble to dig up another book for me. But I couldn't bring myself to read it. All I could imagine was opening it and watching the words twist into someone else's death sentence.

The Nemesis
I Didn't Know I Had

Have you ever been blindsided, Mrs. Tweedy? And I'm not just talking about something unexpected, like finding out you have an extra wisdom tooth. I'm talking about a true, punch-in-the-gut kind of surprise. I didn't know what it felt like until the Friday before our final project was due. It was a little more than a week after I'd had dinner at Drake's house and I hadn't spoken to him since. Every time I spotted him across campus, I'd feel I was on the verge of a panic attack. He always turned away from me as soon as our eyes met.

Though I still spied on him from a safe distance, I tried to avoid running into him. As I headed to third period math class, Jodi cut me off at the cafeteria. Normally I'd communicated with Jodi in some form by second period, but today I'd been in the clouds.

"We've got a situation," she said, wearing her feather earrings and checkered high-top Vans. She flaunted the school's no-gum-chewing policy, smacking it loudly. "It looks like the cat's out of the bag."

"What do you mean?" I asked.

"I just overheard Kristy Draper blabbing to Rosie Yeo and Leigh Green in the girls' bathroom." Jodi crossed her arms. She almost felt worse than I did about Drake discovering the DWOR. Especially since a lot of the notes were in her handwriting. Over the last week, she'd gone out of her way to try to cheer me up.

"You overheard them saying what?"

"You know that Kristy Draper has it bad for Drake, so she's running with the story as far as she can take it." Jodi snapped her gum again.

"What does that mean? What story?" Just then, the tardy bell rang.

"We'll talk at lunch, 'kay?"

Jodi sprinted across the quad as if possessed. She already had four tardies and getting a fifth would mean a detention. I made my way to Geometry. Both Kristy Draper and Rosie Yeo were in that class.

I opened the door to Mr. Marr's classroom. Everyone was seated. I was the last to arrive. I ducked as I crossed the front of the room and slid into my desk near the wall opposite the door. Mr. Marr looked over his glasses at me, but said nothing. He went over his attendance sheet. Rosie Yeo, who sat one row to the right and four desks in front of me, had a blank piece of paper on her desk. She took out a Sharpie, uncapped it, and began writing in large capital letters. Then Rosie turned around and asked if the person behind her could pass the note to Kristy Draper. Kristy sat directly behind me. But as Rosie passed the piece of paper, she didn't fold it or hide the message. She just left it out there for everyone to see. As it made its way down one row, people started chuckling as soon as they read it. When it was immediately on my right, I was able to make out what it said, in large block letters:

LIZZY = DRAKE'S PSYCHO STALKER

I tried not to gasp out loud. I slowly pushed my watch as far as it would go down my wrist. The last thing in the world I needed was someone to discover Drake's name engraved on my hand. Then I reached and grabbed the note out of my neighbor's hand. I crumpled it up into a ball and shoved it into my backpack. I knew that every person in the class was staring at me. My face was burning. I'd never known before what it was like to literally feel I might die from embarrassment. My throat felt like it was closing up and I couldn't keep my feet still. Had Drake told someone about the DWOR? If he had, then there was little doubt that he truly despised me.

The worst part was that Kristy Draper loved every minute of it. Soon, Mr. Marr was handing out quizzes. I tried to concentrate, but I bombed that quiz like I've never bombed a quiz before.

Fourth period, I had European History. Though Kristy, Leigh, and Rosie weren't in the class, it was still painful. I got there early and I was pretty sure a cluster of girls were talking about me in the back of the classroom. By noon, the whole school would think I was some restraining-order-deserving stalker.

I wasn't far off. I waited for Jodi by the planter. On the one hand, this was the worst day I'd ever had at school. On the other hand, though, I had bigger problems than three catty girls out to make my life miserable (such as if and how Vivienne le Mort was involved with Drake's impending death). Of course, Jodi didn't know all that. She had her headphones on and was listening to music, even though that was forbidden, too. She sort of danced toward the planter. When she got to me, she hopped up on the cement bricks.

"So, it's not as bad as I thought, Lizster," Jodi said casually. She took a big bite out of her banana sandwich. "The story going around is that you invited yourself over to Drake's house, saying you needed help on your homework, and then forced yourself on him."

"*Forced* myself on him?" I put both hands over my face, wanting to hide.

"Yeah, it's not great. But at least there wasn't any mention of the DWOR."

"At least."

"Don't worry about it too much, okay? Because Drake has about four hundred girls with crushes on him, so this was bound to happen. You don't tangle with a POI and expect to remain untouched."

"PO what?"

"Person of interest." As she spoke, Jodi began putting a

Bugle on each one of her fingers so that it looked as if she had claws. "Like imagine if all those trashy magazines at the grocery store checkout line had a Crabapple High School version, 'kay? Now say there was news about Drake Westfall making out with someone behind Auto Shop. Well, that would make the front cover because he's a POI. But you or me? We could be making out with Nathan Randall back there and we wouldn't be cover worthy."

"That's gross," I said.

"Oh, calm down, it's just a hypo." Jodi sucked a Bugle off her hand. "I haven't gotten to my point yet." She hopped off the planter and began pacing in front of me.

"You haven't?"

"Of course I haven't. Let's recap, shall we? You go over to Drake's house, right?" Jodi reached into her bag once more. This time, she pulled out a piece of gum and popped it into her mouth. "Somehow a rumor gets started that you invited yourself over there."

"But no one knew about that," I objected.

"Well, maybe Drake casually mentioned it to someone . . . I don't know. The point is, word spreads, of course, and Leigh Green, being the gossipmonger that she is, goes up to Drake during break and asks him if you really *did* invite yourself over. Drake doesn't say anything. So Leigh Green, unwilling to stop until she gets the scoop, asks Drake if you two are dating. Now, what does he do in response? Drake just shrugs his shoulders and walks away."

Maybe you could just stop a dialogue whenever you wanted. "Drake didn't say *no*?" I asked, growing animated.

"Yup, Drake didn't say no. Confirmed by three different people. Anyways, my point is, as soon as Drake did that, you, Lizzy Mortimer, officially became a POI by association . . . a POIBA, I guess." Jodi finished by thrusting her finger at me until she touched my forehead. She smiled.

A lot of people think Jodi is a kook. Her need to abbreviate everything is strange—she's constantly coming up with terms like POI and COT (circle of trust, and it's worth noting, Mrs. Tweedy, that I am officially in hers and she is in mine)—but no one understands high school politics better than she does. It's why she can so easily rise above it. I guess she marches to the beat of a different drummer. Actually, she probably doesn't hear drums at all, but punk guitar riffs instead.

"But what if I don't want to be a poiba?" I demanded.

"Too late. It's not up to you." I spotted Drake out of the corner of my eye. He was eating with Garrett Edmonds and the rest of the water polo team.

"Look, this'll all blow over in a few days when people realize you're not together." Jodi halted her pacing and looked at me squarely. "I'm just sorry that our stalk-him-till-he-loves-you plan backfired so badly."

"It wasn't your fault, it was mine," I said.

"It almost worked." Jodi looked at me sympathetically.

I thought about Drake in the pool house wistfully. "Yeah, almost."

When the bell rang, Jodi dashed off almost immediately. She'd gotten her fifth tardy that morning, and already had one detention looming in her future.

I was gathering up Jodi's trash and my own when I saw a shadow in front of me. Someone was right behind me. I pivoted on the balls of my feet.

"Hey, Lizzy."

Garrett Edmonds, the former captain of the water polo team, stood in front of me. I straightened up and looked at him. Over his shoulder, I could tell that most of the water polo team was watching us from the benches. A few of them were snickering. Drake was no longer with them.

"Hello," I said. I hadn't exchanged a single word with Garrett Edmonds in my entire life. He is a senior and I am a freshman and the fact that he was standing right in front of me worried me more than anything else.

"How's it going?"

"Fine," I said, throwing my leftover half sandwich into my backpack.

"Lizzy Mortimer . . . I have a little proposition for you," he continued, smiling.

I couldn't get my mouth to form any words. Was Garrett Edmonds actually talking to me? Worse, was he flirting with me?

"I hear you're pretty good at math. I also hear that you have a thing for water polo players." Garrett put his hands in his letterman's jacket. I considered just running away from him, but I was paralyzed. With the whole team watching, that might only make things worse. Before I could decide what to do, Garrett began speaking again.

"So . . . if you come and do my math homework for me, I'll let you have dinner at my house," he said, his voice booming. I could tell he was doing it for the benefit of the half-dozen boys gathered twenty feet away at the picnic tables. They began pointing in my direction.

"What do you say?" He didn't bother to stifle his laughter any longer. His body convulsed with one full-body laugh after another.

Sadly, I couldn't think of anything to say. "No, thanks," was all I managed to get out before I turned around and walked away. For the second time that day, my face burned with both anger and embarrassment.

Maybe you remember that Friday, Mrs. Tweedy. I was late to your class. See, I couldn't hang on any longer. I started crying as I crossed the quad. Now that I was a POIBA, I knew that if someone saw me shed one tear, it would be all over school by the time the dismissal bell rang. I wasn't just crying over Garrett Edmonds's cruelty. All of it was too much. So I made a pit stop in the girls' bathroom and waited until the tear-tidal-wave had passed.

I think you called on me that class, Mrs. Tweedy, and I had no idea what was going on. I'm pretty sure you mercifully moved on to someone else, but I want you to know that my poor performance wasn't because I was bored by what you were saying. I just couldn't keep my thoughts on track. Instead, I was thinking about what made someone like Garrett Edmonds do something so spiteful. My thoughts turned to Drake as they often seemed to recently. Was he the one who told everyone I'd invited myself over to his house? If he didn't, then who did?

I was driving myself nuts, constantly checking to make sure that my watch covered my wrist. I remembered all the horrible things I'd said to Bizzy. There was a chance that we wouldn't manage to save Drake at all. I knew I'd feel guilty for the rest of my life.

Halfway through sixth period, I got a slip telling me to go to the office. Once I was there, a secretary told me that I should call my mother from the office.

"Mom?"

"Lizzy! Are you calling from school?"

"Yeah. Everything all right?"

"I'm going to be late picking you up today. So just wait and I'll be there as soon as I can."

"Why?"

"I need to wait for your father to get to the hospital. I don't want to leave your grandmother alone here."

"Bizzy's in the hospital again?" I asked, shocked. "What happened?"

"I'm not sure yet . . . but it's going to be okay." I wanted to believe her. But I knew Mom would have said that no matter what had happened.

Point of View

According to you, Mrs. Tweedy, the point of view is basically a filter. Every detail goes through it and changes slightly depending on whose view it is. Obviously, everything I've told you is from my point of view. Some people might not want to know what everyone's thinking and doing, but I've actually always wanted to be an all-knowing, omniscient narrator. In fact, I get frustrated by how little I know about what other people are thinking, feeling, and doing. One thing's for sure. If I were an omniscient narrator, I would've known that Bizzy was helpless on the sidewalk.

I could have rescued her.

The terrible things I'd said to Bizzy during our last conversation weighed on my conscience. Since then, Bizzy had tried to talk to me, but I'd ignored her and walked away. I wanted her to know the agony I was in.

In the car, Mom explained that Sheriff Schmidt found Bizzy unconscious, with her wheelchair tipped over, on the corner of Kramer and Dolores. Mom thought Bizzy had "wandered off" because she was losing her marbles. When Mom and I got to the hospital, Bizzy and Dad were in the middle of an argument.

"It's not up to you," Dad said, standing with his hands on his hips at the foot of Bizzy's bed.

"Whaddaya mean it's not up to me! A' course it's up to me!"

Bizzy had a fat bottom lip, her leg was elevated in traction, and the left side of her face was cut. Her whole left arm was wrapped in gauze, as was the area above her forehead. There were no tubes in her arms, though. She was awake and clearly very lucid. And livid.

"Phillip wants me to get a kitty-cat-scan so he can get some doctor to certify my brain's demented!" Bizzy said angrily to Mom before spotting me trailing behind. "Sweet Pea! If you ain't all wool and a yard wide, then nothin' is!" Her tone was affectionate. "Tell your mama and pa that I want out of here, pronto. They can't seem to understand what I'm sayin'."

"The doctor hasn't cleared you yet," Dad said, running his hand through his salt-and-pepper hair.

"That doctor ain't worth a hill a' beans!" Bizzy said.

There was a knock on the open door. Sheriff Schmidt poked his head in, not waiting for our response. He took off his hat and walked to the corner of the room. He was wearing large black leather storm trooper boots that came up to his knees.

"Hello, folks," he began, nodding at both Mom and Dad. "I was in the neighborhood and I thought I'd stop by to check on Mrs. Mortimer." Sheriff Schmidt looked at Bizzy. Bizzy turned her face away, toward the wall so that it was impossible for the sheriff to make eye contact with her.

"Thank you so much for all your help today, Sheriff," Dad said, his face beaming with appreciation. Apparently, he didn't dislike the sheriff quite as much as he used to.

"It's no problem, sir. I'm just glad I found her," Sheriff Schmidt said, nodding his head in Bizzy's direction. Bizzy's face was expressionless.

"So are we," Dad said with a sigh.

"You know what? I was wondering if I might have a word with Lizzy." The sheriff looked at me and then at Mom and Dad. "Just a few follow-up questions."

"Of course," Mom said, looking concerned. I stole a glance at Bizzy. The corner of her mouth crept up and she gave me a reassuring wink.

The sheriff led me into the sterile hospital hallway with Mom following close behind. A few men and women in scrubs scurried up and down the hall.

He didn't waste any time getting to the point.

"Elizabeth, I think your grandmother's up to something, and I was wondering if you knew what that is." Sheriff Schmidt played with the brim of his hat, almost nervously. His hair was thinning on top and he looked much older with his hat off.

"I don't know what you mean," I said, unable to focus on him. Mom looked at me anxiously.

"That day that I stopped you and Bizzy by the cannery . . . what did she say you two were doing there?"

"Now wait just a second!" Mom interjected. "When were you and Bizzy near the cannery?"

"We went for a walk, that's all."

"I stopped them, Mrs. Mortimer, because Elizabeth had tied Beatrice's wheelchair to her bike with rope. I thought there were some safety issues."

"You tied Bizzy's *wheelchair* to your bike?" Mom shot arrows of disapproving looks my way.

"It was an awful long walk from Beside the Point when your grandmother was convalescing, wasn't it?" The sheriff's tone was somewhat patronizing. "If I tell you some classified information," Sheriff Schmidt said, lowering his voice, "can I trust you both not to share it with anyone?"

I struggled to subdue the skepticism that was fighting to surface on my face. I recalled one of Bizzy's oft-repeated pearls: *If somethin' don't add up, you most likely don't got all the numbers.*

"Of course you can," Mom said, before I had a chance to answer.

"I've received two different anonymous tips reporting that people have seen Bizzy around the cannery. Dr. Stuhl said she was muttering something about it when she was partially conscious after the fall—"

"What are you implying, Sheriff?" Mom asked. Her defenses were on alert.

"Mrs. Mortimer, I'm not implying anything. I'm only

trying to prevent something more serious from happening to Beatrice. I believe that she knows exactly *who* is staying at the cannery and exactly *why* I found blueprints of the town storm drains and the basement of Miss Mora's place in a tent inside the building!"

I clamped my lips shut. The conversation between Damon and his thuggish friend Randy Maroy replayed in a loop inside my head. I also thought of the dark hole I'd observed within the cannery. Because the sheriff had raised his voice, a few nurses in the hallway turned around to look at us.

"You honestly think a seventy-year-old woman is a part of some plan that involves sewer blueprints? We appreciate your finding Bizzy, but this conversation is over," Mom said.

"Okay, then. Thank you for talking to me," the sheriff said in a phony friendly tone, even though it was obvious that he was seething. He slipped a card out of his pocket and held it out to me. "Feel free to call me night or day." I grabbed it from him and looked at it.

SCOTT SCHMIDT
Sheriff
CRABAPPLE, CALIFORNIA

His phone number was at the very bottom, all in bold.

The sheriff retreated down the hallway. I watched him until he exited through the sliding-glass doors.

"Your father was right about that man," Mom said, her face

hardened. She looked at me. "You don't have any idea what he might have been talking about, do you?" she demanded.

"No," I said, lying through my teeth.

"I don't care if she tells you it's okay; no more trips with Bizzy tied to your bike, all right?" Mom commanded before turning to walk back into Bizzy's hospital room.

Dr. Stuhl had joined Dad by Bizzy's bedside.

"Mrs. Mortimer, I'm afraid you'd be putting yourself at risk if you do anything of the sort. Your elevated blood pressure, in combination with the MRI we did when you arrived, suggests that a stroke is a possibility without any intervention."

"Can't you just give me some medicine and send me packin', then?" I was surprised by Bizzy's casualness.

"You need to be started on an IV immediately and monitored around the clock for at least the next forty-eight hours," Dr. Stuhl admonished sternly.

"Been monitorin' myself for years. I don't see need for any help on that front, thank you very much." Bizzy crossed her arms defiantly.

Bizzy hated hospitals, that's for sure. But I had a feeling her aversion at that moment concerned Drake's predicted day of departure, now just a little over three days away.

I was still standing in the doorway. I had to figure out how to be alone with Bizzy. Away from Mom and Dad.

"Dad?" I said. "Can you come out here real quick?"

"What's up?" Dad asked, stepping into the hallway with me.

"I think if you give me a few minutes alone with Bizzy, I

can convince her to stay in the hospital," I blurted. Dad tilted his head to the side and studied me again.

"Well . . ."

"Bizzy doesn't listen to anyone, I know . . . but she just might listen to me. I'd like to give it a try," I added.

"It's not a secret she likes you best of all," Dad said, tousling my hair like he used to when I was little. "All right. But if you can't do it, I'll understand." Dad walked back into Bizzy's room and announced that I wanted a word alone with her. Mom eyed me suspiciously, but followed Dad out of the room.

As soon as the door was shut, Bizzy's eyes widened and she tried to sit up straight.

"How'd you get the buzzards to stop circling?"

"I told them I wanted to talk to you alone."

"I owe ya one. Seems like Phillip is set on drivin' me crazy," Bizzy said, exhaling loudly.

"Bizzy . . . ," I started, feeling a lump in my throat. "I'm really sorry about the things I said to you after that night at Drake's house. When Mom told me you were hurt and I thought something terrible had happened I . . ."

"Oh, Sweet Pea, shush up now," she said, her voice rich with sympathy. "It's okay, ya hear? This is a lot for anyone to handle. I should've talked with you first before I called over to Drake's house."

"You were just trying to do all you could to save his life and I shouldn't have questioned you. Besides, if you hadn't made me stay for dinner, I wouldn't have found out all the things I did."

Bizzy's eyes lit up. "What sorta things?"

First, I explained what Sheriff Schmidt had told me about finding blueprints in the tent at the cannery of the storm drain system underneath Miss Mora's and of her basement. I then repeated what Drake and I'd overheard Damon and Randy Maroy discussing in the pool house. When I reached the part about the black car and Damon recognizing me from the morning Jodi almost died, I stopped. The fact that it had been Randy's car made me rethink the entire sequence. He was casing Miss Mora's Market that morning. My appearance had caused him to speed away.

Did people only believe in coincidences because, otherwise, fate's grip on all of us would be too horrible to admit?

Bizzy was right there with me, almost instantly. "Dad gum! That's it! Damon Westfall and his miscreant friend are plannin' on robbin' Miss Mora and usin' the storm drains to get in! They were casin' the joint that mornin' of your first specter!" Bizzy's creased forehead became more wrinkled as she grew excited.

"Which means the accident really *was* my fault, wasn't it?" I asked. "By running to Miss Mora's that morning, I caused Randy Maroy to speed away and almost hit Jodi."

"You may have hurried things up a bit, Sweet Pea, but it was Jodi's time no matter what you did. In the end, you also caused her to be saved."

"I honestly don't think I can do this, Bizzy," I said, dejected.

"Oh . . . a' course you can, Sweet Pea! Every Hand a' Fate

worth her salt doubts herself now and again and wonders if she's doin' the right thing," Bizzy insisted. "I still do."

"You do?"

"Every so often, absolutely." Bizzy inhaled and then let out a long sigh. "The most dangerous people in this world are the ones who are always so certain, straight outta the gate. A thoughtful person is gonna be unsure from time to time. Why, it's a sign of intelligence."

"If that's true, then I must be a genius."

Bizzy laughed.

"How do you get over your doubts?"

"Each time, I think of the alternative: stand there like a bump on a log and do nothin' at all? Call havin' death-specters a gift, Sweet Pea, or call it a curse, but it's somethin' and in my mind, we got it for a reason. It doesn't make sense to me that we should just ignore it when we can help a person. We're just fixin' somethin' that got fouled up along the way."

As I listened to Bizzy talk in her unusual but logical way, relief that she was okay washed over me.

"How did you fall?" I asked.

"I lost control of the chair on my way back from the cannery. Thought I'd check things out while you were at school."

"You rolled yourself all the way to the cannery?"

"Actually, I went to Cedar Tree Park right above the cannery first. I guess I didn't leave enough gas in the tank for the ride home. The doctor's convinced I've got Old-Timer's." Bizzy grinned.

"They only want to observe you for a day or so."

"Honest to goodness, I don't know what all the fuss is about. I got a few scrapes and scratches. Never would have happened if I were ridin' Dixie." Bizzy paused. My thoughts returned to Randy Maroy and his threats.

"Don't we need to tell Sheriff Schmidt that we think Damon Westfall is the one who's been staying at the cannery?" I asked. "I'm afraid Damon is going to go through with the robbery and hurt Drake to keep him quiet."

Bizzy began shaking her head violently, gauze bandage and all. "That dad-burned sheriff don't have enough sense to come in out of the rain! Tell him and we might as well broadcast to Damon and his criminal crony that you ratted 'em out."

"But we've got to stop them from robbing Miss Mora!"

"Oh, we will, Sweet Pea. They said they aren't plannin' on robbin' for another two weeks. If we're gonna tell the sheriff, we gotta assemble a shut 'n' open case for him. We got no proof right now. If those dang fools are gonna go after Drake, they'll go after you, too. I ain't leavin' that to chance."

"The cannery fire is supposed to happen on Tuesday," I lamented. "What if the two are connected?"

"That's precisely why I gotta get out of here. You and me have a lot of work to do!" Bizzy wheezed, out of breath. I took one of Bizzy's hands between mine, just like she does.

"You have to stay, Bizzy." She looked confused. I continued. "You have to get better and you can't do that at home."

"A wounded deer leaps the highest!" Bizzy said.

"What?"

"It's another Emily quote."

"No offense, Bizzy, but Emily Dickinson probably didn't know what an embolic stroke even was." I pressed on both sides of her cold, wrinkled hand with my own hands. Bizzy's eyes moved back and forth in her sockets like they were on a working typewriter ribbon. I forged on. "If you don't stay here, you're going to give Dad a heart attack."

"My own son treats me like I'm an invalid! And I ain't leavin' you to fend for yourself in this. It's too big." She put one of her hands through her mound of white hair.

"What if you didn't have to?" I said. "I've been thinking about it. Jodi can help me keep track of Drake while you're here."

"That isn't supposed to be the way—"

"I know I can't tell her about being a Death Catcher, but she'll help me if I ask her to."

"It don't seem right. When Washington crossed the Delaware to attack the Hessians on Christmas Day, I'll tell ya one thing—he wasn't watchin' from the riverbank! Why, he was standin' up in that boat with his troops!"

"I know we're not supposed to involve anyone else, but if I'm going to have to do this for the rest of my life, then I want to do certain things my way."

Bizzy grinned and began to shake her head softly.

"Well, now, Miss Hedgehog . . . I can't argue with that! Been doin' things my own way since birth." Bizzy sighed. "I guess if I tagged along right now, you'd just be draggin' me from pillar to post, and I'd be slowin' you down," she admitted. "You can trust Jodi?"

"I know I can."

"Well, all right then. I'll stay. The last thing we want to do is give your father a heart attack." There was a pause as Bizzy looked down in her lap. "I was gonna wait till we had some real privacy at home, but if I am gonna stay here, then there's one thing I need to discuss before you go."

"What?" I asked.

"Do you know anything about a book called *The Last Descendant*?"

I honestly hadn't thought about the book I'd stolen from Agatha's cottage in weeks. I pictured it resting on my nightstand.

"I took it from Agatha's cottage right after she told me we could never go back."

"Well, Sweet Pea, I ain't ever been good at followin' instructions. I visited her on my way back from the cannery."

My jaw dropped. "Was she there? What did she say?"

"She weren't too pleased to see me, but I told you I'd find out what Vivienne le Mort was after and I wasn't gonna let some old crotchety grave keeper stand in my way."

"What did she tell you?"

"She was sure you stole a book from her called *The Last Descendant*."

"She was?"

"I said I didn't know anythin' about that. But she somehow

knew you'd taken it. And she said if you could see words on the pages, then you were meant to know what Vivienne le Mort was after. She said, otherwise, it weren't her place to tell."

"I don't understand . . ."

"Agatha Cantare is convinced, Sweet Pea, that whatever it is Vivienne le Mort is after . . . that book explains it."

My mind raced as I thought of what I'd learned in *The Last Descendant*. Then it hit me. I'd seen Drake's death-specter a few pages from the end.

I'd become so distraught over Drake, I'd stopped reading.

I never finished the book.

Persuasion

I couldn't wait to get home to read the last pages of *The Last Descendant*, mad at myself for not getting to the end. But before I did any reading, I had a few items of unfinished business to take care of.

Knowing how to write in a way that convinces a person to believe something is important, but I'm not sure I'll ever be good at it, Mrs. Tweedy. You say it's all about using evidence to build a case, but I usually end up sounding wishy-washy. Still, I realized that if I were going to reenlist Jodi to help me watch Drake, I would have to do some major persuading. I needed a better method. So I decided I would leave out the facts that didn't bolster my case and invent some that did.

First, I broke the news to Dad and Mom that Bizzy had agreed to stay in the hospital for the next two nights. I could see the relief on Dad's face. Mom looked at me sort of like I was an alien.

"What did you say?" she asked.

"I told her that she should stay."

"And she *listened* to you?" Mom responded doubtfully.

"Yeah."

"Well, all right," Mom said, shaking her head. "You two have some sort of *special* bond." Mom was acting like she was mad at me.

I rode home with Dad, convincing him I needed to stop by Jodi's to pick up a homework assignment.

The bell attached to the door of Miss Mora's Market dinged as I walked into the store.

"Hello, Lizzy!" Miss Mora said. "How is Bizzy doing?"

"She's going to be fine," I said.

"I'm so glad." Miss Mora came out from behind the counter, wearing her red apron with her hair in a long braid down her back. "Are you looking for Jodi?"

"Is she home?"

"Just walked in a few minutes ago. Go on up."

I took the wooden staircase up a floor to Jodi's. The cramped two-bedroom apartment was decorated with dozens of pictures, and overlapping floor rugs covering the well-worn hardwood floors. Bookshelves filled with records and numerous volumes on topics that included traveling and gardening lined the walls. Jodi complained about not having a TV, but I viewed the Sanchez home as a treasure trove of riches waiting to be discovered.

Jodi was lying on the floor, reading one of Miss Mora's old *Life* magazines from the 1980s.

"Hey!" she said, getting up. "Heard you left class early. What happened?"

"Bizzy's in the hospital again," I answered. "She fell, but she'll be okay."

"She's had a tough time lately," Jodi said. She sat in a shabby Barcalounger in the corner and I plopped in the armchair facing it.

"I have a favor to ask you," I said.

"Anything," Jodi responded.

"I need your help stalking Drake again."

Jodi put her hand up instantly. "Whoa, wait one second. Lizster, I know you may still be hung up on him, but that's going to lead nowhere good. As your friend, I feel like it's my duty—"

"Before you say no, hear me out," I interrupted.

Because Bizzy and I hadn't yet discovered what was going to get Drake to the cannery that fateful morning, we decided I would follow Drake's movements as best I could for the next three days, with Jodi's help, to gather clues. We could easily swing by the cannery both Saturday and Sunday on our bikes. With daily trips, we'd be able to keep track of any changes there, as well. Bizzy had insisted that if we couldn't figure out what would cause Drake to visit the cannery, our best backup plan was to nab Drake right before he got there.

I told Jodi about Sheriff Schmidt's discovery in the cannery of the blueprints to her mother's market. But instead of telling her Damon and Randy weren't planning on robbing the market for another couple of weeks, I said they were going to do it on Tuesday morning, when the cannery explosion was supposed to occur.

"Damon and his friend are going to rob *us*?"

"I think so," I said. "But if we go to the police, it will just be my word against theirs and they'll come after me or Drake. I have no proof. We need to catch them in the act to make sure they end up where they can't hurt Drake . . . or me, I guess."

Jodi's mind was already working. "In the meantime, I'll make sure my mom changes the combo to the safe," she said.

"So you'll help me watch Drake and Damon? You think it's a good plan?"

"I'd help you even if it was a bad plan, Lizzy."

When I arrived home, Mom said dinner would be served in a half hour. I told her that I wasn't hungry and went straight upstairs. Sitting on my bed, I took *The Last Descendant* from my nightstand. I hadn't held the leather volume since I'd seen Drake's death-specter.

My whole world had turned upside down since then.

Thumbing through the book, I found the place where I'd left off: *King Arthur and his passengers sailed from Avalon on the eve of the Feast of Samhain.* I flipped to the end. I'd only left two pages unread. Looking back on it, I wonder if my receiving a death-specter about Drake at that exact moment wasn't Merlin's handiwork. If I'd learned everything about the Last Descendant all at once, there's no telling what I would have done.

In any event, those two pages turned out to be the most crucial of them all.

Not only did they describe the last prophecy Agatha the Enchantress had seen in the Sooth Spring before she set sail with King Arthur and Morgan's child, but they also included a personal plea from the book's author, Merlin Ambrosius.

Agatha's prophecy predicted what would happen to the mortal world if the future proceeded without any interference— Merlin Ambrosius called it Doomsday. Basically, Vivienne le Mort would discover a way to collect the pile of cut threads and weave them into an undead army that would eventually wreak havoc on the mortal world. Death, darkness, and despair would multiply with Vivienne at the helm of her unspeakable army.

After Agatha's prophecy, Merlin Ambrosius then described the only way this eventuality could be prevented.

Before these events take place, *Merlin wrote,* there will be one descendant of Arthur Pendragon left on earth. This last descendant, as it so stands, is scheduled to die before it is his time. However, the Last Descendant is the only one who has the right combination of fearlessness and prudence to defeat Vivienne le Mort. Without him, all hope is lost. Should his untimely death occur, the end of the earth as we know it will assuredly follow.

I, Merlin the Magnificent, write this account during my last free moments, for I have had a vision that I will soon fall under Vivienne's spell and be reduced to nothing more than stone. As my last lucid act, I have enchanted this bound written account and am sending it out into the world, hoping upon all hope that it will find its way to you.

If, as you hold this volume in your hands, you are able to read it, then you are the fated Keeper of the Last Descendant.

Perhaps you have already discovered the identity of the Last Descendant. After all, it is written in the stars that your two destinies will depend on one another, as the destinies of those who came before you once did.

If, by happenstance, the Last Descendant has not revealed himself to you, identify him by the Mark of Arthur. The Mark of Arthur is an eye with two perfect blue halves, divided by a thin band of brown. These two halves represent the ideal balance between reason and emotion, mercy and justice, faith and doubt—all qualities the Last Descendant will need if he is to forestall Doomsday and restore the mortal world to its proper equilibrium.

I hope with all my being that you will succeed where, before you, Guinevere did not.

Remember, peace can only reign when righteousness intersects with fate. I am sorry that the fate segment of this equation has been placed upon your shoulders, but there is no other way. Just as you sought out this book, it has also been seeking you for many centuries. You are the one.

I trust we will meet one day,

Merlin Ambrosius

I sat on the edge of my bed, dumbfounded. My hands went limp and *The Last Descendant* slipped through my fingers and dropped to the floor. I'd pictured Drake's gleaming eyes so many times in my head before, but in the moments after I'd completed *The Last Descendant,* they were even more vivid. He was the Last Descendant and I was his Keeper?

Had I been too dense to see it? Did that mean I was somehow linked to Guinevere? Was I destined to fail, too?

Or was all of it coincidence?

Ultimately, it was too much to take in at once.

Numbly, I wandered downstairs, past Bizzy's dark room. Instinctively, I walked through the back door and out our side gate. From the street in front of our house I could hear the ocean crashing into the rocks below. The air had a gloom to it—the sea fog already had taken its nightly hold on Crabapple. Streetlights on Earle glowed with orange dullness like a row of candles with barely enough oxygen to keep burning.

I hopped on my bike and began to pedal at a maddening pace. I sped along the same hill Bizzy had careened down on Dixie less than two months before, to rescue Jodi.

It was much darker this time.

When I reached Ocean Avenue, Mickey's Music came into view. I jumped off my bike and ran into the store.

Mickey was humming to himself as he read on a stool behind the counter.

"Hey there, Lizzy! I don't usually see you around these parts this late. I was actually about to close up."

"Oh," I said, feeling foolish. "I'm sorry." I turned around, ready to walk right back out the door.

"I didn't mean it that way. Please, stay. Is there something I can help you with?"

Whether I was the Keeper or not, I'd decided there was no time to beat around the bush.

"Mickey, you've read *Le Morte d'Arthur*, right?"

Mickey's eyes lit up behind his thick-framed glasses. "Aha! I'm guessin' you, like many before you, have become enchanted by all things Arthurian!"

"Sort of," I said, resisting the urge to tell Mickey that I may have involuntarily *become* Arthurian.

"Well, King Arthur is one of the most elusive and captivating heroes we have and Camelot is the stuff of legend. You've got the love triangle between Guinevere, Sir Lancelot, and Arthur, you've got the noble Knights of the Round Table. Merlin, Avalon, and the Lady of the Lake . . . so much great stuff! I think that's why the story has stuck around for so long and been retold so many times. Obviously, I went through a bit of an Arthurian phase myself," Mickey said, rubbing one side of his beard as he spoke.

"Well, what really happened, then?" I asked.

Mickey chuckled to himself. "If I could answer that question, Lizzy, I'd probably be a millionaire. Some scholars doubt that King Arthur existed at all."

"What about Guinevere?" I asked. "You said before that she brought down Arthur's kingdom, right?"

"I'm not sure Guinevere's really gotten a fair shake in all the books I've read, to be honest," Mickey said thoughtfully. "But, yeah, she does sort of betray Arthur by taking up with Lancelot. That leads to some pretty disastrous consequences."

"But *Guinevere* was the one who had been protecting Arthur the whole time! And Morgan le Faye was the one having an affair with Lancelot," I insisted.

Mickey raised his eyebrows. "Now that's a interesting take on things I haven't heard before. What book did you find that version in?"

I realized that there was no way Mickey could have possibly read *The Last Descendant*. There was no way I'd be able to explain it to him. Or anyone.

Though I was unsettled by what I'd read in *The Last Descendant*—and what it meant about my role in everything—it also occurred to me that the ending to the version I was living had yet to be written.

There was still time.

After bidding Mickey a quick good-bye, I pedaled quickly until I was in front of Drake's house. Crabapple, as always, was dead this time of night—even on a Friday. I got off my bike and stood in front of Happy Landing. The whole downstairs of the Westfall house was dark, but Drake's light was on upstairs.

I stared up at the window. Drake walked past wearing a white T-shirt. When he walked by the window again, he stopped. Thinking he might see me in the street, I dove behind one of the elm trees that lined the sidewalk.

After catching my breath, I resumed observing. Drake looked above me, out at the sea through the gap between the houses across from his own. I turned toward the sea myself.

The silver moon spilled enough murky light on the bay that I could make out the outlines of waves and rocky cliffs.

I turned back around.

Drake was still. His little notebook rested in the palm of one of his hands. In the other, he held a small pencil. His right hand hovered above the book. He closed his eyes for a moment and then his hand began to move quickly across the open page. His face wore an expression of extraordinary concentration.

Drake was drawing, using nothing more than his memory and moonlight.

I'd always expected that somewhere within Drake, there was something that made him different from most of the kids at Crabapple High. *The Last Descendant*, if it was true, was proof of that. I realized why I'd come out into the street. I had to see him, to see Drake now that I knew who he was. Or maybe I had to see him now that I knew who we *both* were. I thought about the passage I'd just read.

It is written in the stars that your two destinies will depend on one another.

Was I really Drake's Keeper? Was what was written in *The Last Descendant* true? Could Morgan and Lancelot's affair really have set in motion everything that had happened leading up to this point, including Drake and me?

I wanted to talk to Drake . . . to tell him all that I'd learned. For the first time, I felt the pang of longing.

I resisted the urge to yell up at his window that he needed to stay as far away from the cannery as possible. I thought about what had happened when I'd tried to warn Jodi. If I told Drake to avoid the cannery on Tuesday, that's exactly where he'd end up. I'd never be able to forgive myself and if what Merlin wrote about Agatha the Enchantress's last prophecy was true, neither would the rest of the world. Vivienne le Mort would do everything she could to ensure Drake died the way he was supposed to. She'd approached Drake across the field that day and looked into his eyes to confirm that he had the Mark of Arthur. I was sure of it.

I'm not quite certain how long I stared up at Drake before the chill in the air grabbed my spine and began climbing down it. Within a moment, my whole body shivered.

In the distance, I heard Mom's anxious voice, wondering where I'd gone as she called out my name.

The Personification
of a Secret

The true meaning of Merlin's words became apparent when I decided to show Bizzy *The Last Descendant* at the hospital that night. When she opened the book she gave me a puzzled look.

"What in tarnation kinda writin' is this?" she asked.

In Bizzy's hands the text, which had been perfectly clear to me, turned into a jumble of meaningless symbols. Merlin had written, "*If, as you hold this volume in your hands, you are able to read it, then you are the fated Keeper of the Last Descendant.*"

Could this really be? Once I caught my breath, I took back the book and read to Bizzy the words I saw, clear as could be, on those ancient pages. Bizzy and I went over and over the meaning of the last pages, but neither of us was certain what the future held for me. Even though I was able to read the book, was I really the Keeper? Would I be the Keeper forever? I'd just started to adjust to being a Death Catcher, but how would I ever cope with this? I didn't sleep much when I finally went to bed that night.

The next day, breakfast, lunch, and dinner came and went. Even though I could see the concern on Mom's face as I pushed the green beans around on my plate without eating them, I couldn't force any down. I tried, for Mom's sake, but I felt nauseous and it wasn't just from Mom's cooking this time.

That night, Jodi and I figured out a perfect way to keep tabs on Drake and Damon. We found the ideal elm tree. It was Bizzy's idea. She suggested we track the Westfalls by climbing up a tree so we could see inside their rooms. It sounds creepy, I know, Mrs. Tweedy, but we had good reasons—Jodi was doing it to protect her mom's store and I was doing it to protect Drake (and, just maybe the whole world by keeping Doomsday from happening). When I objected to Bizzy's suggestion because I thought someone would be able to see us, Bizzy laughed.

"Pick one at an angle," she said. "Why, if people were horses, they wouldn't need blinders. We got the self-imposed kind. People are too busy lookin' straight ahead of 'em to ever look to the side. They'll never see ya, trust me." I let out a mischievous laugh. Had Bizzy climbed a tree to get a look in someone's window before? I could see her in her purple nightgown and slippers hanging from an elm branch. It wasn't all that hard to imagine.

Jodi and I met outside the Westfall house at 10 p.m. I hadn't climbed a tree in about five years, but I soon learned it was like riding a bike—it came back quickly. I hugged the trunk. Squeezing it between my thighs, I scooted up one inch at a time. Finally I could reach the lowest branch with my hands.

I grabbed it and swung my legs over. The tree leaves rustled in the dark night. I moved from one branch to another until I was across from Drake's second-story window, a few feet above it. I could hear Jodi's muffled laughter from below as she watched me watch Drake. She moved three trees down and climbed to a spot for viewing Damon's room.

I could see everything clearly. Drake's desk lamp was on, his bed was unmade. He was lying on his back on the floor, mindlessly tossing a water polo ball from one hand to the other. I studied his features. His square chin, his wide chest, his long, lean arms. The ball pounded against the flesh of one of his palms, then the other. *Bong, bong, bong,* in perfect rhythm. Drake's eyes stared up at the ceiling. His lips were in the shape of a small *o* and his eyes brilliant blue—like someone had put two bits of shimmering ocean in his sockets. From that distance, I couldn't make out the brown streak in his left eye, but I knew it was there.

He got up and sat down at his desk, opening a textbook. Yawning, he made his hand into fists. He rubbed his eyes with them, turning his hands in his eye sockets. I couldn't help but smile at the childlike act. Especially coming from Drake, who could now grow facial hair and was all hard, wiry muscle. I wanted to reach out and grab him. As soon as I thought it, I became self-conscious.

I pulled my eyes away from Drake to the empty street below. I hopped down from one branch to the next, jumping the last four feet before tumbling onto a neighbor's front lawn.

"You okay?" Jodi whispered. She'd already gotten down from her post.

"Fine," I said.

"I don't know why I got stuck with spying on Damon and you got Drake," Jodi said.

"That's because I'm a POIBA," I answered. Jodi rolled her eyes.

"Did you see anything?" I asked.

"Damon was sleeping. You?"

"No," I responded.

"See you at the cannery tomorrow?"

"Yup," I said. Jodi turned on the light attached to her fixie and hopped on the seat. She pedaled into the darkness.

Scrambling across the street, I reached our backyard in moments.

Sleep that night once again battled with restlessness. Restlessness won. Morning came, but my anxiety was undiminished. Saving Drake's life would have been enough to keep me awake, but my mind kept returning to *The Last Descendant*. Was it true? Was Drake's premature death going to bring on some kind of apocalypse? Was I really the one who had been chosen to stop it?

In the past I'd impatiently waited for a particular day to arrive—Christmas, for instance. But this was different. Unlike Christmas, all that waited for me wrapped under this tree was uncertainty and dread.

The walls of my bedroom seemed to be closing in on me.

On Sunday afternoon, after Jodi and I had checked out the cannery, which was still deserted, I decided I needed to get out of the house. I followed the sandy path that was a switchback down the cliffs to the beach. It was another in a long line of gray, foggy, cold Crabapple days. I walked a ways down the shore and then sat on the beach. I lay flat on my back. The thicket of clouds above didn't seem to be moving at all and the sand was cold on my back and neck. Even the cypress trees had a slanted sogginess to them.

My mind wandered. I thought of the dozens of my Hands of Fate ancestors. I marveled at the fact that they'd managed to pass down certain stories and legends all these years, through oral tradition alone, over fear of being discovered. Maybe it was better that way. Of course, it would have been nice if there was some structure to it—like maybe a website or a convention. Or a support group.

I wondered who they'd saved. I also wondered what kind of trouble they'd seen as Death Catchers. So far, I'd had my hand involuntarily tattooed twice, saved my best friend, been kissed and then ignored, and been threatened by thugs. Maybe the whole thing wasn't changing *me*, but it sure was changing my life.

Bizzy seemed to bask in the weirdness of it all. Perhaps it was the strange power that came with knowing people's fate before they did. But Bizzy and I were different. Bizzy was stronger. And louder. If life gave her lemons, I had no doubt she'd throw them at whoever stood in her way. But that wasn't really me, was it? I was more likely to tire myself out searching for someone who liked the tart taste of lemons.

I wasn't cut out to be a Keeper of anything. What if I failed?

"Lizzy?"

I opened my eyes and felt the sting of my own tears. So lost in my own thoughts, I hadn't even noticed I was crying. I wiped the tears away quickly. Mom's face hovered a few feet above mine. Her reading glasses dangled from her neck. She was wearing a bulky knit sweater, sweatpants, and furry clogs—very much the crunchy librarian.

Without a word, she dropped to the sand and lay down right next to me. From Lookout Point, it must have appeared as if we were taking naps right next to each other. Or sunbathing. Except there was no sun and we were fully clothed. I could feel the mist from the crashing waves gather on my eyelashes, making them heavier.

The tide was coming in.

As on most cold and dreary December days, the beach was deserted.

"What are you doing out here?" Mom asked. The left side of her body was about an inch away from my right.

"Thinking."

"About?"

"I don't know." Of course, I did know. I could see Mom's chest rise up and then flatten out as she exhaled a large swallow of air. We lay there for minutes without speaking, like two people who'd finally run out of things to say to one another, on side-by-side rafts, adrift in a sea of sand.

"Did you know that your father wakes up early on Sundays and goes into the backyard to smoke?" Mom blurted it out like she wanted to get the thought out before she lost the courage to say it at all.

I pushed my head back a little so that I could see Mom's face without moving my eyes. I knew I was raising my eyebrows at her, but I couldn't help it.

"Really?"

"Yes. He keeps a pack of cigarettes in his underwear drawer." Mom put her hand under her cheek, lifting her head up ever so slightly.

"You're okay with that?" I asked. In truth, Mom hated smoking. As with a lot of other things, she's pretty judgmental about it, actually. She rolls her eyes and hacks when someone lights up in front of her. I usually try to distance myself when she starts into her don't-smoke routine.

"Oh yes. He doesn't think I know, and he'd just about die if he knew I was telling you."

"I'm surprised you didn't kick him out of the house or something when you found out."

Mom's tone turned serious. "Your father is so good in so many ways, Lizzy. His sense of duty is sharper than just about anyone I know. He works so hard. Sometimes I think he'll drown in responsibility. I've thought about it and, honestly, I think it's a release for him. I may not love the habit, but I just don't have the heart to take it away from him." Mom let out a small sigh. I must have looked puzzled because Mom readjusted and pointed her face straight at the sky again.

"He smokes—as a release?" I questioned, looking at Mom's profile. With her glasses off, she looked younger and prettier. It wasn't hard to imagine how Dad could've fallen in love with her.

"That's my guess."

"Why don't you tell him to stop? Or at least tell him that you know about it and that it's okay and that he doesn't have to hide it anymore."

"I guess that's my point, Lizzy. It's *his* secret. And secrets are a part of life," Mom said. Her words startled me. I turned my head toward her and could feel the damp sand on my cheek. Mom turned toward me, too, so that our faces were inches apart. I had no idea what she was getting at, but I was growing uncomfortable with the direction. "Everybody has at least one," she continued.

"But it doesn't bother you that Dad's never told you? That he thinks he has to keep it from you? What if he isn't telling you about a bunch of other things?" I began to wonder if Mom and Dad's relationship was as rock solid as I thought it was.

"I think sometimes people need their secrets to be exactly that—secret. Communication is important, of course, but we all need a private life . . . We all need something that's just ours and ours alone." Mom lifted up her head and put both hands behind it, like she was relaxing on her imaginary raft. Maybe I hadn't given her enough credit.

Was it possible that Mom knew I was a Death Catcher? That Bizzy was?

"I have my share. Have I ever told you that when I was little, I never learned how to read?"

"No." I was shocked. I always figured Mom came out of the womb with a book in her hand.

"I never learned and then I got left behind. As each semester passed, I lived in constant fear every day that my teacher would find me out. It was torture. Finally, I broke down one day and told my mother everything. I thought she'd spank me or yell at me, or worse. Of course she didn't. She only marveled that I had been able to fool everyone for so long. The next morning, my mother woke me up an hour before everyone else in the house, and brought me down to the kitchen table. She began my first lesson—teaching me how to read, until my father woke up. Then she would stop, hide the books we were working with, and pretend that we'd both awakened moments ago. I caught up before long. No one ever knew." Mom wasn't a natural storyteller, but under the dark gray clouds, there on the sand, her words came out smoothly. Her voice had a different quality to it than it normally had—like she was thinking out loud.

"Is that why you love to read? Because you couldn't for so long?" I asked.

"I'm sure that's part of it. It's funny. Years later, I asked my mother if she was upset I never told her I couldn't read for so long. I'll never forget what she said. 'All secrets have wings,' she told me. 'Your secret just wasn't ready to fly until that afternoon in the kitchen and there's no way I can blame you for that.' My mother was right, but I think I just didn't realize early enough that mine was ready to fly . . . all those anxious nights I spent crying in my bed. All those days I spent cowering in the classroom. Everyone needs a private life. I truly believe that. But I also believe that saying something out loud to someone who loves you can make all the difference. Sometimes, the hardest thing to do is to recognize when you need help and then ask for it."

A single seagull flapped its wings in the sky above us. I stared at it and I could feel hot tears on my cheeks. I wasn't sure what Mom knew and what she didn't. But she'd been watching me. i mean *really watching* me. She'd noticed. Maybe she'd noticed everything. It was frustrating because as much as I wanted to tell her all of it, starting with that first day when I saw Jodi's death-specter in the paper, she couldn't possibly understand.

Sure, *most* secrets have wings. But this one I was keeping from her had been born deformed, I was sure of it. Either that or it was so big and heavy that its wings could never lift it—like an ostrich or an emu.

Mom sat up so that she was sitting with her hands around her knees. The back of her sweater was covered with sand. She stared out at the ocean waves making their way to the shore.

"I have a secret now, Lizzy. I don't want it to be a secret anymore. I want to say it out loud to someone I love." Mom turned to look at me. I could see all the worry lines on her face. "I'm more concerned about you now than I've ever been," she said. Her words were coming quicker now. "You're not eating, you mope around most days. You keep leaving the house and going off by yourself. I can't sleep because I think about you. I don't know what it is, but I know you. You're not the same Lizzy. The only person you talk to is your grandmother. I know Bizzy Bea's one of those magnetic people, but I'm not sure that a teenager's closest confidante should be a woman sixty years her senior." Mom never took her eyes off mine. They started to pool with tears of her own. "As much as I want you to be safe, to intervene and protect you, to force you to tell me whatever it is that's inside you, I also want you to know I trust you, I love you, and most of all, I'm here for you, always, whatever it is."

Silently, my mother raised herself out of the sand. Without brushing the grains stuck to her back, she turned toward the sandy path that led up the hill and back to our house. I didn't get up, but I shifted my head so I could see her walk away. When she'd traveled a few feet, she turned around once more. "Hopefully this goes without saying," she started. Her voice had none of the tentativeness it had had when she was talking about Dad's secret and her own. "But just because your father smokes does not mean that you should start, under any circumstances."

Almost in a flash, she left and my tears returned.

Suspending Disbelief

When I was in fifth grade, Mom gave me my first fantasy book to read, *The Lion, the Witch and the Wardrobe*, from the Chronicles of Narnia. She let me know that most children were crazy about the series and read every single volume. I think she wanted me to believe *I* was crazy if I didn't like the book.

I read a couple of chapters, but I couldn't get into it. In my mind, there was no way some kid could travel to a magical world full of talking lions and goat-men, simply by going through a wardrobe in the closet. It didn't make much sense.

When I told Mom, she laughed and suggested that I needed to work on *suspending my disbelief.* She explained that it meant I should "buy into the story" and let my imagination do the rest. She said that if I went with the premise, imagining it was possible, even for a moment, I'd enjoy the story. It's still hard for me to let go of the belief that magical worlds don't exist at all, yet alone in wardrobes.

Which is to say that I had it coming.

Because a few months ago, I never could've imagined who was waiting when Bizzy finally came home from the hospital. I knocked and stood outside Bizzy's door, anxious to discuss our evolving plan.

"That you, Lizzy-Loo?" I heard Bizzy shout through the door.

"Yes," I responded.

"You alone?" she asked. I could hear her wheeling around in her room.

"Yes," I answered, growing curious. Bizzy unlocked the door and cracked it open for me.

"Quickly," she whispered, beckoning me inside.

I closed the door behind me.

Then I gasped.

Sitting on Bizzy's bed were two women cloaked in hooded satin frocks, one blood red and the other canary yellow. Both sat upright, unflinching, when I entered. I couldn't judge how old the women were, but their eyes were clear and bright. The one in yellow smiled at me. The one in red, with long dark locks spilling from the hood of her cloak, peered at me curiously. Bizzy's room smelled like apple-cinnamon oatmeal.

"Lizzy." Bizzy wheeled to the side of the room so that she was facing both the women and me. "It's my pleasure to introduce you to two women who have traveled a very long way to see us." Bizzy motioned to the woman in red. "This is your great-grandmamma, many times over, Morgan le Faye, and her sister, Fial," she said nodding at the woman in yellow.

Facing Morgan le Faye and Fial, I knew it was time to suspend my last shred of disbelief. A few months ago, I would have assumed I was dreaming—that there was no way I was actually staring at two satin-cloaked women who were my ancestors from a mythical and magical island. But after two death-specters, Jodi's near death, Drake's being revealed as the Last Descendant, and Merlin's appointment of me as Drake's Keeper, life was beginning to seem like one big suspension of disbelief. Heck, my disbelief hadn't been suspended. It'd been expelled.

"Hullo," Fial said, looking squarely at me. Her voice was high pitched, sweet, and smooth. She spoke with an accent that I couldn't quite place. Her rosy cheeks, in combination with her stout frame, made her seem like the friendlier of the two women. Fial removed her hood. Her pale hair was swept into a bun on the top of her head. "Please forgive us for arriving so suddenly, but it could not wait a moment longer."

Morgan le Faye looked at the brainstorming wall and then back at me. Though she was seated, I could tell she was quite a bit taller than Fial. She had the greenest eyes I'd ever seen—like piles of freshly cut grass floating atop two glasses of milk—set deep within her face.

"What do you know of us, Elizabeth Mortimer?" Morgan le Faye asked. Her voice was deep and rich, with the same accent as Fial's.

"Um," I said, trying not to stutter, "I know that you live on the Isle of Avalon, that you are a gifted sorceress, you once saved King Arthur's life, and—"

"Wait a moment!" Fial insisted. "*I* am the one who nursed Arthur back to health. Morgan had very little to do with it!" Fial stomped her foot on the floor. When she did it, I saw a golden sandal poke out from beneath her yellow robe.

"Fial, we do not have time for your petty concerns," Morgan admonished.

"Easy enough for you to say. You're the one who's been getting undeserved credit for the last thousand years!"

Morgan rolled her eyes as if she'd heard Fial's complaint hundreds of times before.

"What else do you know, Elizabeth Mortimer?" Morgan questioned.

"The legend goes," I said, trying to remember exactly what I'd read in *The Last Descendant*, "that your half-mortal daughter was the first Death Catcher."

"Death *what*?" Morgan said, rising from her seated position. She put her hands behind her back and began pacing. Her ebony hair and pale skin made her appear as if she'd never spent a single minute in the sun.

"It's just a name we came up with, Bizzy and me, for the Hands of Fate," I explained, growing nervous.

"I see," Morgan said disapprovingly.

Fial nudged her sister playfully. "I think it's clever," she said. Morgan ignored her sister. Her eyes narrowed as she scanned Bizzy and me.

"Is that all you know of our legacy?" As she spoke, I assumed Morgan le Faye was looking at us wondering where the gene pool had gone off the track in the generations between herself and us.

"Oh, Morgie, you're scaring the poor child with all this legacy talk," Fial said, coming over and wrapping her arm around me. Though I appreciated the gesture, her arm was heavy and dry-ice cold.

"I've read about you in *The Last Descendant*."

"What is this now?" Morgan said, clearly confused.

"Merlin Ambrosius, right before he was turned to stone, wrote down everything about Avalon's history and King Arthur, hoping it would reach the person destined to protect the Last Descendant."

"That sly dog!" Fial said, clapping her hands excitedly. "Perhaps he's not as dim witted as I once thought!"

"Let us not forget he was dim enough to allow himself to be turned to stone by Vivienne," Morgan said coolly.

"Well, at the end of the day, he is still a sorcerer, and we all know a sorcerer can be quite gull—"

"Where did you come across this book?" Morgan le Faye interrupted.

"Agatha's cottage," I responded. "So it's all true?"

"I'm not sure you can trust any story a sorcerer tells . . . we all know Merlin was a little off-kilter when he wrote whatever is in *The Last Descendant*."

"That is quite enough, Fial," Morgan commanded. She turned to me. "If Merlin's little account imparted all of this to you, then you may also already know part of the reason we are here."

I turned to Morgan le Faye, trying to drum up all the confidence I had in me. "Are you the one who sends Bizzy and me the death-specters?"

Morgan le Faye sat back on Bizzy's bed. "I am, indeed," she said. Fial put her hand to her mouth and murmured something in a language I couldn't understand.

"Why?" I asked.

The sisters of Avalon each took a deep breath and locked eyes. Morgan le Faye, still wearing the hood to her red satin cloak, removed it. Her hair had an unnatural shine to it and her pale skin seemed to glow in the dim light of Bizzy's bedroom. She was quite beautiful, even if she was over a thousand years old. She focused her green eyes on me.

"Perhaps you are aware from Merlin's account that there was a time, long ago, when I desired to be free of Avalon forever. I had come to care deeply for a mortal named Lancelot du Lac. When Vivienne cut his thread before his time . . . it changed me." Morgan's voice grew quieter. "You must understand my whole life has been in the service of death and the transition between this world and the next, and yet I never understood it before I lost Lancelot. When Vivienne cut his thread, I realized why death unleashes such despair. It is not the loss or transition of the mortal's soul itself that causes pain, but rather the uncertainty and longing of those who remain behind. Soon after my daughter arrived here in Crabapple more than a thousand years ago, I discovered my special skills would allow me to communicate with my own flesh and blood while I was still in Avalon."

"Just a minute," I interrupted, "so Crabapple *is* more than a thousand years old? Is Old Arthur in the cemetery actually King Arthur himself?"

"There are most likely many things about Crabapple you do not know. We will not have time to discuss them all," Morgan said dismissively before moving on. "As I was saying, at first I sent the specter to spare my daughter some of the suffering I had experienced. Each time I realized someone close to a descendant of mine, no matter where they were located, was to die unnaturally, I sent a death-specter.

"But I have continued sending death-specters for a much more important reason. I realized that, although I could not leave Avalon because of the Great Truce, by communicating with my lineage, I would always have a representative here in this world, able to save the Last Descendant when he arrived . . . someone perfectly equipped to protect him. Someone who would not fail in the way Guinevere did. Sending the death-specters helped me feel I was atoning for my offense of leaving Avalon for Lancelot." As Morgan finished, her voice wavered slightly. "The time has finally come for me to right my wrong."

Fial placed her hand over Morgan's, gazing at her sister sympathetically. "There is no use assigning blame, Morgan. Vivienne broke the laws of Avalon as well, by cutting Lancelot's thread prematurely," Fial said. She turned to Bizzy and me. "What is important for you both to realize, though, is that Agatha's prophecy about the Last Descendant was a direct result of Morgan's and Vivienne's actions. The world has been put on the path toward Doomsday and we must now fix it. The first step was initiating the Hands of Fate equipped to deal with Arthur's descendant when he arrived. That descendant, as you may know, is Drake Westfall."

I had already realized as much, but to hear it said out loud was another thing entirely. It knocked the wind right out of me.

"Before Agatha's last prophecy . . . long before my actions, as well as those of Vivienne, had altered fate permanently, the boy with the Mark of Arthur had already been destined to bring peace to the land during a time of darkness and great upheaval," Morgan said.

Fial perked up. "Agatha's last prophecy also revealed how my sisters' interference so many years ago changed fate, leading to Drake's premature death."

Morgan peered at me with a startling intensity. "Did Merlin's account impart what Vivienne le Mort is planning? Her evil plans for the threads she has cut?"

"Yes," I said, shuddering at the thought of Vivienne le Mort and her army of lost souls. "But how in the world is Drake supposed to stop all that?"

"Drake is necessary because only the one with the Mark of Arthur can wake Merlin from his stone slumber. That is all you need to know for now," Morgan said.

"He has the perfect balance necessary to lead," Fial explained, ignoring Morgan's dismissal of the subject. "First, although I hate to admit it, we will need Merlin. Personally, I find Merlin Ambrosius to be insufferable, with an ego the size of Pangaea, but he knows of Vivienne's weaknesses, and his power and knowledge will be of immeasurable value to a king."

Bizzy, who had been unusually quiet, her eyes on me, chimed in for the first time. "I'm sorry, ladies," Bizzy said. "I hate to break it to ya both, but you've been gone a while and we don't really have many kings anymore."

"Perhaps a different name is used today," Fial said, "but so long as the world turns, there will always be kings or leaders— the most righteous of which, like Drake, possess a perfect balance of logic and feeling. He will assemble the Round Table and defeat Vivienne le Mort."

"I'm not sure I get it," I said. "What exactly do you think is going to happen? Are you two going to equip Drake with the Excaliber, give the water polo team some spear guns, and let them have at it?"

"Foolish child, of course not!" Morgan said. "The sword never makes the man. It is the man who makes the sword. The Excaliber was only a powerful tool because Arthur possessed the judgment necessary to make it most effective."

"Well, does Drake know any of your big plans for him?" I asked.

"Of course not." Morgan frowned. "It is not time for him to know and you must not tell him. For now, he must just stay alive."

"Agatha only granted us leave to spend a few minutes here and I am afraid our time is running out, Morgie," Fial said, wearing her concern on her unlined face. "You best get to it."

"The true purpose of our trip here is to warn you about Vivienne. As you may know, our sister does not want to restore fate to its proper balance. Once Arthur's last descendant dies, there will be no one left to stop her. When she has an army of evil souls to do her bidding, she will be the most powerful of all the sisters. Thus, if you do not save the boy, nothing else will matter, because the earth will be on a course for Doomsday, I assure you."

"You have to excuse Morgie. Sometimes she plays up the fire-and-brimstone aspect of all this a bit much," Fial said. "We honestly came to warn you. We believe that Vivienne now knows you Hands of Fate exist," she said as she looked knowingly at me, "which is why Agatha allowed us to leave Avalon and come here."

"If Drake's death is that important, why doesn't Vivienne just kill him now?" I asked, fearful that Drake might be in immediate danger as I spoke the words. "Why hasn't she killed him already? Why wait?"

"Mortals always have a tendency to see the world as a series of discrete incidents," Morgan said, sounding impatient. "But destiny is a most delicate pyramid of the smallest of circumstances." My eyes connected directly with those of my distant great-grandmother, for the first time. Her expression wasn't warm, but it wasn't cold, either. "You see, Vivienne is, and will always be, beholden to fate. She cannot be sure cutting a thread before its time will not alter fate once again—and perhaps send the world on a different course entirely."

I may have suspended my disbelief for a little while, but it was back. I didn't care if Morgan le Faye was two thousand years old or whatever, she was talking absolute nonsense. Drake Westfall of one-thousand-year-old Crabapple, California . . . the key to the world's future? And me, Lizzy Mortimer, high school freshman, the one responsible for his well-being? The whole thing was suddenly hard to stomach.

Bizzy, on the other hand, didn't seem to be sharing my doubts any longer.

"So if the Westfall boy dies unnaturally when he's scheduled to, we can kiss our messy ole world good-bye?" she asked.

"I am afraid so. Which is why we came to tell you that Vivienne is sure to be tracking Drake Westfall right now. Watching his every move very carefully," Morgan le Faye said, looking directly at me. "If she finds out you two are the ones trying to prevent his death, she will find a way to destroy you."

Morgan le Faye stopped in front of me and paused.

"So, are you gals goin' to help us save Drake, then?" Bizzy asked.

"I strayed once from Avalon's rules and caused pain and a great rift among my sisters. I will never do so again," Morgan le Faye said. "We cannot violate the Great Truce. You already possess all that you need to save Drake Westfall."

"I hate to say this, Morgie," Fial said, her eyes shifting around the room, "but we have really already been here too long for anyone's well-being." Fial got up and put her yellow hood over the pile of blond hair on top of her head.

"You are correct, Fial. Our presence here only serves to put you both in more danger. Agatha has only allowed us to warn you because she believes the epic contest must be fair. Avoid Vivienne at all costs." Morgan le Faye began moving her right hand in a circle, at first slowly and then gathering speed. She closed her eyes. Red haze surrounded her, as if her moving hand conjured it. Fial produced her own cloud of yellow smoke. Morgan le Faye's voice thundered out of the thicket of red and yellow, sounding as if it was coming from all sides like some giant surround sound.

"May fate be on your side. And if it is not, may you make it so!"

As if it were being sucked from Bizzy's room with a vacuum, the vapor disappeared out Bizzy's open window in one single whoosh.

When the colorful haze was gone, only Bizzy and I remained, sitting across from one another in her bedroom, growing more certain by the minute that unless we found a way to stop fate and Vivienne le Mort, Drake Westfall had less than forty-eight hours to live.

Revision

Look, I know it's important, Mrs. Tweedy, but rewriting something after you've already finished it is not the easiest task. Writing can be a painful process. Sometimes revising feels like using an already-sore muscle.

After Morgan le Faye and Fial visited, I began to realize that life is one big revision. We are constantly rewriting the stories we tell others about ourselves. Even the Death Catcher part of me keeps changing and morphing. Maybe the only difference between language arts and life is that when you revise an assignment, it's supposed to improve it, right? But when life gets revised, there are no guarantees it will. In fact, sometimes it gets a whole lot worse.

When I found out that Drake's death didn't just affect his life and my life, but according to Morgan le Faye, the entire world, I wished I could edit the knowledge out of my brain. If I could hit the delete key, I thought, the information would be gone and I could adjust to being a Death Catcher first, before

I dealt with things like being the Keeper, Doomsday, and the Doomsday maniac, Vivienne le Mort. Yet, I knew, there was no way to separate any of it—one thing bled into another.

Fortunately, there wasn't much time to dwell on it with Drake's life hanging in the balance and with our supposedly united destinies. Bizzy and I discussed the details of our plan that night. Monday arrived on schedule. Drake's body would be discovered in the cannery on Tuesday.

I thought the school day would pass slowly, but first and second period flew by. As soon as recess rolled around, I tried to get a visual on Drake. He was at the picnic tables, hanging out with his teammates.

Jodi met me by our planter. She was wearing a large polka-dotted headband, a homemade feather earring in her right ear, and braided sandals.

"What's the plan for tonight?" Jodi said, watching me watch Drake.

"Bizzy is planning some kind of stakeout," I said without taking my eyes off Drake.

Jodi and I both jumped up from the planter as the word "FFFIIIIIGHT!" echoed across the quad.

A crowd had gathered by the picnic tables.

"Over there!" Jodi pointed. Instead of running toward the group, Jodi hopped back onto the brick planter. I joined her. From our bird's-eye view, we could see the entire scene.

In the middle of the mob, two students were tearing at each other in one huddled mass of clothing and flailing arms.

I spotted Garrett Edmonds first. He was bobbing and weaving, crouched close to the ground, holding someone in a headlock. Drake's head appeared as he freed himself from the headlock.

Simultaneously taking a step back and winding up, Drake took a massive swing at Garrett's face. His fist connected with Garrett's jaw, followed by a loud pop. The crowd murmured and lurched backward, creating space for Garrett to topple over onto the concrete. His groan echoed through the crowd. Garrett thrashed on the ground. I stood on my tiptoes to get a better look at Drake. He was bleeding from his lip and his T-shirt was torn.

Soon, Mr. Thompson, the assistant principal and football coach, was pushing students out of the way, trying to disperse the crowd so he could get to Drake and Garrett. He blew his whistle repeatedly. Finally, he had a direct path to the boys. By that time, most of Crabapple High had assembled around the fight area.

Mr. Thompson reached out and collared Drake.

"Step back!" he yelled at the crowd, waving his free arm at the students. After a few seconds, Mrs. Rios, the theater arts teacher, reached Garrett. She kneeled next to him, asking if he was okay. Garrett hopped up defiantly, still clutching his jaw. Suddenly, he lunged at Drake in a rage. The murmur of the crowd spiked once again. Mr. Thompson stepped between the boys, pushing against Drake, forcing him out of Garrett's reach.

After another minute, the commotion ended. Mrs. Rios led Garrett to the office while Mr. Thompson ushered Drake from the scene. The quad was alive with the leftover buzz from the fight.

Jodi and I looked at each other, speechless, from our perch on top of the planter. We watched students cluster together, reenacting and recounting portions of the fight. The noise grew. Jodi was the first to notice a group staring at us. She nudged me. Some students pointed at us and then resumed talking. Soon other groups did the same.

"Are they looking at us?" I asked with disbelief.

"No, they're looking at *you*," Jodi said. The ringing of the bell sent students scattering, though dozens of pairs of eyes still followed me as I walked across the quad.

I waited impatiently for two more periods to pass so that I could meet with Jodi again. I was sure she'd have more information for me. She did.

"Looks like I was right," Jodi said confidently.

"Right about what?"

"People were staring at you after the fight." Jodi took her cherry ChapStick out of her burlap shoulder bag and coated her lips.

"They were?" I said, dismayed.

"Uh-huh. Apparently Garrett and Drake were fighting *over you*."

I had to stop myself from toppling over into the planter. There was just no way it was true. I said as much to Jodi.

"I've heard it from multiple sources. Garrett said something to Drake about how Garrett invited you over for dinner . . . Garrett started teasing Drake about stealing Drake's girlfriend. Which, I guess, is you. Drake exploded or something. Word is he kinda went agro on Garrett."

"He did?" I asked in disbelief. "That's awful."

"Um, that's one way of looking at it," Jodi said, extending her hand and patting my shoulder.

"What do you mean?"

"If Drake was defending your honor, or whatever, I'd take it as a very positive sign that he doesn't hate you. I think it means the opposite." Jodi smirked at me. "It looks like you guys can't seem to escape one another."

"Maybe Drake fought Garrett because he was upset that Garrett was associating me with him," I said. Could Drake really have been defending me? Though I tried not to, I thought about Merlin's words about Drake's and my intertwined destinies.

"Gee, Lizster. And maybe we'll all die in an atomic bomb blast tomorrow. But I prefer to think positive."

I almost laughed at Jodi. She was closer to the truth than she knew. None of this would matter if Drake wound up inside the cannery tomorrow morning.

"Anyways, I'm sure Drake will be suspended, so you'll have a few days to think of something to say to him when you see him next," Jodi said, taking a bite out of an apple she pulled from her bag.

"How do you know I want to say something to him?"

"Don't you want to talk to him again?" *More than anything,* I'd wanted to respond. My feelings about Drake were a muddled mess. Between the combination of the death-specter, his behavior at school, his name engraved on my hand, and my new role as his Keeper, I had no idea how I felt, just that I wanted to spend more time with him.

I had to focus on the most immediate of the concerns. I considered Drake's possible suspension. Would he still be able to play in the last couple of water polo games? If not, Mr. Westfall would be furious. Furious enough to lose his temper and do something destructive? Was that what Drake was trying to tell me pre-kiss in the pool house?

When the dismissal bell rang, I headed straight for my bike. Jodi split off, promising she'd meet me at Cedar Tree Park at midnight. If she was nervous, she didn't show it.

I don't think I've ever pedaled as fast as I did the rest of the way home that afternoon. I knew Bizzy would be waiting anxiously for me when I got there.

Ὀπομᾰτοποεῖᾰ

You're always encouraging us to use onomatopoeia—words that sound like what they describe—to make our writing "sing." Most of them are fun words like *buzz* and *growl*, but there's one onomatopoeia I will remember above all others: *rumble*. It wasn't until Bizzy and I heard the low rumble that we figured out how Drake was going to die.

I should explain.

Bizzy's last trip to the cannery shaped the final part of our plan. The reason she'd traveled all the way to Cedar Tree Park was that, at one hundred feet above and two blocks away from the cannery, the park provided the perfect lookout point.

Since Bizzy and I still hadn't figured out why Drake was going to be at the cannery on Tuesday morning, we'd decided we would sneak out and spend Monday night camped out under the cedars at the park. From there, we'd be able to see someone approaching the cannery. There was a clear view of Mission and Ocean avenues, as well as the streets in the surrounding area.

From the park, we could intercept Drake before he even got close to the cannery. While Bizzy watched from the hill, Jodi and I would monitor the storm drain entrance and the Westfall house.

I wasn't supremely confident in our plan the way Bizzy was. Then again, Bizzy had been in the death-catching business for sixty years. I hadn't even been doing it for sixty days.

Regardless, the moment to put our plan into action had arrived.

While I was at school, Bizzy had been living up to her name. She'd gathered the camping equipment we would need from the garage, hidden it underneath a patch of bushes at Cedar Tree Park, and tracked down a blueprint of Crabapple's storm drain system.

"How did you get to the park and back by yourself?"

"I drove," Bizzy said. Since her first accident with Dixie, Bizzy's old Buick Roadmaster station wagon (complete with wood paneling on the sides) sat in the driveway unused. The doctor had warned that it would be impossible for Bizzy to drive with her leg straight out in a cast. But by extending her leg into the passenger's foot well she'd figured out how to do it.

"Did the doctor clear you to do that?"

"I cleared my doggone self!" Bizzy said. "I'll just need help with my chair." I looked on Bizzy's bed. She'd started collecting another pile of supplies. There were two headlamps, three thermoses, a large Maglite, two blankets, a map of Crabapple, a bag of groceries, handcuffs, and a compass.

Bizzy pointed to the brainstorming wall. The covering photos were pulled back.

"Take a good last look, Sweet Pea—you may need every scrap of information—no predictin' what might happen out there tonight."

I leaned against the bottom of the bed and started at the top of the wall. **Drake Westfall**. Followed by tomorrow's date. It was hard to believe it was almost here. My eyes followed the lines from Drake's name to **the cannery**, to **foul play?**, to **art**, to **Mr. Westfall's temper**, to **Damon**, to **robbery**, to **Miss Mora's Market**, to **basement**, to **storm drains**.

I thought of all the things that weren't listed on the wall that were so intimately related to those that were there: Morgan le Faye, Vivienne le Mort, the Great Truce, Old Arthur, and *The Last Descendant*.

We'd learned a lot in the past few weeks. But it still hadn't been enough to figure out what would cause Drake's appearance at the cannery.

"How are we going to sneak out?" I asked. Bizzy wheeled up next to me.

"Honeychile, ya tellin' me you never snuck out of here at night, not once?"

"Well . . . no . . . I mean," I stammered. Bizzy cut me off with a laugh. Leave it to Beatrice Mildred Mortimer, my seventy-four-year-old grandma, to make me feel completely lame.

"It's simple. Your parents fall asleep 'round ten. Meet me

out back at eleven sharp. Wear dark clothes and dress warm. Yur first stakeout's always yur longest." For dinner, Mom had made beef stew, which was my favorite and one of her few edible dishes. We hadn't really talked since our conversation on the beach the day before. I knew she'd be watching me, so I forced myself to down a small bowl of stew, even though I felt queasier with every spoonful. When I asked to be excused early, Mom looked anxiously over her glasses at me.

I spent the rest of the evening pacing, mostly, back and forth in my room, and trying on different shades of black clothing. I settled on a black fleece and Dad's old ski pants that I sometimes wore when I rode my bike in the cold. When it was ten minutes to eleven, I checked my room for anything else I thought I would need. Sheriff Schmidt's business card was sitting on my desk. I grabbed it and slid it into my pocket along with my cell phone. Although reception was poor around Crabapple, it did get better at night.

When I got out to the driveway, Bizzy was waiting in the Roadmaster. I loaded the rest of the supplies in the back, including my bike. As soon as I was buckled in, carefully avoiding her leg—which was extended into my foot space, Bizzy put the car in neutral. The Roadmaster coasted out of the driveway and into the street.

How many times before had Bizzy snuck out secretly on her way to save someone whose thread was about to be cut? We glided farther down the street. Bizzy was careful not to start the engine until we were a safe distance from the house.

"Better do your first check a' the night on Drake and Damon," she said, motioning with her head to the row of elm trees on the opposite side of the street.

Climbing the elm tree was easier the second time. Scrambling from branch to branch, I was level with Drake's window in no time. The lights were out in Drake's room, but I could still see inside. He was a big lump on his bed, asleep. The carrot-colored light of the streetlamps filtered in. I could barely make out the slight cut on his lip. He coughed and turned over. I gripped the tree tightly, hoping Drake wouldn't open his eyes and look right out at me. He didn't. He was asleep.

He was alive.

I climbed down a few branches and hopped back onto the sidewalk. When I scaled the other tree to look at Damon, I was relieved to find him asleep, as well. He wasn't supposed to rob Miss Mora's Market for another ten days, but I couldn't help but think he was involved somehow.

We arrived at Cedar Tree Park about two minutes later. Bizzy stepped out of the car, her legs shaky, and beckoned for her wheelchair.

"You're late."

I turned around and spotted Jodi emerging from behind a tree. She was wearing a beanie, black leggings, and an oversized black cashmere turtleneck. The outfit actually made her look stylish. As I unfolded the wheelchair from the backseat, I got my first look at Bizzy's ensemble. A black bandana covered most of her white hair. She'd managed to find black sweatpants big enough to fit over her leg cast. But the sweats' tight fit made her appear to have one huge leg and one small one. She wore old-school black Reebok high-tops and a sparkly black long-sleeve top—probably something she used to wear out on the town back in Louisiana. A black scarf was wrapped around her wrinkled neck, clear up to her nose. With her face still cut, and in her strange garb, Bizzy resembled a battle-worn grandma ninja.

I was completely out of breath by the time I wheeled Bizzy up the grassy hill to the top of the park. Jodi had offered to help, but pride kept me from accepting. The wet grass was slippery and I kept losing my footing.

The opposite side of the hill had a steep side. At the top there was a low wood railing and a sign warning people about the sheer drop to the water below of over a hundred feet. People called it Deadman's Drop, though I had never heard of anyone who had died falling from it.

The grove of cedar trees loomed like towering sentinels watching over all of Crabapple. We helped Bizzy retrieve the gear she'd dropped off and laid out the tarp over an out-of-the-way spot under one tree. In the middle, we set up two beach chairs, a small gas grill, and a battery-powered clock. We took the blankets, flashlights, and remaining supplies out of the car. Bizzy wheeled over to the portable gas grill and ignited it. It clicked on. Then she rifled through one of her bags and found a kettle and some marshmallows wrapped in tinfoil. Realizing that the beach chairs were for us (Bizzy had her own chair, after all), Jodi and I sat back in the creaking seats and huddled under one of the blankets. I could see my breath in the cold Crabapple air. I watched Bizzy work. She poured water from a jug into the kettle and began heating it over the grill after she lined it with aluminum foil. It was remarkable how well she'd learned to move around in her wheelchair in just a few short weeks. It wasn't long before she'd filled three thermoses with piping hot water and chocolate powder, topping them off with marshmallows. She had packed some Creole seasoning and sprinkled a little in her own thermos. Then she wheeled over next to Jodi and me, and the three of us stared out over the cannery.

The stars seemed brighter up above the trees, like hundreds of lit pinholes. Down below, I could make out the stone building that housed Miss Mora's Market in the dim light of the lampposts that ran along Ocean Avenue. I spotted the pharmacy and, off in the distance on the south side of Crabapple, the widely spaced streetlights on the road that led in and out of town. What struck me most, though, was the sea behind us. Where shore met ocean, the gleam of Crabapple dropped off into a great blackness. The dark waters rippled in the distance, reflecting little of our town's glow. The bay and the ocean beyond looked like one giant oil slick.

The warmth of Bizzy's chocolate concoction passed through my lips and into my core. I wondered if hundreds of years before this moment, granddaughters had sat up with their grandmas and best friends, drinking hot drinks much like the three of us were doing. For a brief moment, as I sipped, I felt content.

As soon as we were settled, we began the first of our hourly checks. Jodi and I decided that one of us would check in on the Westfall house and the other would head to the storm drain entrance on Delores Avenue and look for anything suspicious. I chose Drake's house for my first mission. Whizzing through the streets of Crabapple, I felt like I was flying through the night air. Bizzy made us wear the lit headlamps, in case a car approached and couldn't see us. She also insisted we ride on the sidewalk and keep our phones on in case something happened at the cannery in the meantime.

When I got to Drake's, I climbed up to the second-story level of the elm tree. There Drake was, sleeping peacefully, completely unaware that fate had made an appointment for him at the cannery. I climbed the elm on the side of Damon's room. The room was dark, but I could make out a Damon-sized lump under the covers of his bed. I didn't linger at Damon's window like I had at Drake's.

I zipped back to Cedar Tree Park in under eight minutes, which was a one-way record.

Hours passed that way. Jodi and I both nodded off a few times. But in each instance, my head would snap up and I'd wake to find Bizzy, fully alert, scanning the perimeter of the cannery. The three of us were alone together, with only the crickets and night owls for company.

"So far, all remains quiet on the cannery front, eh?" I asked Bizzy softly when I realized Jodi had fallen asleep again.

"Yup," she said.

We were silent for a few minutes. I looked down at the clock. It said 4:35. Morning was around the corner.

"Can I ask you a question, Bizzy?"

"Shoot. That's what nights like this are for," Bizzy said, smiling at me through the shadows.

"Do you think Drake is actually going to grow up to be some kind of hero? I mean, do you think the world *needs* him or whatever?"

"To tell you the truth, I ain't sure. If he is, he's sure gonna need you as his Keeper. I found Morgan le Faye pretty convincin'. But you know him. Do you think he's heroic?"

I thought about it. I'd always been convinced there was something different about Drake—he was intelligent, genuine, and independent. He stuck up for people like Roger. He'd liked me even though there were dozens of girls that were more popular than me who threw themselves at him. "What makes someone heroic?" I asked Bizzy.

"Lots of things. I'm not sure about Drake, but I am sure about you, Sweet Pea. No matter what happens this mornin', I want you to know that. It makes perfect sense that you could read that book a' Merlin's. You've got more courage in your pinkie than most people have in their whole bodies. That makes you a hero. It's been an honor watchin' you come into your own." Bizzy's eyes misted over. "I love you and I'm gonna miss you."

"What do you mean you're going to *miss* me? Where are you going? What's wrong?" I asked, glancing at Jodi, who was still fast asleep.

"I only meant when I finally do pass on. But I'm sure that won't be for a long time, so don't mind me. 'Fraid I'm turnin' into a sentimental ole woman more and more each day."

As Bizzy wiped her eyes, I heard the sound of the birds nesting in the park taking flight all at once—a noisy chorus of flapping wings. Before I could comment on it, my chair began to sway from side to side. There was a low rumble, like the earth itself had a bellyache. The trees swayed eerily above us in the half light. Soon I could hear the rattling of buildings, glass, and concrete.

Bizzy looked at me wide-eyed.

"It's a doggone shaker!" she screamed, raising her hands over her head for protection as cones from the cypress trees pelted the ground.

Pathetic Fallacy

You may not appreciate my telling you this, Mrs. Tweedy, but when we learned about pathetic fallacy in *Macbeth*, I thought the whole thing was pretty bogus. When Duncan is about to get murdered, the lightning and thundering outside is supposed to foretell the upcoming violence, but I found it silly. Shakespeare did this, you said, to scare the audience and give them a general uneasy feeling so that they're doubly terrified when all the violence and murder happens, right?

Well, I don't think it's bogus anymore, Mrs. Tweedy. Now I'm certain there's nothing pathetic about it. After the earthquake hit Crabapple, at around five in the morning, I'd never been more scared. The rumbling must have gone on for a solid minute. We've had real shakers before in Crabapple, but this one was more of a roller, like the earth was one giant water bed.

After the temblor, a few lights went on in houses down below. Bizzy and I could see several people out in the streets through a pair of binoculars she'd brought along. I was glad

I'd left a lump of pillows under the covers in my bed. If Mom peeked in she'd think I'd slept through the whole thing. The lights in the southern part of the city were out completely. A few car alarms sounded briefly before being silenced.

It was ominous. I scanned the area around the cannery. Jodi was disoriented from being jolted awake and Bizzy tried to calm her down. She dispatched me to Drake's house, and Jodi to the entrance of the storm drains, warning us to "be extra careful." When I went to check on Drake on my bike, I swore I made the round trip in about twelve minutes. I had such an adrenaline rush, I was pedaling at lightning pace. I saw a light on in one of the first-floor windows of the Westfall house. Creeping to the window, I watched as Mrs. Westfall picked up a few picture frames the earthquake had knocked to the floor. I ran back across the yard to the elm tree. I looked at my palm. DRAKE WESTFALL. His name was still there, same as ever. Whether he lived or died was coming down to a matter of hours. Drake's light was on. I peered into his room.

His bed was empty. Drake was gone.

I took a few nervous breaths and climbed up the elm next to Damon's room. I gulped. Damon was missing, too. Down the street, I spotted a black sedan.

Fearfully, I looked down at my palm once more. Drake's name was still bright red. That meant he was really *close*. I tried to calm myself, wondering if maybe I was overreacting and Drake was in the bathroom or something. I crossed the Westfall yard once more and snuck around the side gate into the backyard. Drake's name grew slightly brighter. When I approached the house, the letters dimmed. I turned toward the pool house and the letters brightened. I surveyed the Westfall backyard. The surrounding sky was no longer black—it looked like the inside of a toaster when it's just beginning to heat up.

The door to the pool house was ajar. As I slipped through the cracked door, Drake's name began to tingle, then burn and light up on my palm. I was getting closer.

The pool house was dim and as I pressed against the closest wall, I heard voices coming from the other side of the room. I ducked behind a stack of brown boxes and listened.

"Calm down, man. It was the only way we could be sure he wouldn't rat on us." I recognized Randy Maroy's voice immediately.

"I'd already convinced him we weren't going through with it!" There was no mistaking the second voice, either. It was Damon Westfall's. Loud and clear.

"Yeah, well, the earthquake must have woke him up and he *saw* us in here, with the plans. He probably heard us talking about it, too. So we can't wait. We're all ready, anyway. We'll hit Miss Mora's this morning."

"We're going to have to do something with Drake so my parents don't find him here. What about dumping him at the cannery—and getting him there using the storm drains?"

"The drains lead to the cannery?"

"I've used them before when I stayed there. They lead right to a grate underneath it. No one'll see us go in and no one'll find him there until we're long gone," Damon explained.

"Good. And I think we made it pretty clear before I knocked him out that if he tells anyone, we'll come back for his little girlfriend. It'll shut him up," Randy said coldly.

"Let's get to it then. We've only got an hour before Miss Mora's opens."

I froze as the rustle of movements and footsteps intensified. I peered around the side of the stack of boxes and saw Damon and Randy struggling with Drake's limp body. Randy had a grip on Drake's legs while Damon grasped him under his shoulders. As the two moved forward, Drake's head bobbed up and down and his torso swayed back and forth, as if he were in a hammock.

Damon and Randy passed inches from me as they cleared the door. I huddled close to the ground, hoping they wouldn't see me. After they'd carried Drake's unconscious form completely out of the pool house, I counted to sixty before moving again. I heard a car door slam and sprinted around the side of the Westfall house.

Grabbing my bike, I raced up Earle toward the park. I had to reach Bizzy. I couldn't stop imagining Drake stashed somewhere in the cannery.

When I got to the park, I hopped off my bicycle and pushed it to the top of the hill, to our makeshift campsite. As I looked out, I realized morning had arrived.

"Bizzy!" I said. I looked around. "Where's Jodi?"

"I sent her to check on you when you didn't come back on time," Bizzy said.

I told her what I'd just seen. "They've changed their plan,

Bizzy. They're robbing Miss Mora's this morning." When I finished, Bizzy gasped out loud.

"By gum! A leak!" Bizzy's voice was so loud, I thought she might wake up someone in Crabapple.

"What?" I said, following her gaze to the portable gas grill right in front of us on the tarp. "I don't understand."

"The earthquake, Lizzy-Loo! That's the explosion. Gas leaks contributed to almost fifty structure fires during the Northridge quake alone." I'd never heard Bizzy talk so quickly. "Gas leaks are the cause of a lot a' earthquake-related casualties!"

"So?" I said, still confused.

"They've deposited Drake in the cannery by now. If someone lights something there, smart money says the whole place'll go *kaboom*!"

"Oh no . . . his lighter!"

"What's this now?" Bizzy questioned.

"Drake has this lighter. It was his grandfather's. He carries it wherever he goes and—"

Bizzy didn't wait for me to finish. The wheels were spinning in her head.

"You still got Sheriff Schmidt's number?" I handed his business card to Bizzy.

"Good. I'm gonna call straight away about Damon and his miscreant friend. After that earthquake, the sheriff is sure to have sent several squad cars out on patrol. If one of 'em sees you near the cannery at this hour, we're done for. You've got to get into the cannery without anyone stopping you, okay?"

"I'll go in through the storm drain," I said.

"That's far too dangerous. Stay outta sight for as long as you can, then go in through one a' the windows."

"Someone might see me. The storm drains are the only way!" I exclaimed, my heart pounding. After a night of slow-motion observation, suddenly everything seemed to be happening in hyperspeed. Bizzy paused for a second.

"Well, all right then. Run as fast as you can. Take the compass. Once you're in, you'll need to keep goin' north to get underneath the cannery." Bizzy switched my headlamp back on. "Shouldn't be too far. Once you're in, do whatever you have to do to make sure he doesn't use his lighter or anything else. I'm gonna wheel down to the cannery and try to see if I can't do somethin' from above ground. If you can't wake up Drake, you can holler to me and I'll get help to get him out of there."

I was about to dash to the corner of Dolores and Kincaid when Bizzy grabbed my wrist.

"And Lizzy," Bizzy said, almost quietly, "Damon should be long gone and on his way to Miss Mora's. Remember that I'll be up here doin' what I can."

As I tried to leave, Bizzy wouldn't let go of my wrist. She was staring intently at my right hand. She couldn't take her eyes off it. I looked down.

On the base of my right hand, a new name had appeared in red.

BEATRICE MILDRED MORTIMER

I looked at my left hand. Drake's name was still there. But I hadn't seen any kind of death-specter about Bizzy.

I felt like my lungs were deflating. I couldn't get enough air.

"Bizzy," I said. "Bizzy . . . your name!" I thrust my right hand in her face. "What does it mean?"

"I . . . I . . . don't pay no attention to that just now," Bizzy stuttered.

Bizzy and I both turned toward the sound of a small voice coming from within the cedar grove.

A banshee emerged from the trees looking almost exactly like the one that had appeared to take Jodi in front of Miss Mora's, wearing a black dress, with white hair and the blackest eyes.

"*You have a date. A date with fate. We shall not be late,*" she sang in her high-pitched robotic drone. She repeated it again, skipping toward us as if she were half asleep, her face expressionless. "*The time is here. There is nothing to fear. You have a date, a date with fate.*"

Soon, the banshee was a few feet away from us, staring through the moonlight with her dark vacant eyes.

"Bizzy," I whispered, my voice trembling with terror, hoping the banshee wouldn't hear me. "Bizzy, what is she doing here?"

Bizzy waited a few seconds to respond, looking only at the girl.

"Judgin' by your hand," she said, her voice filled with resignation, "she's here for your dear ole grandmamma."

I turned my open palms up toward the sky. I looked at Drake's name and then at Bizzy's. One on each hand, with Bizzy's name glowing much, much brighter than Drake's. Bizzy glanced at my wrists, then at the little girl in black lace, still chanting softly, and then finally up at my face. There were tears in Bizzy's eyes. "Dyin' . . . ," Bizzy began, choking up a little, "is a wild night and a new road." Her once-strong voice was now weak under the weight of sadness. The words filled the space between us. *Dying is a wild night and a new road.* I recognized the phrase immediately—it was from an Emily Dickinson poem. "No one . . . ," Bizzy continued, "gets to choose her time, Sweet Pea."

"What are you saying, Bizzy?"

"You best be gettin' goin' after Drake."

"I'm *NOT* leaving you—not with your name on my hand and that banshee here," I said.

Bizzy grabbed my hands.

"If you care about me even a little, Elizabeth Mildred Mortimer, you will go save that boy!" Bizzy said, commanding me over the eerie chants of the banshee.

"*You have a date, a date with fate. We shall not be late,*" the girl singsonged cheerfully, swaying back and forth.

"No! I *can't* leave you here to fend off whatever's coming by yourself!"

"You don't understand," Bizzy said. "This is the way it must be, Lizzy! The last death-specter I ever had in the ocean—it was about *me*. My own name didn't appear on my hand because it was my last one, just like what happened to my mama. Morgan le Faye had the courtesy to give me ample warnin' that I was goin' to be leavin' this world helpin' you. It's my time. Please . . . it's the only way."

"But . . . I . . . can't . . . ," I protested as tears spilled onto my cheeks.

"You mustn't think of me. Think of the countless others dependin' on you. We'll see each other again. It may not be soon, but it'll have to be soon enough . . ."

Bizzy rolled forward and shoved me backward. She nudged me again, closing her brimming eyes.

"I love ya to pieces and back again," Bizzy whispered, giving me one last push away from her. "May fate be with you. And if it ain't, make it so."

She spoke them as if they were last words.

Seconds later, I was running downhill, stumbling and sobbing as I made my way toward unconscious Drake and the cannery. I didn't look back at my grandmother. I knew that if I saw her on the top of the hill, left to face her fate alone, I wouldn't have the strength to stop myself from going back to save her.

†HE CLIMAX

You call the climax of a novel the "turning point," Mrs. Tweedy, but I still think that's not very easy to identify. For me, the only way you really know you've gotten to the climax is when you've got a thin stack of pages left and you're at a part where you can't stop reading because you need to find out what happens. I don't have much left to write, so I should probably get to it.

Halfway down the hill, on my way to Drake, I fell hard, hitting the ground with a thump. I moaned as I tumbled the rest of the way to the bottom. Thinking I tripped on a tree root, I tried to get to my feet. I had to get to Drake or all of it would be for nothing.

Soon, I felt myself being lifted up off the ground. My vision blurred as my body screamed out in pain. I bounced up and down, traveling faster than if I'd been on my bike going downhill. Things came into focus for me once again and I realized that someone—or something—was carrying me back up the hill and toward Cedar Tree Park. Toward Bizzy.

I was wrapped up tightly in some kind of black silky material and was being held so firmly, I couldn't even move my head to look up to see who or what was carrying me. When we reached the top of the hill, the mysterious presence threw me to the ground once more.

Dazed, I got up, trying to process what was happening. My shins burned from the impact.

First I saw Bizzy, her back to me as she sat in her chair, facing Deadman's Drop.

Bizzy's head leaned to the side as if she were asleep.

"I cannot imagine why you would want to leave before the main event," said a commanding voice from behind me. I whipped around.

There stood Vivienne le Mort, in her black robe, against the red-yellow light of sunrise, a few feet from me.

Vivienne le Mort pointed one of her long, spindly fingers at me. "You see," she said, "I have been waiting a long time for this day to arrive. But it wasn't until I saw you with the boy that day in the field that I realized you and your brainless little grandmother had set out to save him. That it was *you* Morgan was communicating with. I've been watching you very closely since then, carefully planning how best to stop you. You nearly spoiled it all by running off like you did!" Vivienne le Mort's shrill voice grew louder in a dreadful crescendo. I thought about Drake, who could wake up at any moment, pull out his lighter, and ignite it. Vivienne le Mort stalked up the hill and grabbed Bizzy's wheelchair, pushing her closer to the edge of Deadman's Drop.

"What have you done to Bizzy? What do you want with her!"

"Your grandmother is only temporarily incapacitated. I have done so to ensure that the banshee," Vivienne le Mort said, "retrieves what she came for."

The banshee stood silently a few feet to the side of us, blinking her black eyes.

"What do you mean?" I asked.

"All you have to do is look down at your palm, and you should be able to figure that out yourself. I believe my dear sister has tried to send you one of her pathetic warnings about your grandmother. Hasn't she?" Vivienne le Mort asked in her most patronizing tone. "The banshee has come for your *grandmother*." She smiled devilishly, revealing all her yellow teeth.

I charged full speed toward Vivienne le Mort and Bizzy, near the cliff's edge.

"I would not travel one more step in this direction unless you want to see your grandmother plunge to her death immediately!" Vivienne snapped

I skidded to a stop.

"Why are you doing this?" I asked.

"I am not *doing* anything," Vivienne le Mort said, seemingly amused by my question. Her red eyes sent electric shivers down my spine. "That is what you descendants of Morgan le Faye fail to understand! To think that, all this time, right under my nose, you have spent your lives fighting against that which you cannot possibly hope to defeat . . . fate!"

"I will do whatever you want if you let Bizzy go," I pleaded.

"You are even weaker than I imagined!" Vivienne le Mort squawked. "I know you are aware of the prophecy concerning the boy, and yet you stand here, distressed about saving a decrepit old woman who has reached the end of her thread. Not that I am surprised to find a mortal who cannot see beyond her own selfish interest!" Vivienne le Mort looked at me with the purest form of disgust.

"You don't have to do this," I said.

"There is no point delaying the inevitable," Vivienne said, moving one of her long fingers to her dark lips. She turned Bizzy's wheelchair around. Bizzy's expression was blank. "I want to see your grandmother's face as she plummets to her death!"

In the emerging sunlight, I could see that Bizzy's eyes were closed. It was as if she was sleeping peacefully. Vivienne grabbed the arms of Bizzy's wheelchair and began to roll her to the absolute edge of the cliff.

I scanned the ground around me and spotted a fallen branch. I estimated Bizzy was ten feet away.

I had to act quickly.

"Nooo!" I sprung forward and picked up the branch in one hand. Leaping off the ground, I spread my arms out in front of me and jumped toward Bizzy and Vivienne. Vivienne continued moving the wheelchair toward the cliff as I made a straight path toward Bizzy.

The banshee stood silent next to Vivienne, her eyes growing wide with excitement.

"Biiiiizzy!" I yelled, extending the branch in front of me as

I crashed into the ground and slid into Vivienne, inches from the base of Bizzy's wheelchair. I saw the edges of the chair's two wheels dip below the cliff's edge. With every bit of strength I possessed, I jammed the branch through the spokes of the wheelchair.

Then I held on for dear life. I felt Bizzy slipping over the precipice, dragging me with her through the slick muddy grass. I groaned as I tried to anchor myself with my heels. Slowly, we slid together, my grandma and me inching over Deadman's Drop. The banshee's eyes grew wider, as if someone had placed a heaping plateful of food in front of her and she hadn't eaten in days.

Bizzy was tipped at an angle over the cliff. My heels caught on something—a rock, maybe. Using the leverage I had, I clenched my teeth and began to pull on the branch. The branch creaked, nearly splintering from the weight of Bizzy and her chair. But it was working. Inch by inch, the wheels of Bizzy's chair returned to solid ground.

With my final tug, I tipped the chair completely away from the cliff, and Bizzy, still unconscious, fell on me. The chair followed on top of her.

Bizzy's weight on me meant she wasn't tumbling down the cliff. I wanted to hug her, but there was no time. I rolled her off me carefully and quickly scrambled to my feet, covered in grass stains and mud. In the meantime, Vivienne le Mort stood to the side. I panted, clutching my aching sides.

When I finally focused on Vivienne, I was shocked.

She was staring at me, laughing. She clapped her hands. The banshee, less than half her height, stood next to her, looking sullen.

"What a show! Right on cue, too. Saving your grand-mother at the risk of your own life . . . If I had a mortal heart, I might find the whole thing rather touching. But I must ask you, foolish girl, did you really think about the consequences of such an action? Even after you saw your grandmother's name on your hand?"

"I . . . I . . . don't understand . . . ," I said, still gasping for air.

Vivienne le Mort took a step toward me. "It may not be exactly how your grandmother was scheduled to die, but it will be close enough to ensure fate marches on as planned. I knew that if it unfolded right in front of you, because of your attachment, you would not stop until you saved her."

"You *knew* I would save Bizzy? You brought me here to *save her*?"

"You honestly think after watching this dreadful little town so carefully, I would just let you go rescue the boy? I've heard you read Merlin's foolish little account and now you fancy yourself the boy's Keeper, do you? Well, you will fail just as Guinevere failed! You cannot possibly fathom how long I have waited for this day. Imagine never knowing when you would be relieved of the task of overseeing imbeciles such as yourselves! My dear sisters may not see it my way, but they soon will. To finally be in control, I would have stopped at nothing!" Vivienne le Mort punctuated her remarks with a nasty snort. "The most impressive part of my brilliant plan, of course, is that I *knew* a banshee would arrive to take Beatrice Mortimer when you saved her. Because you have inherited Morgan's silly intolerance for the wail of the banshee, only one question remains: Who will die first? You and your decrepit grandmother here on the hill? Or the boy-who-would-be-king in the cannery? I suppose it does not matter, but perishing at the hands of the banshee's cry is very painful . . . ," Vivienne said, ending in a cackle of laughter.

I focused on the banshee. She skipped to Bizzy, who was curled up on the ground next to her wheelchair, slowly, surely, silently. Upon reaching Bizzy, the banshee placed a pale hand on her. Bizzy's chest rose and fell under it.

First the banshee whimpered. Her dark eyes grew bigger and wider. They turned into black whirlpools, dominating the top half of her face. She let out a small cry. After a few seconds, the cry swelled into a deafening shriek. It wasn't long before my lungs and brain sizzled as if they had been set on fire, firmly under the spell of the banshee's wail.

As I crumpled to the ground in pain, I thought about how close I'd come to rescuing everyone—Drake, Bizzy, and myself. Now we were all at the mercy of a devilish banshee spirit, in the midst of throwing the deadliest of tantrums.

"I must leave you now, to ensure the Last Descendant perishes according to fate's plan. Good-bye, Elizabeth Mortimer. You can be certain another banshee will arrive to collect your soul soon enough."

A Metaphor Before Dying

The pain I felt as I lay dying on the grass next to Deadman's Drop is hard to put into words. It felt like someone was trying to force my brain through a really sharp cheese grater. I'd never experienced anything like it. I lay there, paralyzed by the banshee's scream, as I watched Vivienne le Mort float away, down the hill. She was headed to the cannery, to make sure Drake's demise went according to plan.

I twisted my body, writhing in the wet grass.

Bizzy groaned. Dragging myself with my arms toward her and the banshee, I rose to my knees, then to my feet. The earth seemed to be wobbling with me, like I was straddling a teeter-totter. I could barely keep my balance. Concentrating, I lunged at the ground where I thought I saw a metallic gleam. There, among the trash, lay a crumpled remnant from Bizzy's hot chocolate preparation. Dizzily, I smoothed the discarded scrap and held the shiny sheet of aluminum foil in front of the wailing banshee's face.

Whoosh. The blast of sand ripped right through the shiny square, hitting my face, knocking me over.

It had worked.

Without waiting to catch my breath, I stumbled to Bizzy.

She was awake now, no longer under the spell of Vivienne le Mort. Bizzy grimaced in pain.

"Sweet Pea," she said. She tried to get up, but faltered.

"Hold on," I said, lifting her frail body back into the chair.

"Where'd she go?" Bizzy asked, confused. She put her arm at the side of her wheelchair and came up with a handful of sand. "A banshee? For me? How did you . . ."

"I used the aluminum foil. I held it up and the banshee saw her reflection in it."

"My oh my. Those banshees'll never learn not to mess with a Mortimer!"

"Vivienne went down the hill," I said, "after Drake."

Bizzy became agitated as the gravity of the situation hit her all at once. "There's no time to lose! We've got to go after 'em!"

Without any delay, I began pushing Bizzy down the hill. My legs felt like Jell-O and my head still pounded from the banshee's wail. Bizzy noticed two figures in the distance and commanded me to stop. Under a canopy of cedar trees at the base of the hill, I spotted the unmistakable black robe of Vivienne le Mort. Facing her, a few feet off, was a woman in a white robe.

We rushed forward and hid in some bushes only a few yards from the two women.

"It's Agatha the Enchantress!" I whispered to Bizzy upon

recognizing the woman in white. We were close enough to overhear their heated conversation.

"Please get out of my way, dear sister." Vivienne le Mort's voice dripped with sarcasm as she addressed Agatha. "I must go ensure the boy's thread is cut in fulfillment of your prophecy."

"Have you even considered the possibility that by cutting Lancelot's thread before his time, *you* caused my prophecy about the Last Descendant?" Agatha asked.

"And what of Morgan's wrongs? It was *she* who caused the rift. I am only following the truce you agreed to, Agatha," Vivienne said, scowling.

"Morgan's mistake was born out of love. But yours was one spawned by hatred and contempt. That makes all the difference. Look at what you've become, Vivienne, I beg of you. You were once beautiful, but this obsession with Doomsday has transformed you into a ghoul!"

"I will have to take comfort in the fact that I do not look as bad as the poor girl and her grandmother did when left to die at the hands of the screaming banshee!" Vivienne le Mort cackled.

"I beg your pardon!" Bizzy said, leaving our concealment and wheeling herself between the sisters. "I don't take too kindly to people reportin' my passin' before it happens . . . I may be gettin' up there, but I ain't dead yet!"

Agatha turned toward Bizzy and at the same time spotted me standing in the bushes. I detected the slightest smile forming on her face. It was obvious that Vivienne le Mort was shocked to see us.

Agatha gazed intensely at me. Our eyes connected and I could hear her voice in my head.

"*Go after the boy*," Agatha's voice echoed as I stared back at her. Her lips didn't move. "*I will handle this.*"

"How did you, a feeble old woman . . . ," Vivienne said, almost growling. Frenzied, she descended on Bizzy, with her hands out as if she was going to strangle her.

Agatha raised both of her arms in response. "It is time to reset fate!" White lightning shot from Agatha's palms, hitting Vivienne and knocking her off her feet backward, away from Bizzy. Bizzy wheeled out of the way. Vivienne sprung to her feet. She raised her hands at Agatha, snarling as black smoke–colored beams projected from her hands. The two Ladies of the Lake had their hands raised, their faces studied with concentration, as bolts of light continued to shoot from their palms.

The beams met halfway between them in one big bundle of gray light, rising up into the sky. It was almost as if a huge transformer was blowing up, splattering the Crabapple sky with bright light.

Bizzy wheeled toward me, over the loud popping of the colliding currents.

"Go, Sweet Pea!" she screamed. "Run like the wind!"

Knowing I didn't have a moment to lose, I raced down the hill of Cedar Tree Park to Delores Avenue, thinking of Drake the whole time, wondering if I was already too late.

LEGENDS, OLD AND NEW

I understand that legends and myths teach us important lessons or explain phenomena in the world that are hard to fathom, Mrs. Tweedy, but now, I wonder how many legends are actually true.

At least one of them is.

I'd heard several Crabapple urban legends about the kids who used to hang out in the storm drains that run underneath the town. There were stories that a gang of high school kids graffitied all eight miles of them. Other rumors suggested that a group of boys would take baseball bats and go "batting," which involved shining a bright light into the cavernous concrete pipes and swinging away in the hopes of connecting with a bat flying out of the dark tunnels.

At the storm drain entrance I hopped the barrier fence, landing in an area about eight feet below ground level, surrounded by concrete on three sides. I was in the open-air part of the storm drain, standing in front of the tunnel where the giant pipes descended completely underground. I couldn't see very far into the drain, but it was similar to an enormous concrete tube. The bottom was mossy and water slicked.

I stood there, on the fringe of total darkness, shaking with fear. I wasn't sure if I had any adrenaline left. Turning on my headlamp, I took a deep breath. I started with an all-out sprint. The beam of light from the headlamp bounced off the walls in front of me. A scurrying rat ran off into the darkness, soon joined by two more. I could've sworn they were crawling up my spine with their little clawed feet. Still I kept running. The spray-painted letters of legend appeared on some walls, though I didn't stop in one place long enough to see what they depicted. Instead, I kept running.

I ran and ran and ran, farther and farther into the black hole ahead of my small beam of light. I looked down at the compass. I was still headed north. Then I checked my left hand. Drake's name was getting brighter. It was dark. It was cold and damp. And it smelled like dead animals.

Suddenly up ahead, a concrete wall loomed in front of me, turning the passage hard to the right. I skidded to a stop in front of it.

Just then, I heard a bone-chilling screech. I turned around. A bat was flying straight toward me, flapping like a demon. I screamed. My yelp echoed off one concrete wall and then the other, over and over again. I waved my arms and fell over, back into a puddle of rank, reeking water. The bat passed and I got up and bolted in another direction. I didn't think about which way I should go. I lost track of my location in the darkness. For a moment, I thought I would die right there in the storm drain. Were the walls closing in? With only my small ray of light to guide me, I couldn't really tell. I was damp with sweat and puddle water, but I didn't stop running. I headed deeper into the storm drain network.

After a few more minutes, I slowed down. There was another concrete wall ahead, which meant another turn. The compass indicated I was headed west. I stood in front of the wall and turned left. I felt Drake's name tingle on my hand and knew I was headed in the right direction.

I made the critical mistake of looking back into the darkness. I'd come a long way by now, which meant it would be a long way back if I ever wanted to see daylight again. I wasn't sure I even remembered the way back. I forced myself to keep going. I swallowed my nausea and pounded ahead, splashing more scummy water on my jeans with each step.

Finally, I reached another bend. I felt as if I'd traveled several miles. I took a deep breath, scanning the walls with the light of my headlamp. There it was—a rusty ladder hinged to the concrete wall. Drake's name glowed in the darkness as brightly as if he were in the next room.

I looked up.

The ladder led directly up to a grate. It was partially pushed aside, revealing an opening big enough to crawl through. I listened, hoping to hear sounds of Bizzy yelling at Drake to get out of the cannery. I smelled the faint odor of natural gas.

Without hesitating, I climbed the ladder, one rung at a

time. It was corroded and felt gritty on my hands. I reached the top. The grate was directly above me.

I pulled myself up through the small opening. When the top of my body was halfway into the cannery, I realized my hips weren't going to fit through the opening. Damon and Randy must have slid the grate back when they left. The odor of gas was sharper now that I was partially inside.

I grunted, trying to move the grate so I could squeeze through.

"Hello?"

It was Drake's voice, coming from the far side of the room. "Drake, don't move!" I screamed. I was stuck. My legs dangled below, still in the storm drain.

"Drake, you can't move!" I wiggled and struggled but I couldn't free myself. "Don't move! There's a gas leak!" I screamed, suddenly realizing that Drake, with his chlorine-impaired sense of smell, had no clue what danger he was in. I heaved the entire weight of my body against the grate. I felt a sharp poke as the metal edge of the grate shoved into my ribs. But ever so slightly, the grate had slid to the side.

"Lizzy?" Drake sounded very confused. "Lizzy? Is that you?"

"Please don't move, Drake," I cried.

I heaved again against the iron. I felt another piercing jab and cried out in pain. But I could feel it move again. Just an inch. But it was enough. I began to struggle through.

"Hold up, Lizzy!" I heard Drake say. "Let me make some more light so that you're not stumbling through the dark."

"Don't do that!" My fleece caught on one of the grate's sharp edges. But I didn't care if it ripped apart entirely. I took a deep breath and pushed off the top rung of the ladder. Exploding like a rocket out of the storm drain, I clanged into the giant metal machine above the opening. Then I ran. Straight for Drake's voice coming from the distant corner. Blind with fear.

The light from my headlamp was growing dimmer now, but as I got closer I could make out Drake's form hunched in the corner, right next to the makeshift tent. I didn't take my eyes off him. I felt as if I were running in slow motion, little by little getting closer. I could hear each one of my footsteps pound in my head.

When I was near him, I jumped up. I flew through the air, spreading out my arms.

I crashed into the tent, tearing through the old ratty blankets, causing the wood beams to collapse. I plowed through it and onto Drake. My chest collided with his back, my head bumped into his head, my legs slammed into his legs. He groaned under me. I was squarely on top of him. I squeezed him with my arms, as hard as I could. We were a tangle of clothing, wooden beams, and tent fabric.

I looked down at his hands, spread out in front of him. He was holding his grandfather's Zippo lighter with the black crackle finish. I grabbed it.

"What *is wrong* with you?" Drake asked from beneath me, his voice a mixture of pain and confusion.

Every bone in my body ached. Wearing half a torn fleece, with blood soaking through my shirt from the grate, I held

Drake tightly in my arms. I didn't let go. For a few moments, he let me hold him. He was absolutely still. I closed my eyes, and for the briefest second, I imagined that he wanted to be like this with me, that I hadn't just run like a maniac and tackled him like I was a defensive end and he was a running back trying to reach the end zone from the five-yard line. The strong smell of gas made me feel dizzy.

My left hand throbbed from the impact. I flipped it over. There was nothing there. Drake's name was nowhere to be found.

I wondered if I'd ever be able to explain to him how I'd known he was in mortal danger. At that moment, I didn't care.

Vivienne le Mort had failed. I hadn't.

Drake was safe.

According to Bizzy, Agatha the Enchantress battled Vivienne le Mort just long enough to distract her so I could save Drake. Bizzy said a thick gray cloud filled the park and then the two sisters were gone. Agatha's white light had attracted spectators to the area.

After I disentangled myself from Drake, I tried to explain what I was doing at the cannery.

The one thing I've learned about gathering information about someone is that it makes it a whole lot easier to lie to that person. I told Drake I woke up and realized he might be using the cannery as his place to paint. Bizzy had told me over and over again about the danger of gas leaks after earthquakes, so it wasn't difficult to convince her that we should check and make sure no one was at the cannery. I said it was a "premonition." Fortunately, the light had been so dim, he hadn't seen me explode out of the storm drain. He thought I jumped in through a window.

Once Drake and I climbed out through the back window of the cannery, my adrenaline was used up and I realized I was having trouble breathing. Bizzy called the gas company to report the leak. She informed us that Damon and Randy had been taken into custody. Though Bizzy thought Drake should go to the hospital to make sure the blow he'd been dealt hadn't done serious damage, Drake insisted he was fine. Bizzy informed Drake that head trauma was a lot more threatening than most people realized, quoted some scary fatality statistics, and made Drake promise that if he had any symptoms, like blurred vision, he would go to the doctor. We rode silently in the Roadmaster to Drake's house, dropped him off, and then Bizzy took me to the hospital. Bizzy told the emergency room nurses that I'd hurt myself prying open the cannery window after becoming convinced that there might be a gas leak there which put the citizens of Crabapple at risk. Of course, I knew my struggle getting through the grate from the sewer was to blame for most of my injuries.

The nurses bought the story, hook, line, and sinker. So did Dad. But Mom was a tough sell. Especially after the doctor told her that it was "quite unusual for a young person to break two ribs from a fall like that." I didn't even get a brace or a splint.

The doctor said I just had to rest and take Advil for the pain. Dad and Mom didn't argue when I told them I didn't want to go back to school that afternoon. I skipped the rest of the day.

The newspaper headline the next morning was very different from the one I'd seen as my death-specter. It read:

MORTIMERS SMELL GAS LEAK, PREVENT CATASTROPHE

The article went on to talk about how Bizzy and I, out for an early morning walk after the earthquake, had noticed a smell coming from the cannery and called the gas company.

"Those folks sure did their part as good citizens today," the gas company man said in the article. "If someone had so much as lit a match near that place, I think half of Crabapple might have gone up in flames." The article also mentioned that Beatrice Mildred Mortimer was no stranger to heroics. In addition to saving a friend from drowning a few years back, she'd also prevented a house from burning down two years ago by wandering in with an extinguisher because she had smelled smoke from a block away. It went on to recount her recent rescue of Jodi Sanchez from the path of a speeding car.

The reporter had asked Bizzy if she felt that she had heroic qualities. "Nah," Bizzy was quoted at the end of the article. "Plain and simple, some folks just got more luck than sense. And that's one of Bizzy's pearls, free a' charge."

Mom read the whole article out loud at the breakfast table.

She eyed Bizzy and me suspiciously, especially in light of my bizarre trip to the hospital. Another article reported on a thwarted burglary of Miss Mora's Market by Sheriff Schmidt. In the paper, he said that he'd received an "anonymous tip."

"Your first battle wounds," Bizzy said, looking years younger, after we were finally alone. "I'm proud a' you, Lizzy. You're a full-blown hedgehog!" If anyone else in the world had called me a hedgehog, I would've been very insulted. Coming from Bizzy, though, I knew it was her greatest compliment.

Just then, tinted fog seeped in from the open window of Bizzy's room. In a matter of moments, the room filled with yellow-and-red haze. The colored fog began to clear and, sure enough, Fial and Morgan le Faye appeared in Bizzy's room.

Fial wasted no time. She wrapped me up in her cold arms and yellow robes. "You are the most precious girl! So brave for someone so young!"

I thought she might break another of my ribs. As I looked over her shoulder, I saw Bizzy smiling at the two of us. After Fial released me, she sat in a chair by the window. The four of us stared at one another. The silence lasted more than a minute.

"So Drake is safe now? Does this mean the world will . . . go on?" I asked.

"Yes. When the time comes, he will be called to free Merlin and lead the Round Table. No doubt, you will also be right by his side as—"

"That is quite enough, Fial," Morgan said with a renewed sternness. "The one thing all of this should have taught us is that we cannot be certain about what the future holds. Elizabeth already knows too much of her destiny as it is."

From where I sat, I felt as if I knew nothing of what was in store for me. Other than that Drake was going to help find Merlin and free the cursed sorcerer to defeat Vivienne le Mort before she made the world crumble, I didn't know anything.

"You'll have to excuse Fial," Morgan le Faye said, addressing me, "she gets quite carried away." Fial and Morgan le Faye kept gazing at me. Finally, Bizzy spoke.

"We're honored by the visit 'n' all," she said, "but what brings you ladies back to Crabapple?"

"Oh yes, of course," Morgan said, growing embarrassed. "We, you see, procured Agatha's permission, to come here to . . ."

"What Morgie's *trying* to say," Fial said, rolling her eyes at her sister, "is that we wanted to properly thank you two. The boy is alive and though the world does not know it, every mortal owes a large debt to you."

"Such is the way of fate," Morgan le Faye added matter-of-factly. "Sometimes the bravest acts are the least recognized. We are sorry your courage cannot be more widely celebrated."

"Where is Vivienne le Mort?" I asked. Now that things had settled down, I kept thinking she'd appear behind me at any moment.

"She has been taken care of," Morgan announced.

"But what about her army and the threads and all that?" I asked.

"Do not torment yourselves with thoughts of her reappearance," Fial said in a reassuring tone.

"It should also be mentioned that if Drake is to carry out his fate," Morgan added, changing the subject, "it is important you do not reveal his destiny to him."

"I'm not planning on it, don't worry," I said. Drake had stared at me the entire ride home from the cannery as if I'd just landed from outer space. There was no chance I was going to tell him anything else that would only confirm his suspicions. Drake's status as the Last Descendant was one secret I wasn't sure would *ever* be flight ready.

"There is one last question I must ask you," Morgan said, beginning to pace with her arms folded behind her back. She stopped in front of me with her gleaming green eyes. "My reason for sending the specters—to both save people from untimely deaths and to allow my descendants the practice and experience to be ready when it came time to save the boy with the Mark of Arthur—has vanished. My sisters and I have decided, however, that as a reward for your courage, you should be permitted to decide whether or not you want to continue to have them."

Speechless, I hesitated.

How could anyone possibly make that choice?

"If you do choose to remain a Hand of Fate, you will only see the specters of preventable deaths of those you care about, as you did before."

"Does she have to decide now?" Bizzy asked, her voice filled with concern. "Can't she have some time to cogitate on it?"

"I'm afraid we must return to Avalon shortly with an answer," Fial said.

I thought of the extraordinary burden that came with knowing the details of another person's impending death. Someday, I would grow tired of having death-specters. But the fact that I would *have* a someday—hopefully many somedays—was a pretty spectacular thing. My next death-specter could be Mom or Dad or someone else I cared about. How could I turn down the chance to give them more somedays?

In the back of my mind, thoughts of Drake emerged. Morgan and Fial hadn't mentioned my role as his Keeper. For some reason, I couldn't shake the idea that my job was not done. If he was as important as everyone seemed to think he was, chances are he'd be in danger again. Was it delusional to think he still needed me, even when he was probably never going to talk to me again?

"I want to keep having death-specters," I declared. I doubted my decision as soon as I said it out loud.

"Are you sure, Sweet Pea?" Bizzy said, growing emotional. She grabbed one of my hands in between hers. "You don't have to do this!"

"I know I don't, Bizzy. But it's what a hedgehog would do, right?" I asked, staring earnestly into her eyes. "And you'll be here to help me."

"You betcha I will," she exclaimed, lifting my hand up in the air with hers.

"I told you, Morgie," Fial said, elbowing her sister. "We

gave her the choice this time. She really is the Keeper we've been waiting for."

"Waiting for?" I asked, nervous energy pumping through me in light of my enormous decision.

"Never mind," Morgan said. For the first time, she smiled at me. "Our paths may cross again, but for now, we wish you well, Beatrice and Elizabeth. May fate be with you, and if it is not, may you—"

"Make it so . . . yes, yes, we get it, Morgie." Fial said, laughing as she interrupted her sister. She stood up as a yellow cloud began to creep into the room. "Morgie's all for the formal good-bye, but sometimes I cannot help but think a hug is in order."

With that, Fial put her arms around me once again and squeezed tightly. It was all I could do to keep from crying out as pain shot through my broken ribs. She moved on to Bizzy.

"It was a pleasure meeting you," she said earnestly to my grandmother. "You watch over our girl!"

"Count on it," Bizzy said with a wink. Soon the haze was so thick, I couldn't see Bizzy a few feet away from me.

"Good-bye, Death Catchers!" Fial said, as she disappeared within the cloud she produced.

After a few seconds, with a whooshing sound, the fog rushed out the window, leaving behind nothing but the now-familiar smell of apple-cinnamon oatmeal.

Bizzy and I were alone again.

"Do you think we'll ever see Morgan le Faye and Fial again?" I asked, breaking the silence.

"Dunno, Sweet Pea. The one thing I've learned in all this is that the word 'never' is the most useless one in the English language."

Bizzy, I knew, was prone to exaggeration, but in that instance she was probably right. It had been a little over two months since I'd learned I was a Death Catcher. The sheer number of things I *never* thought would happen that, in the past months, had happened was astonishing.

"What are you thinkin' about?"

"Nothing really," I answered Bizzy.

"Cogitatin' on your gift?" I could no longer roll my eyes every time Bizzy called death catching a "gift." It was now a choice I'd made. I hope I didn't live to regret it.

Emily Dickinson had it pegged all along. *Find ecstasy in life; the mere sense of living is joy enough*, she wrote in one of her poems. Maybe Emily meant that if fate is a delicate balance of occurrences and circumstances, where any slight change drastically alters a person's course, then the real "gift" was life itself—a life full of choices, beauty, love, and most of all, people to share it with. Death is so scary to all of us, I realized, because it seems like an unknowable end to all that. Perhaps doling out life extensions was a gift after all.

That night, we stayed in Bizzy's room for several hours, gossiping about the people in her life she'd saved. She recounted some of the stories she'd collected over the years. I grew excited about what the future held. It was two o'clock by the time I stumbled upstairs and into bed.

I don't think I'll ever be that exhausted again in my life.

When I woke up the next morning, my ribs were killing me, so Mom let me stay home again. Jodi visited me after school and told me that if I wasn't a POI before, after the article in the paper, I was now. Although she protested at the time, she was grateful that Bizzy had insisted she go home for her own safety when she returned to the cannery from her watch at the storm drain. Fortunately, she'd been able to sneak back into her bedroom without Miss Mora ever realizing she'd been gone the night of the quake.

On the third day of my recuperation, Mom insisted I go to school.

Because of my ribs, Mom said she would drop me off. As we made our way out to the driveway, I heard a familiar voice calling my name.

Drake was running down the street toward our house.

The Paradox

If I had to define my relationship with Drake Westfall, I'd say it was a paradox. Maybe the word doesn't precisely apply to two people, but our relationship certainly seems contradictory. I've had a little time to get used to it and I still think it defies logic.

When Drake crossed the street that morning before school, I had no idea what he was up to.

"Good morning, Mrs. Mortimer," Drake said. His golden hair flashed though there was no sunlight to be found in the gray Crabapple morning. I wished our relationship could go back to what it had been before he found my journal.

"Hello, Drake," Mom answered.

"I wondered if I could give Lizzy a ride to school," he said, putting his hands in his pockets. "I'm headed that way." Drake smiled brightly at me.

"Well," Mom considered, "that would be a huge help. I've got a book inventory to do this morning because of the end of the semester."

"Great," Drake said. "By the way, I wanted to let you know how much I liked *Fever Pitch*. It's really funny."

"I'm so glad to hear that," Mom said, positively beaming. "I'd bet you'd like Nick Hornby's other books, too."

"I'll have to check them out," he replied. I rolled my eyes at Drake. He only smiled in return. "Stay put," he told me, "and I'll run and get the car. I don't want you putting any more strain on those ribs than you have to."

Mom, still grinning, put her hand on my shoulder. "Have a good day at school," she said, raising her eyebrows knowingly. I tried to analyze the look on Mom's face. What had gotten into everyone? Drake was talking to me again, Mom was smiling at me, completely ignoring the California Vehicle Code, and letting me ride with Drake to school . . . I honestly felt I had entered the happy Twilight Zone.

Drake helped me into his car. I imagined he let his arm linger around my waist a few seconds longer than he had to. We drove silently up Earle toward school. I stared at his tan, muscular arms. He was wearing a plain green pocket T-shirt and dark jeans, but he still looked like a model. Wanting to end the silence, I began with the first thing that popped into my head.

"You know, now that you told my mom you liked *Fever Pitch*, she's going to bring you a stack of every single book the author has written."

"I've been looking for something new to read," Drake said, beginning to laugh.

"Fine, but don't go complaining to me when you want the book avalanche to stop."

"I wouldn't dream of it," Drake said. After he responded, the conversation stalled. I tried to think of something to keep it alive.

"Is your suspension over?" I asked.

"Yup. First day back," Drake answered.

"Oh," I said. "I'm sorry about Damon, by the way." Damon and Randy had been moved to the county jail, where they had been officially charged with attempted burglary.

"Don't be," he said. "I would have called the police myself if he hadn't knocked me out."

"Drake," I said, "I need to explain to you about the journal. You have to know that I wasn't trying to—"

Drake took one hand off the steering wheel and gently covered my mouth with it briefly. He laughed and turned off Ocean Avenue and onto a side street next to the steep cliffs guarding Crabapple against the crashing waters of the Pacific. The cypress trees along the bluffs jutted at strange angles along the edge of the road. He put the car in park.

We both stared off into the horizon. With the thick cloud cover, Crabapple and the ocean beyond almost looked like a black-and-white photograph. It was beautiful.

"One of the things I like the most about you, Lizzy, is that you'll talk about anything—you say what you think. But right now, I just want you to listen for a minute, okay?"

"Okay," I said.

"I'm sorry that I didn't react better when I found the journal," Drake said, his eyes perfectly matching the blue of the ocean below us. "Honestly, it scared me. I'm glad Jodi told me

the truth in her letter. But even if it *had* been your journal . . .
I'm not sure I'd be able to stay away from you. There is something about you that I can't explain. When Garrett Edmonds
said those things about you . . . the thought of you with him . . .
it made me fly into a rage like never before. And that was *before*
you saved my life. I guess what I'm saying, Lizzy . . . is that I
like that you care about me enough to pay attention. You notice
the things I want noticed. You get me in a way other people
don't. I'm tired of trying to stop thinking about you. I recently
realized that I don't even want to try to stop anymore."

Drake reached into his backpack. "This is for you." He
handed me a rolled-up canvas. I unrolled it. It was about twice
the size of a piece of notebook paper.

I let out a gasp when I looked at it. It was a brightly painted
portrait of Bizzy, her tousled white hair piled carelessly on her
head. Dozens of pearls surrounded her neck. Drake had splashed
her face with colors. She looked like she was in the middle of a
giant laugh.

A smile spread across my face.

I'm not quite sure how he did it, but Drake had captured
the very essence of Beatrice Mildred Mortimer—her stubborn
joy, her dizzy quick-wittedness, her harsh affection, her passion
for life.

It was beautiful. Stunning even. I looked at Drake, not
knowing what to say.

"She'll love it."

"It's not for her . . . it's for you," Drake said, his blue eyes with their brown slash glistening. "Something to always remind you of her."

"Oh," I said softly, staring down at it.

Drake put his arm on my headrest. He leaned in closer. I grew nervous, staring out at the endless Pacific in front of us—the jagged cliffs reminding me of how close I had come to losing Bizzy.

"I've had some time since I was suspended, and I didn't know how else to thank you for that morning in the cannery."

I looked up at Drake. He moved closer. He shut his eyes.

His lips met mine with a gentle forcefulness. I felt like I might melt into a pool of happiness.

I let myself lean in to him.

"Ack!" I yelled, straightening up, pulling away from Drake. Pain shot through my torso.

"What's wrong?" Drake said, his eyes wide open. "I'm sorry . . . I guess I got carried aw—"

"No, no. It wasn't that. It's my broken ribs . . . the bending hurt more than I expected," I explained, mortified that I'd cried out in pain in the middle of the most pivotal romantic moment of my life so far.

Drake's concern turned into a smile, which turned into laughter within seconds. "One day soon, I promise, we'll get it right . . . without being interrupted by extreme pain or someone planning a robbery."

His eyes looked into mine. I wondered if my face looked as hot as it felt. At that moment, the paradox of me, Lizzy

Mortimer, sitting in the car with Drake Westfall, the supposed Last Descendant, admired by all, struck me as ridiculous.

Soon, Drake and I were back on the road to school. When we neared the parking lot, he took his right hand off the wheel and reached for me. I got goose bumps as his warm hand squeezed mine—the very hand that had had his name emblazoned on it a few days ago.

"Hello, stranger!" Jodi said, already sitting on our planter. "Am I glad to see you. I had to eat lunch with Opal Greenstone's crew the last two days. Talk about boring."

"I missed you, too," I said. "You wrote Drake a letter?"

Jodi cocked her head to the side. "Um, yeah. And I also already know it worked. It's all over school. Lizzy Mortimer and Drake Westfall are official."

"How do you know that?"

"I mean, if you wanted it to be a secret, maybe you shouldn't have been HHIP-ing within a mile of the school."

"What?"

"Holding hands in public."

"What was in the letter?" I asked, hardly able to contain my curiosity.

"You mean Bizzy didn't tell you?"

"What's Bizzy got to do with this?" I asked, growing more confused. I took a moment to scan the picnic tables for Drake. Our eyes met and he waved at me as if it were the most natural thing in the world. It was surreal.

"*Bizzy* is the one who asked me to write the letter. She came into the market the afternoon of the earthquake. I told her I'd find a way to pay her back for saving my life that day, and I meant it. Plus, I thought it was a pretty good plan. Your grandma is kind of a genius. I assumed you knew all about it."

"The first I heard of it was when Drake mentioned it on the way to school this morning. I had to pretend I knew what he was talking about. What in the world did you say in it?"

"Well, I wrote that the journal was mine, basically. That I got it into my head that you two were perfect for each other, like star-crossed lovers and stuff, so I started feeding you information about Drake, which I was collecting without you knowing it. Bizzy said there was some book, I don't know, where there's a girl obsessed with setting her friend up, and that she thought it would work for our situation. Anyway, I explained that I'd put the journal in your backpack to hide it at lunch. Before I could get it back, it fell out in his pool house that night."

"I don't know what to say," I said, amazed that Jodi had been willing to take the rap for the DWOR. "Thank you."

Jodi smiled and put her checkered Vans on the planter, leaning back. "Don't mention it. It was really all part of my plan. But remember, now that you and Drake are in *loooove*, you can't go forgetting about your best friend, Jodi."

"Like you'd ever let me," I said. "And we're not in *loooove*, by the way."

Soon, the bell rang and Jodi and I headed to our respective classes.

Mrs. Tweedy, I honestly didn't even remember that your final project was due until the second I walked into your classroom that day.

When I saw everyone's projects sitting on their desks, I almost fainted. Remember, you asked me where mine was? I know you were shocked when I said that I hadn't finished. I didn't even have time to come up with some lame excuse.

Please don't think that I wrote this down to have you feel sorry for me or to make excuses, but I wanted to explain why I didn't turn in my project. I better stop writing now and go down to dinner. Lately, Mom's been watching me like a hawk. Spending all this time in my room writing probably hasn't helped my cause.

In conclusion, for the aforementioned reasons, I believe I should pass English even though I did not turn in my final project.

Very sincerely yours,
Lizzy Mortimer

P.S. Maybe that last sentence is a bit over the top. It's certainly not Emily Dickinson quality, but I read a Supreme Court opinion once that ended that way. I found it very persuasive. Even if I don't pass your class, I hope you have a happy New Year.

The Epilogue

Dear Mrs. Tweedy,

I don't think I've ever been as happy as I was the day you handed me back my defense paper and told me that I was going to get an A for my semester grade. Honestly, at first, I thought you were joking. It really is a small miracle. That's my best grade this year. Heck, it's my best grade this life.

Mom's going to flip.

I also want you to know that I followed your instructions. I took my paper and I locked it away. I haven't shown it to anybody, just like you told me.

You said that all you wanted in return for showing me leniency with my final project was an update in two months' time on my "story."

How exactly did you phrase it again?

I think you said, "No story is complete without closure, and yours is missing an epilogue."

So here it is. I guess, after thinking about it, I agree with what you said about my lack of resolution. You said that I was the protagonist of the story, even if I didn't want to be, and that you wanted to know how things were left with Mom. I think you used the term "short shrift" when referring to how I left things. Yes. That's what you said. I remember now. You said readers don't like to get the "short shrift" when it comes to major relationships in a story.

Actually, I have Mom to thank for straightening things out with Drake. See, she was pretty frantic after I broke my ribs. When she asked Bizzy what had gotten into me lately, my grandma felt like she had to tell Mom something.

I can't really blame Bizzy—Mom was starting to get permanent worry lines on her forehead every time she looked at me. So, Bizzy told her about the DWOR and my crush on Drake, leaving out all the stuff about the Death Catchers and Morgan le Faye and *The Last Descendant*. Mom was the one who came up with the whole plan of Jodi writing the letter to Drake. She and Bizzy figured out the details together.

We were sitting at the kitchen counter a few days after I returned to school when it popped out.

"I'm sorry I've been acting like such a crazy person lately, Mom," I said. "Bizzy told me it was your idea to have Jodi write the letter. Thank you."

Mom smiled over her cup of tea. "You're quite welcome. Judging by the amount of time you've been spending with Drake lately, I'm assuming everything worked out?"

"Things are going good," I said.

"*Well*," Mom corrected. "Things are going *well*." I rolled my eyes. Mom continued. "Have you started reading *Pride and Prejudice* yet?"

I shook my head.

"I only ask because if you had read it, you would've realized yourself that there are very few misunderstandings a well-written letter can't fix."

"Really?"

"Absolutely. The idea came straight out of *Pride and Prejudice*, though I suppose there was a dash of *Emma* thrown in. You see, Mr. Darcy writes Elizabeth this incredible letter that clears up her misconceptions about that rascal, Mr. Wickham." Though I was quite used to Mom talking about characters in books like they were real people living down the street, it still made me laugh.

"You laugh, Lizzy dearest, but one day you will see it my way. The solution to every one of life's problems," she said, pausing dramatically. I knew the end of the sentence by heart and jumped in.

"Can be found within the pages of a good book," we said in unison. Though I often made fun of Mom's favorite phrase (Bizzy called it Mom's *only* pearl), I was beginning to think she was right. Mom hadn't even read *The Last Descendant*. If she only knew. At the end of the day, I've realized, when you have a problem or a question, a book is certainly a safe place to explore your options (as long as you don't encounter a death-specter, of course).

"Well, I'm so pleased you seem happy again," Mom said.

"I'm sorry I told Bizzy about the Drake stuff before I told you," I added quickly.

"I understand your grandmother is very easy to share things with. But you should try me out sometime. If you let a secret fly to me, I won't shoot it down."

"I know that. In fact, I'm pretty sure you'd never shoot anything, ever. Except maybe someone who burned books."

Mom laughed loudly. "I suppose it would depend on which books the person was burning."

That night, on a whim, I started reading *Pride and Prejudice*. Not only did I read it, but I didn't even skip any parts. I finished it in three days.

It might be my Right Book! I'm as shocked as you probably are. But my namesake, Elizabeth Bennet, is a fictional character I can really get behind, you know? Mom was thrilled, of course, and she keeps giving me romances to read, but I don't like any of them as well as I liked *Pride and Prejudice*. It may be some time before Mom finds me another Right Book. Part of me, though, thinks that she enjoys the chase more than anything else.

I kept my promise to Jodi. See, though I'm seeing a lot of Drake these days, she and I are still best friends. Occasionally, she even manages to talk me into visiting the cemetery. When we do, I can't help but stare at Old Arthur's tomb. Sometimes I wonder if he always knew when he set sail for Crabapple so many years ago that his lineage would once again fatefully intersect with Avalon's.

I like to think that he did.

As for Bizzy, she's still as nutty as ever, but I can't imagine life without her.

The Death Catcher/Keeper thing is still not normal to me yet, but it's getting there. In fact, just this morning I had my third death-specter while I was reading the comics.

But don't worry, Mrs. Tweedy. It's not you. Of course, I couldn't tell you if it were. Life's a gift, so why waste it thinking about all the bad things that might happen? I can't help but believe whatever time we have here together is better spent thinking about all the good things we can *make* happen.

I guess you could call that one of Lizzy's pearls, free a' charge.

Anyway, even if my latest death-specter were about you, Mrs. Tweedy, I wouldn't worry too much. The Die-namic Duo's on the case, after all.

Acknowledgments

I want to thank my parents, Clare and John Kogler, for the countless story conferences and their unflagging enthusiasm. I am, indeed, the luckiest.

A number of people were incredibly helpful as first readers as I wrote *The Death Catchers*, including Lizzy McCloskey (whose name I borrowed as well), Kristy Cole, Jodi Wu, Mary Steffens, Lisa Hart, and Bradford Lyman. Marnie Podos helped me deliver the knockout blow.

Though my first introduction to all things Arthurian was most likely *Monty Python and the Holy Grail* on television, I would be remiss if I didn't mention the many wonderfully talented authors who made the Arthurian legend their own before I did. These books have inspired me as both a girl and an adult, including Geoffrey of Monmouth's *Historia Regum Britanniae*, Thomas Malory's *Le Morte d'Arthur*, T. H. White's *The Once and Future King*, and Marion Zimmer Bradley's *The Mists of Avalon*.

When I began to write this story, I was making a number

of appearances at middle schools across the country. I want to thank the long list of welcoming librarians, English teachers, and other educators, who do vital and greatly underappreciated work, as well as the many bright students I met along the way. I hope Mrs. Mortimer, Jodi, Lizzy, and the gang do you all proud.

Many thanks to my wise editor, Emily Easton, for all the guidance and faith and, finally, the magnificent Faye Bender, without whose help affording health insurance would be a mere pipe dream.